"If you take me against my will, you will be guilty of a crime," Gabriella warned.

"I have no intention of taking you against your will," the baron said truthfully. Then another need that had been so vital for so long arose inside him. He must be in control, of himself, of her, of everyone around him.

"You cannot deny that you want me, Gabriella," he continued. "I could taste your desire. I could feel the excitement in your body. When you come to my bed—and you will—it shall be of your own free will."

She stared at him with horrified disbelief. "The only way I shall go voluntarily to any man's bed will be when I am married, and I can assure you, Baron DeGuerre, that if you were the last man in the kingdom, I would not marry *you!*"

Dear Reader,

Whether you're a longtime fan of Margaret Moore, or meeting her for the first time, her new medieval novel, *The Baron's Quest*, is sure to please. This captivating story of a rough-edged Saxon who falls in love with the refined gentlewoman whom he has inherited as part of his new holdings is full of the warmth and humor readers have come to expect from this very talented author. We hope you enjoy it.

Badlands Bride from Cheryl St.John is the story of a newspaper reporter who goes west pretending to be a mail-order bride, only to find herself stranded in the Dakotas for one long cold winter. *Pearl,* from Ruth Langan, is the next in her new series, THE JEWELS OF TEXAS, featuring four sisters who are brought together by their father's murder.

Liz Ireland rounds out the list with *Millie and the Fugitive,* a lighthearted Western about a spoiled rich girl and an innocent man on the run.

We hope you'll keep a lookout for all four titles wherever Harlequin Historicals are sold.

Sincerely,

Tracy Farrell
Senior Editor

Please address questions and book requests to:
Harlequin Reader Service
U.S.: 3010 Walden Ave., P.O. Box 1325, Buffalo, NY 14269
Canadian: P.O. Box 609, Fort Erie, Ont. L2A 5X3

Margaret Moore

The Baron's Quest

Harlequin Books

TORONTO • NEW YORK • LONDON
AMSTERDAM • PARIS • SYDNEY • HAMBURG
STOCKHOLM • ATHENS • TOKYO • MILAN
MADRID • WARSAW • BUDAPEST • AUCKLAND

ISBN 0-373-28928-6

THE BARON'S QUEST

Copyright © 1996 by Margaret Wilkins.

MARGARET MOORE

confesses that her first "crush" was Errol Flynn. The second was "Mr. Spock." She thinks that it explains why her heroes tend to be either charming rogues or lean, inscrutable tough guys.

Margaret lives in Scarborough, Ontario, with her husband, two children and two cats. She used to sew and read for reasons other than research.

To the readers,
my humble and hearty thanks.

And to those who wish to write romance,
for the goal is worthy.

Chapter One

Warwickshire, 1223

The anxious servants of Castle Frechette and the tenants of the surrounding estate should have been about their business this sunny September day, either preparing for the harvest, sowing the winter grain, laying in a store of wood, or any of the other tasks associated with Michaelmas. Instead, the large crowd gathered in the castle's inner ward stood as silent and subdued as if they awaited a public execution. Considering the true reason for their presence, the comparison was not so farfetched.

The Earl of Westborough had been dead only four weeks, but already the young king had contrived to strip the Frechette family of their land and give it to an upstart noble of no great family, the infamous Baron DeGuerre. He was to arrive after the noon.

Standing motionless in the inner ward of her family's castle, Lady Gabriella Frechette attempted to convey an aura of calm serenity that was not com-

pletely successful, for she had heard many things of
Baron DeGuerre, few of them good.

Men called him the devil's spawn and a host of
other unflattering names. He had appeared out of
nowhere and risen to prominence by winning every
tournament he entered. He had been awarded a title
when he allied himself to William Marshal. Two very
advantageous marriages to older women of wealth and
title had enriched him. His vaulting ambition was no
secret, nor was the rigor of the rule he exerted over his
many tenants.

It was said women found the combination of Baron
DeGuerre's physical strength and aloof arrogance
nearly irresistible. A widower now, he had for his
mistress the most beautiful woman in all of England,
and he lived openly with her in mortal sin.

Gabriella clasped her hands tightly within the cuffs
of her simple homespun gown to still their trembling
when a loud cry went up from the battlements. The
baron's entourage had been spotted on the ridge.

What was going to happen to her people with a man
like Baron DeGuerre for their lord? she thought as she
surveyed the murmuring crowd.

Her lip curled with slight scorn as she watched
Robert Chalfront, the bailiff, hurry about excitedly,
making sure all was in readiness for the baron's men,
troops and servants. No doubt *some* would feel no ill
effects. Chalfront would surely do whatever was necessary to retain his privileged position here, and she
wondered how the baron might respond to Chalfront's obsequious manner—or if he would see the
dishonest rogue lurking beneath the fawning mask.

Unable to bear the sight of the bailiff, she looked at William, the village reeve, who stood with Osric the hayward and Brian the woodward, the men speaking in hushed and wary voices with an occasional glance in her direction.

Her father had always impressed upon her the necessity of taking care of the tenants, and the peasants had appreciated the kindness of their lord and his family. Both her sweet, long-dead mother and her generous father had been truly mourned by everyone on the estate, from the knights in his service to the poorest peasant begging alms at the castle gate.

The knights were gone now, of course. They had taken their leave singly at first, then in greater number after her father had died. They needed to find some other lord to feed and house them, for apparently that was the only basis for their loyalty.

The outer portcullis rattled upward and the large gates swung inward. The crowd looked expectantly toward the entrance as a boisterous cortege rode into the courtyard of Castle Frechette.

Despite her resolution to be strong, Gabriella's knees started to tremble and her mouth went dry, her attention immediately drawn to the man sitting upon a prancing black stallion at the front of the company. She had heard of the baron's long hair and handsome face, and this tall, commanding man could be no one else.

His chestnut locks brushed his muscular shoulders, and no beard covered his cleft chin. On another man, such a fashion might have conveyed an aura of effeteness. Not the baron. His hair gave him a savage air, like one of the barbarian Celts who still roamed the far reaches of the land, and he had the broad shoulders and posture of a born warrior.

He wore a cloak completely black, and underneath that she could see an equally long black tunic. His boots were plain leather, as was his sword belt. The only ornament he sported was a simple brooch to fasten the cloak about his throat, although the hilt of the dagger stuck through his sword belt was of finely wrought gold.

All in all, Baron DeGuerre emanated invincibility and complete control.

Behind Baron DeGuerre came his knights, their horses adorned with colorful accoutrements. The metal of their armor and weapons shone in the sun. Numerous banners, carried by mounted squires, floated in the slight autumn breeze. Then the foot soldiers and hounds, and finally several baggage carts entered the inner ward, which was rendered as noisy and overcrowded as a marketplace.

The baron swung down from his prancing horse as if it were the calmest, mildest mare in Christendom and strode to the center of the courtyard. Surprisingly, he did not seem pompous or proud, but removed and aloof from the commotion behind him and the castle servants before him. To Gabriella, he looked completely, utterly alone, even in the midst of this chaos.

Just as she had felt the day her father had died.

The baron slowly turned on his heel, surveying the buildings as if he were a merchant here to offer the cheapest price, and Gabriella remembered exactly why he had come.

As she looked at the buildings around her, her heart filled with pride at this monument to her parents, nearly overpowering the pain that one such as the Baron DeGuerre would be the possessor of it. Surely he would not care about this place beyond its strength as a fortress.

But there were other strongholds as well built. What was unique about Castle Frechette was its beauty. Her father had not been content with Norman utility when it came to his home; he had decorated and embellished wherever possible and insisted upon the finest materials. The stone frames of all the doors and archways were wonderfully carved, and even the simple stone hearth in the kitchen had been decorated with the shapes of fruit and braided loaves of bread. The chapel in the north tower boasted a lovely stained glass window, and her father's solar in the south tower had three of plain glass. The apartments above the great hall were spacious and paneled with oak. The walls of the hall had been plastered and painted, so that even without tapestries, they were glorious to behold. All of the outer stones of the castle had been whitewashed with lime and today they gleamed in the September sunlight like the lovely marble used to pave her parent's bedchamber.

Before she could look away, the baron's gaze fastened upon her. Her breath caught in her throat, and her limbs seemingly turned to stone, although his face betrayed neither pleasure nor displeasure, pride nor scorn—indeed, she had never seen an expression so unreadable. He simply stared, his long hair and an-kle-length tunic stirring slightly in the breeze.

She was the daughter of an earl, she reminded her-self, so she stared back indignantly even as a heated blush flooded her face and warmed her body.

Without a change in his expression, Baron De-Guerre pivoted and continued his survey of the cas-tle.

She had harbored a hope that the rumors about Baron DeGuerre were exaggerated and that she would be able to ask this man to allow her to stay in the only home she had known. In her most desperate fancies, she had even dared to imagine that he would welcome her superior knowledge of the castle, the land and the tenants.

She knew now, and with more disappointment than she cared to acknowledge, that these hopes had been completely ludicrous.

In a deep, dispassionate voice, the baron began to issue orders to the servants, grooms and squires to stable the horses and unload the wagons. As he did so, she forced herself to look at the others in his retinue with the same impartial scrutiny with which he had regarded her home, and her.

There were several knights, some clearly more im-portant than others, and it was to the two pairs riding nearest to the baron that she gave her closest atten-tion. The first twosome was composed of a sleek, dark-haired man who also wore his hair long, but un-like the baron, it was brushed back from his high, pale forehead. He had what could have been a handsome face, except that his eyes were narrow and shifty as a ferret's, overshadowed by heavy dark brows. As for his smile, it was a scornful, arrogant, sneering slash. His clothing and accoutrements were very fine, and she wondered if his favored position in the retinue meant he had influence with the baron. Woe betide her tenants if he did!

Beside this man, however, and in contrast to him, rode a blond-haired, merry individual in a tunic of very bright scarlet. At first sight, Gabriella thought him little more than a youth. When he dismounted and moved closer, she discerned subtle wrinkles around his mouth and eyes, and guessed that he was nearly of an age with the baron himself.

Gabriella found this man's presence comforting. If the baron was as evil as men claimed, would such a pleasant-faced man be in his service? Or perhaps any man of Baron DeGuerre's power and reputation would attract many followers, both good and bad.

Behind these two rode a pair of young knights. One was a slender, thoughtful-looking fellow, the other big and brawny. When they conversed, it was through the simplest of words and gestures, as if they had been friends for so long, nothing else was necessary.

Then Gabriella saw the woman who had to be Lady Josephine de Chaney. She was astonishingly beautiful, with a heart-shaped face and a perfect complexion, her pale, smooth cheeks having a very slight tint of pink; large green eyes fringed with incredibly lengthy lashes; rosy, full lips; delicately arched brows that were slightly darker than her blond hair; and a long, slender neck. She wore a cloak of rich blue and a headdress that sparkled in the sunlight over her bountiful blond hair. It was no wonder songs had been composed celebrating her classic beauty and graceful deportment, and that men had died vying for her love.

Gabriella smoothed down her simple brown homespun gown, and for an instant wished she had not sold all her fine dresses. But that was a vain thought, unworthy of her, and one quickly subdued.

Her self-evaluation was interrupted by the baron's quiet yet commanding voice, which carried to every corner of the ward. "Where are the late earl's children?" he demanded.

Now it comes, Gabriella thought. If only Bryce were here beside her instead of somewhere in Europe, ignorant even of their father's death. Surely her brother would have been able to prevent this terrible situation. Or if not prevent, delay by going to the king himself when the true state of her father's treasury became known as he lay dying. Instead, there had been no time, and no money to send another to intercede for her.

Gabriella blinked hard to subdue the weakness of tears and raised her chin, gazing upward at the soaring walls and battlements of her family's home. She alone represented her family now, and she alone stood between her people and the Baron DeGuerre. She would not be afraid of an immoral, ambitious parvenu.

"I am Lady Gabriella Frechette," she announced, slowly moving toward him and curtsying. "I bid you welcome."

Etienne DeGuerre had many years of practice in masking his emotions, so now he easily kept the surprise from his face. He had noticed the young woman standing among the servants, of course. He had been struck by her uniqueness immediately: her steadfast gaze, which conveyed an attitude of strength at odds with the softness of her other features that made her pretty, her face surrounded by its dark corona of thick, wavy hair, and the simple gown that did more to emphasize her bountiful natural gifts than the finest garment might have. He had thought her a maidservant, possibly another example of the luxuries the late, profligate Earl of Westborough had enjoyed.

He should have noticed the proud, graceful carriage of a woman raised in wealth, a poise undiminished by the recent unfortunate events. He never should have surmised that since the earl's daughter was unmarried, she was a child.

Her voice was also curiously intriguing, for it was low for a woman, even husky. No simpering, breathy helpless tone to her words, but an almost masculine forthrightness that was most unusual.

Etienne DeGuerre had met very few members of the female sex who impressed him, and those who did so usually had outstanding physical beauty, like Josephine. In all of the baron's experience, there had been only two others who seemed to possess such calm determination and confident self-possession as this young woman. One had been his mother. The other was the new wife of his trusted liegeman, Sir Roger de Montmorency.

Nevertheless, Etienne's expression did not alter as he magnanimously ignored her impertinence and walked toward her. "Where is your brother?"

"I wish I knew," she retorted bluntly, "for he would not have allowed this to happen."

Etienne halted. For years no one had had the effrontery to talk to him in such a manner, or use such a tone.

Then Gabriella Frechette made another mistake, for she obviously took the baron's silence as an opportunity to continue. "Have you not forgotten something, such as the simple courtesy of a greeting or an expression of sympathy for my father's demise?" she asked with a scornful politeness. "Or perhaps a thanks for how his untimely death has enriched you?"

For a brief instant, indignation raged through Etienne with the speed and fierceness of a summer's grass fire. His emotional response was quickly quelled, however, and none of that indignation showed on his face. Instead he regarded her impartially with the coldly measuring stare that had made many a brave knight cower before him, a look that came from the knowledge that he had seen, done, experienced and survived more than most men had or ever would.

Gabriella Frechette did not flinch under his scrutiny. She did not start to weep. She did not even lower her eyelids. She simply stood there and faced him.

Etienne was not often confounded, and he did not like the sensation now. Either Gabriella Frechette was a stupid, foolish woman ignorant of the true meaning of her reduced status, or she had the spirit to maintain her personal dignity in spite of it.

Then, out of the corner of his eye, Etienne saw the mocking scorn of Philippe de Varenne's smirk. Sir George de Gramercie, conspicuous in his customary scarlet, was simply and understandably studying the woman and finding her fascinating. Donald Bouchard, whom Etienne always thought of as "the monk," was patiently waiting to see what would happen next; his friend, the stolid Seldon Vachon, was openly shocked. The castle inhabitants were unabashedly staring.

Suddenly he knew that this one lone woman represented a threat to his authority here. But Gabriella Frechette's father had lost this estate by spending too freely on frivolities, and by raising a quarrelsome son who had argued and run away. *He* was not in the wrong to accept his reward. *She* was in the wrong to stay. She must be made to see that she was no longer the lady of the manor, just as he had to make clear to the rest of the servants that he would brook no disobedience or rebellion of any kind.

He considered his opponent, knowing not every weapon need be held in the hand. For a woman as proud as she, the best attack would surely be humiliation. Strangely and most unusually, he felt a twinge of regret that it must be so. But it was. He had fought and sacrificed too long to have his power corrupted in any way, by anyone.

"What are you doing here?" he asked with the dispassionate calm his enemies had come to fear.

The wary servants and tenants shifted uneasily and exchanged anxious whispers. Etienne noticed that Josephine, standing off to one side waiting patiently, looked at the young woman with sympathy in her lovely eyes. Philippe de Varenne no longer smiled, and Sir George was, for once in his life, looking grave. Donald and Seldon wisely went about their business.

"This is my home," the late earl's daughter answered.

"Not anymore," he replied quietly. Very quietly.

There was a flash of grudging acknowledgment in her eyes, and a deep flush spread over her smooth cheeks. Etienne realized he had achieved a measure of triumph over her, yet did not feel overly triumphant. Well, it was never as enjoyable defeating a woman in a battle of words.

"My lord, if you will excuse me," Sir George said with very slight reproach in his usually merry eyes, "I will assist your lady with her goods."

"As you wish," Etienne replied, telling himself George's disapproval was nothing, and Josephine should see to making their bedchamber a comfortable haven. With a silent curtsy, Josephine took George's arm and walked toward the large building that had to be the hall. Others in his retinue took their cue from them and sauntered away, all except Philippe de Varenne.

"Where is the bailiff?" Etienne demanded, momentarily ignoring Gabriella Frechette.

A moon-faced man of short and stocky stature burst out of the remaining crowd like an arrow from a bow, bustling toward the baron with a curious mixture of humility, self-importance and fear. "I am Robert Chalfront, my lord," he said in a rather high-pitched voice. "I have been the bailiff here for ten years."

Etienne glanced at Gabriella Frechette. She did not like this man, although she was trying not to show any emotion at all.

Nevertheless, Etienne had spent years gauging reactions, so he was quite certain that she hated the bailiff. Yet he had been in her father's employ for ten years. That was most interesting, and possibly another tool for him to use. "You may remain bailiff, Chalfront," the baron announced, his decision made in that instant. "Your continued presence should ease the transition to my rule."

A subdued murmur ran through the crowd, whether of approval or not, Etienne did not trouble himself to consider.

Chalfront did not stifle the relieved sigh that broke from his lips as he bowed to the baron. "I will serve you well, my lord. I give you my word. The reeve is here, my lord, and the woodward and the—"

"I expect nothing less than my due, from you or any of my people," Etienne replied. "As for the reeve and the others, I will see them another day. Tell me about the late earl's son."

Her brown eyes gleaming with defiance, Gabriella Frechette stepped forward. "Baron, is this not an inappropriate place to discuss such matters?"

Etienne regarded the young woman with the mildest of disdain. "I do not recall addressing you."

She flushed, and after a moment's hesitation, looked down at the ground.

Etienne immediately turned back to the bailiff. "Answer my question, Chalfront," he commanded, his voice still calm and unruffled.

"My lord, the present Earl of Westborough is—"

"There is no longer an Earl of Westborough," Etienne observed.

"Yes, well, um, my lord, Bryce Frechette is somewhere in Europe at the moment, we think, and—"

"Where in Europe?"

"Nobody knows, my lord. Naturally we tried to locate him when his father fell ill, but to no avail, I'm afraid."

Etienne listened impassively, although he had been informed of this before. He wanted to hear how the local people interpreted the childish action of the son of their late lord. It was quite obvious his sister did not condemn him for it—more fool her! "He did not say where he planned to travel before he left?" Etienne asked, already knowing the answer.

Chalfront cleared his throat nervously and gave a sidelong glance at the blushing Gabriella.

"He, um, left home rather abruptly, my lord," Chalfront said, "after a quarrel with his father. His father claimed he did not care where his son had gone. When it became clear that the earl's illness was mortal, Lady Gabriella sent men to find him. Unfortunately, by the time they returned with no news of her brother, the earl was dead. Lady Gabriella could not afford to send the men again and, being wiser in her handling of money than her father, she did not."

Gabriella Frechette stiffened, but said nothing.

"This Bryce Frechette...what do you think he would do, should he hear of his father's demise?" Etienne inquired.

Chalfront looked down at his hands, then glanced at Gabriella Frechette. Her expression was murderous, and Chalfront's tone changed to one of angry defiance, aimed not at the baron to whom he spoke, Etienne guessed, but at the woman beside him. "I cannot say, my lord. He was something of a wild youth, if truth be told, impetuous and spoiled. Some—nay, most—felt it was better that he had gone, although of course it is regrettable that any son should quarrel so with his father."

"*You* felt it was better he was gone!" Gabriella Frechette cried impetuously, her hands drawing into fists at her side. "You were glad that there was no one to watch over you except my sick father! No one who might see your dishonesty!"

"Dishonesty?" Chalfront squeaked, growing red in the face.

"My steward has examined the account rolls of Castle Frechette and found nothing amiss," Etienne said, believing Gabriella Frechette's accusation was made of haste and hate. He had every confidence that Jean Luc, his steward of many years, would have noticed had anything been amiss with the castle's financial records. "And I should not have to remind you again that you will speak only when you have been addressed," the baron said to the young woman. He spoke not loudly, but with unmistakable firmness.

Rather impressively and contrary to the reaction he had anticipated, she quickly regained her self-control. Her eyes still flashed with angry fire and she did not look at the bailiff, but it was clear she was capable of subduing her emotions when it was necessary. A most rare quality in a woman, and one completely unexpected.

"Why are you not married?" he asked suddenly, trying to confound her. When she did not answer, he said, "Well?"

"Excuse me, my lord, I did not realize you were addressing me."

She was playing a dangerous game, this pretty woman with the defiant eyes standing before him in wounded pride and unbowed majesty. But she would lose. He would win this first test of his authority, because he must always win. "Why are you not married?" he repeated, and no one who heard the stern tone of his voice would have dared refuse to answer.

"Because I did not wish to be," Gabriella Frechette said, some of her defiance replaced by obvious fear.

"My lord, if I may say so, Lady Gabriella tended to her parents most devotedly," Chalfront stuttered, clearly terrified. "She said she would entertain no suitors while she did her duty to them."

"I did not ask you for your opinion, bailiff," the baron noted dispassionately. The man looked about to collapse, but that was of no concern to Etienne. He spoke only to the young woman. "Apparently your father was more shortsighted than I had been told, since his lack of concern for your future has left you on my hands. Is there no other family to whom you could go?"

"No."

"You will address me as 'my lord' or 'Baron,'" he said.

"No, *my lord,*" she replied with undeniable scorn in her dark brown eyes.

What kind of creature was this? The boldest knights in England were more easily dominated than this wench. "Who fostered you?" he demanded.

"No one, *my lord.* My parents wished to raise us."

"If you are as devoted to God as you were to your parents, you should go to a convent."

"Excuse me, my lord?" Chalfront interrupted again, his voice like the squeak of a mouse.

The baron turned his impartial gaze onto the bailiff. "What is it?"

Chalfront cleared his throat nervously. "Lady Gabriella is penniless, my lord. It would cost some money for her to be accepted into a convent, and there is nothing left."

"There are debts still unpaid, too," Baron De-Guerre noted.

Suddenly Gabriella realized he had known more of her family history than he had indicated.

Obviously his questions, embarrassingly posed in front of the assembled servants and tenants, had but one purpose: to reveal her penniless state to everyone and shame her in public. He was a cruel and heartless man, worse than even the rumors had led her to believe!

She must have been mad not to see immediately the unfeeling creature he was. How could she have been so impressed with his strength and commanding presence when he did not temper those qualities with mercy? How could she have thought there was a hint of vulnerability in his aloofness? How could she ever have found him attractive, unless she had felt the same fascination for him that Eve had experienced for the snake in the Garden of Eden?

They were engaged in a battle, and Gabriella would not admit defeat, especially when Baron DeGuerre took a step toward her and made what she supposed was his idea of a smile. "However, I can be generous."

The look in his eyes assured her that his idea of generosity was not one she would share.

Chapter Two

The baron reached into the wide, plain brown leather belt about his waist and produced a leather purse.

Gabriella had very little doubt what he might expect in the way of recompense for his "generosity," this vain, arrogant bully who had tried to humiliate her in the courtyard of her own home. What kind of woman did he think he was dealing with? One like Josephine de Chaney, who had abandoned her morals for the sake of money? "I want nothing from you, my lord," she said contemptuously.

Not a muscle moved in the baron's handsome, impassive face.

"You...you have been most munificent, my lord," Chalfront said anxiously, reminding Gabriella of his odious presence. "Surely everyone understands that."

"Except this person," the baron replied, his gaze still fastened upon her. "Whether you accept my gift or not, you will leave this castle and the village at once."

"No, I will not. This is my home and—"

"If I order you to go, you will go." The baron said the words quietly, but the menace was unmistakable. Then he smiled again. "You may stay in the castle if the tenants' *feelings* are so vital to you. As a servant."

It took a mighty effort, but Gabriella straightened her shoulders and said, "The tenants will be most upset if you make such an order."

"The tenants?" he asked with a very slight hint of incredulity. "What care I for the feelings of the tenants?"

At his arrogant words, the mood of the crowd changed from one of dread to defiance.

"If they wish to remain on my land, they would do well to try to please me, not the late earl's daughter," Baron DeGuerre said. Then he slowly surveyed them, his impartial, chilling scrutiny resting for a brief moment on every person there.

They all fell silent and averted their eyes from his, their insolence gone as if he had physically taken it from them. One by one they silently went out the gate. "I will speak with you later, Chalfront," the baron said, and Chalfront, obviously dismissed, joined the departing crowd.

"Goodbye, Gabriella Frechette," Baron DeGuerre said before he turned on his heel and strode toward the hall, clearly convinced by her stunned silence he had won this skirmish. The other knight who had remained smiled cruelly and followed his master into the hall like a dog on a lead.

Gabriella stood in the courtyard all alone, feeling more abandoned than she had by her father's death and even Bryce's absence.

If she stayed, she would have to be a maid, humbled before the servants and tenants she had known all her life, the very people she had been raised to believe she had a duty to protect.

Was it so humiliating to be a servant? Had her father not praised many times the labor of his people and the worth of his hirelings who had built this place? Was it worse than being driven from her home?

The Frechettes were not cowards. This was her family's home and had been for generations; Baron DeGuerre could not force her to leave, however he tried. Besides, there was the very real chance that Bryce would return one day, and who could say what might happen if she were not there? She could not count on Baron DeGuerre or Robert Chalfront to tell her brother where she had gone.

Also, as the baron surely knew—to his discredit—it would be too dangerous for a woman with no money and no escort to travel. She would quickly find herself in a worse predicament, and at the mercy of villains even more loathsome than the baron.

If she remained, she might yet be able to help her people. Clearly the tenants would need any and all assistance she might render.

If she fled, that would allow the baron to think he had triumphed over her.

Therefore, there really was only one thing she could do. She must stay.

With the fierce pride in her family name to sustain her, Gabriella turned on her heel and marched to the kitchen.

Despite what had passed in the courtyard, the room was abustle with preparations for the evening meal, a feast she herself had ordered and that would use the last of the stores her father had purchased. Both she and the cook had wanted this meal to make them proud, if for slightly different reasons. She had thought of her family's honor; Guido wanted to retain his position by impressing his new master.

One of the maids spotted Gabriella and gasped, her mouth an "O" of surprise as she colored. Then the others realized who was in their midst and there was an awkward pause before Guido came toward her with outstretched, floury hands.

"My lady!" he cried, his Italian accent strong because of his indignation. "This is a terrible business! The baron is no gentleman! Sit here." He indicated a pile of bags filled with flour.

Gabriella smiled, sure again of their affection and that she had made the right decision. "No, Guido," she said, "if I am to be a servant, I had better begin to work."

The other servants exchanged shocked glances. "My lady!" James the baker began. "Your sainted mother—"

"Is mercifully in her grave," Gabriella said, subduing a pang of sorrow. "The baron has given his ultimatum and I have made my choice, with no regrets. Now," she continued briskly, "have the flowers been spread upon the tables yet?"

"No, my lady," a girl named Alda replied quietly, nodding toward cut stems of late-blooming campion.

"Very well," Gabriella said. "I will do that." She picked up the flowers and headed toward the corridor leading to the great hall.

"Alda, you help her," Guido ordered, and Gabriella heard the respect in his voice.

It made her feel . . . good. Before, they had always deferred to her, but never had she been so aware of their respect. This time, too, it was not because she was her parents' daughter, but for herself alone.

As she waited for Alda to gather together more flowers and join her, Guido went back to peering into a bubbling pot, like an alchemist waiting for lead to turn to gold, and the spit boy turned an enormous boar as if the fate of the kingdom rested on the performance of his duty. James fussed over the exact shape of the sweetmeats, but paused to give her a genial smile.

And the baron thought she would leave!

During the evening meal, Etienne DeGuerre permitted himself a very small and very rare smile of satisfaction. The king had not lied when he said that while the Earl of Westborough was not a fighting man, he was no fool when it came to the building of defenses. This castle was as strong as any fortress Etienne had ever seen. The outer curtain wall was nearly twenty feet tall, and over two yards wide. The inner wall was even taller and wider, built to allow archers to protect or defeat any soldiers caught between the two. The gate house was nearly as large as the stables, and well fortified with an oak portcullis tipped with iron in front of a heavier solid oak door strengthened by iron straps. Above and behind the portcullis was the murder hole, through which stones or boiling oil could be poured, the bane of any enemy trapped between the portcullis and the outer door.

The late earl also had a canny eye for picking a good location. The castle had been built on a low rise at the meeting of two rivers, a spot of unmistakable strategic significance. If the decorations were rather lavish, that was something new in Etienne's experience, and he found them not unpleasant. For so many years he had survived with the barest of necessities; the external beauty of this fortress seemed to say that all those years of struggle were finally behind him. Not that he could rest content even now, he thought, watching Philippe de Varenne talk to George.

The young knight was an ambitious braggart and a bully, but he was from a wealthy family of great rank, and Etienne didn't doubt that the man would soon leave his company for a lord with more to give. That being so, he was willing to tolerate Philippe's presence—especially since Philippe was free with his money and often paid for meals in taverns for himself and his friends, thereby sparing the baron's larder.

George was a good and loyal knight, if a trifle indifferent to everything except his clothing and being the wittiest man in any hall. He could be counted on in a fight, if necessary; however, more often than not he prevented the others from expressing their disagreements physically.

In contrast, Donald Bouchard, from a poor but ancient family, was rather too serious. That surely came from his training under the strict eye of Urien Fitzroy, a teacher becoming famous from his students' skills and moral rectitude.

Seldon Vachon had profited immensely from Fitzroy's guidance. Etienne knew the young man's family, a bunch of brawling braggarts. Thanks to Donald's steadfast friendship and Fitzroy's example, Seldon was a fine exception to his family's reputation.

The other knights and squires were all rather similar, each ambitious and anxious to please their overlord by distinguishing themselves. Some were rich, some were poor, but all wanted more, whether it was wealth, power or fame. All expected to achieve those ends by associating with Etienne DeGuerre.

He did not begrudge them their aspirations, for he, too, had harbored similar ones himself—as long as they did not try to succeed to *his* detriment.

As his gaze returned to the interior of the great hall, Etienne noticed at once the discrepancy between the beautiful carving on the door frame and hearth, the polished paneling and painted walls, and the meager nature of the furnishings. Surely other, more lavish trappings had been sold to pay off the bulk of the earl's several debts. However, with some initial expenditure and Josephine's exquisite taste, this hall would soon be a showplace for his wealth and power.

Already he detected Josephine's touch in the flowers upon the table. He turned to her, pleased as always to think this beautiful creature was his and that men envied him all the more because of her. "Wherever did you find the flowers?"

His mistress gave him a surprised look. "That was none of my doing, Etienne," she replied in her soft, dulcet tones. "I was too busy seeing to our baggage. Some of the servants must have done it."

"Ah. No matter." Etienne reached forward to take another piece of bread and allowed himself to enjoy the extravagant feast. It would be quite some time before he would authorize such a meal, so he might as well indulge at the late earl's expense.

The bread was excellent, the meat spiced to perfection, the fruit fresh and the pastries light, proving that the late earl had an excellent cook, and that the victualing of this castle had not been done with an eye to expense. The servants did their jobs quickly and competently; obviously, they had been well trained.

What a place this must have been when the earl and his wife were still alive and wealthy! It was easy to imagine the luxury, the bustle, the many guests, the music and laughter. Easy, too, to envision a spoiled daughter unaware of the change about to befall her. But that was not his concern.

How different from the wattle and daub building that had been his lonely childhood home, presided over by his bitter, domineering mother, the only guest being the memories of his father.

That didn't matter now. He had risen above his past and the earl had died impoverished.

Etienne turned his mind to the other things the king had told him: the depletion of the stores caused by the late Earl of Westborough's generosity to anyone who arrived at his gates, whether noble or the poorest of beggars; the earl's careless treatment of illegal activity, especially poaching; the astonishing amounts of money—indeed, all that he had left in his coffers—that the earl had given to the church for masses and prayers. Not that there was much to give, after the disastrous harvest last autumn.

If Castle Frechette was a masterpiece, it was because the earl had promised his masons and carpenters lavish wages, and they had worked with a will. Unfortunately, when the true state of the earl's debts became clear at his death, all the furnishings had been sold to pay these wages, for the work could not be taken away.

Etienne had also noted the fine state of most of the peasants' dwellings as he had ridden toward the castle. The injustice of it had struck him immediately, that the earl should have lost his land while his tenants prospered.

He had heard, too, of the earl's wastrel son who had left the country in a fit of pique. Perhaps the young man had not known of the sorry state of his father's affairs, or the man's ill health, but he should have ensured that they knew how to reach him.

Because of Bryce Frechette's selfishness, his sister was in serious difficulty and completely alone. Yet, apparently, she did not condemn her brother for such childish behavior. Outside in the courtyard, she had been upset to hear the truth discussed in the open, in front of the tenants.

He leaned back thoughtfully, watching his men enjoy their meal. He supposed Gabriella Frechette would say, in her defiant, husky and compelling voice, that she loved her brother. It was distressing to think an otherwise formidable woman could be so blinded by an emotion.

Gabriella Frechette's predicament was already a thing of the past. She was surely already gone, and he would be left in possession of this, his tenth estate, the number he had set himself so many years ago when he was poor, and starving and freezing in the winter's snow. At last he had reached the end of the quest.

Etienne DeGuerre permitted himself another small, satisfied smile as he reached out to grasp his goblet. When it was halfway to his lips, he halted for a barely perceptible moment. Gabriella Frechette had just entered from the kitchen carrying a platter of meat, which she proceeded to serve to a delighted George de Gramercie.

God's teeth! He had thought she would gather her things and be gone before an hour had passed after her public humiliation. What would possess a woman to remain after that?

A new sensation tore through Etienne, one he had not felt in years upon years. He was suddenly ashamed that he had tried to humiliate this bold and fiercely proud woman.

He quickly subdued his reaction. Obviously she was not easily humbled, nor did she fully appreciate how precarious her new position was.

His gaze flashed around the hall. The other servants were guarded and watchful, but clearly just as proud of their former lord's daughter's defiance as she surely was of herself.

Philippe de Varenne was watching her, too, with a greedy look in his snake's eyes and a hungry smile on his thin lips. Even the usually jovial George was eyeing the wench with serious speculation.

Fortunately, Donald Bouchard could be counted on not to—but the young man was staring at Gabriella Frechette as if an angel were serving his dinner! The only man who seemed oblivious to Gabriella's presence was Seldon, who gave all his attention to his food.

Etienne's scrutiny returned to the provocative movement of Gabriella Frechette's shapely hips. Was it deliberately done or was it simply a gift of nature? Either way, if she stayed, she was going to cause trouble.

This situation could not continue. She must be made to leave before his men started quarreling over her and the other servants began to believe they could defy him with impunity.

"Gabriella!" he called, his voice slightly louder than usual.

She turned and walked toward him, a questioning look in her eyes, her dark, shapely brows lifted just a little, her pale, smooth cheeks tinged with a hint of a blush.

He could not go back on his ultimatum. That would be a sign of weakness that he simply would not permit. When he considered the state of his men, it occurred to him that she might be engaging in a different sort of battle, one that started with covert rebellion.

The little fool! He had seen campaigns of many kinds, including those waged by women, and he knew different attacks and defenses. He always got what he wanted. She should have heard enough about him to know that.

What did he want from her? To caress that shapely body? To crush those ruby lips against his own? To have her yield, willingly, fervently, with all the passion of her hate turned to burning desire...

His glance darted to Josephine, who was wiping her rosebud lips daintily with a napkin. God's wounds, he must be going to mad to even think of kissing this wench when he had Josephine de Chaney to share his bed. What kind of spell was this dispossessed noblewoman beginning to exert over him?

Gabriella halted, her full lips pulled into a thin line of strength and she bowed her head in acknowledgment.

He must and would control this estate, this castle, this hall and most of all, this woman. "Fill my goblet," he ordered.

Gabriella did as she was told, trying not to look at Baron DeGuerre's lean, handsome face illuminated by the many flambeaux set in sconces in the walls. Despite her self-confidence in the kitchen, she had dreaded meeting him again, and with good reason. His pale blue eyes were so intimidating in their inscrutability! The man was like a statue, betraying nothing of his feelings. Indeed, it was as if he were not quite human, but some kind of supernatural warrior put on earth to remind others that they were weak, frail vessels of humanity.

While she bent to fill his goblet with hands that *must* tremble, he moved not at all.

No, not a statue, she thought as she poured his wine slowly to avoid a spill. He was more like a cat sitting before a mouse's hole. She was aware of the others in the hall, but all her attention was focused on the man in front of her although she did not look directly at his face.

She had already seen enough of it. The baron's features, lean and battle-hardened, presided over by his cold, unrevealing eyes, might have belonged to a martyr. She doubted even being burned at the stake would make the man flinch. But he was no holy man. It was not hard to envision the baron's slender, strong fingers, grasping the goblet before her, around a man's throat, squeezing the breath from his body.

Gabriella forced herself to concentrate on her task so that she could finish and be gone, away from his intense eyes and unreadable face.

At last the baron moved, to lean back leisurely in his straight-backed chair with a motion of sinuous grace.

She tipped the vessel of wine up and backed away. Before she could leave, however, the baron smiled slowly, slyly, seductively, and said, "Go to my bedchamber."

"Etienne!" Josephine de Chaney gasped. Suspicion and pain appeared in her lovely green eyes, her reaction giving Gabriella a confirmation she did not want.

"Being a servant is new to you, so this *once* I will repeat myself," he said deliberately, ignoring his mistress. "Go to my bedchamber."

Gabriella could only stare at him, shocked, aghast and horrified. Surely he didn't—couldn't—mean it!

She felt as if she had been stripped naked in front of everyone. A wave of hot shame washed over her as she hoped against hope that he would rescind his order. She may be no more than a servant now, but she was a free woman. If he took her against her will, it would be rape. He would be committing a crime. She would go to... whom? Who would stand up for her against the powerful Baron DeGuerre, favorite of the king, the terror of tournaments, a man who had once fought for ten straight hours simply to win a bag of silver coins?

While he continued to regard her with those implacable blue eyes, she began to understand that she had engaged an enemy whose power and influence she had never fully considered.

But she had power and strength on her side, too. He would be a criminal if he touched her, and all would know it. And if he thought it necessary to stoop to such tactics, who had the upper hand then?

With her back as straight as an arrow's shaft, her carriage as regal as any queen, Gabriella turned and headed toward the wide staircase leading upward, toward the north tower and the bedchamber.

"Well, well, well, what are we to make of that?" Philippe de Varenne asked, gesturing with his head toward Gabriella as she disappeared inside the tower and those assembled in the hall broke the silence with a flurry of murmurs and whispers.

Sir George de Gramercie, usually so quick with a witty remark, could only raise his shapely, patrician brows and shake his head.

"I mean, I think we can all understand his intentions," Philippe went on before taking a large gulp of his wine. "I know what I'd do if I had a wench like that at my service."

"He's not going to hurt her," Donald said, both shocked and defensive.

"Oh, no, I never said he would *hurt* her," Philippe replied with a wink. "I'd give a purse of gold to know what Josephine is thinking at this particular moment."

The men glanced at her. Both the baron and Josephine de Chaney were eating as if nothing at all unusual had happened, which was very far from the truth.

"She'll never question him," George said with absolute certainty. "She's far too clever for that."

"Which makes her the perfect mistress, eh?" Philippe noted. "That and other talents."

"You are speaking of a lady," Donald said severely.

"A soiled dove of a lady," Seldon observed with more honesty than tact before shoving a large morsel of beef into his mouth.

"But a *lady* nonetheless," Donald answered. "Nor do I think it fitting to bandy about the name of the baron's lady, or to make such jests."

Seldon, who usually agreed with Donald and followed his lead, shrugged his shoulders. George grinned and Philippe clicked his tongue in disgust.

"Pardon me for offending your delicate sensibilities," Philippe said, "but no matter how beautiful she is, Josephine de Chaney is still a—"

George held up his hand. "Not exactly, and I believe the distinction is worth noting," he warned the impetuous young man beside him. "And she *is* a noblewoman."

"Yes, she is," Donald said firmly.

"Aye!" Seldon seconded, wiping his lips with his large hand.

"Oh, very well," Philippe grudgingly conceded. "However, that Gabriella, she's not anymore." He smiled, and it was not a pleasant sight. "Let us drink to the impertinent Gabriella," he said, raising his goblet. "I daresay she'll be taught a lesson she won't soon forget, eh?"

Donald looked appalled. Seldon did, too, but it was George who was the first to speak. "Philippe," he said with a touch of anger in his usually mildly amused voice, "you know the baron will not harm her."

"Then why did he order her upstairs?" Philippe demanded.

George chuckled ruefully. "He probably has something he wants her to do."

"That's precisely my point," Philippe said as he sullenly surveyed the others.

"I meant *work*," George chided. "Maybe something to do with his boots or his cloak. He has no body servant, you will recall."

"So you think he's planning on having a female body servant? A most fascinating concept, I grant you."

"All I'm saying is," George replied, "the baron has never dishonored a woman in his life to my knowledge, and I see no reason for him to start now."

"You don't? Are you blind, man? She's got the roundest, most delectable—"

"We noticed," Donald interrupted, blushing like a boy.

"Did you?" Philippe asked Donald. "I thought you concerned yourself solely with the life to come."

"And my duty here on earth," Donald said stoutly. "It is our duty, as knights of the realm, to protect women."

"Besides, why would the baron risk a charge of rape when she's so skinny?" Seldon asked solemnly.

"You would dare to fight the baron over a serving wench?" Philippe demanded, ignoring Seldon.

"Yes, I would," Donald replied with conviction.

"God's holy heaven!" Philippe chided as he looked at Donald. "You *should* have been a monk."

"That little bailiff didn't look at all happy, poor fellow," George remarked, obviously attempting to defuse the tense situation. "He ran out of the hall like he was pursued by one of the hounds."

"What's he got to be upset about?" Philippe said as he filled his goblet again. "He's still the bailiff. For now."

"I daresay he's been harboring a tender feeling for his late lord's daughter, if I'm any judge, and I think I am. He's probably been pining in secret. Poor fellow, I don't think he'd stand a chance with a woman of such spirit."

"He didn't defend her," Donald said. "If he truly cared for her, he would."

"Come now, Donald," George replied. "He isn't a knight. I wouldn't be surprised if he's completely terrified of Baron DeGuerre. She wasn't, though. Whoever would have imagined a woman standing up to Baron DeGuerre?''

"He's not a god, you know," Philippe said scornfully. "You all treat Baron DeGuerre like he's the second coming!"

"You say that because you're new to his service," George said affably. "You've never seen him fight. By God, you'd change your tune fast enough then."

"Perhaps," Philippe said, clearly unconvinced.

"Our Donald's still suffering the effects of being trained by Fitzroy," George said with a sad smile and laughing eyes. "That man's notions concerning the fairer sex are even more strict than the baron's."

"Ah, yes, the famous Fitzroy," Philippe said. "I wouldn't mind facing him in a tournament someday. You fought him once, didn't you, Seldon?"

Seldon looked away. "Yes."

"And you lost?"

"Yes."

"It wasn't quite a fair fight, I believe?"

"Shut your mouth and leave it," Donald snarled, rising. "That was a long time ago, and he's made up for it since."

"Of course, of course, calm yourself!" Philippe declared. "I simply asked."

"Come now, we are getting far too worked up. It must be the fine wine," George said. "We are all friends here."

Donald was not appeased. "I've had quite enough of you for one night," he said to Philippe, his teeth clenched. "Good night!"

He marched from the hall, followed a moment later by Seldon. "That wasn't very nice, Philippe," George said coldly. "Seldon was a boy when he did that unwise thing."

"He's still a dullard," Philippe replied, reaching out for more wine.

George raised his wine in a salute. "Let us drink to women in general, eh, Philippe? Will that satisfy you?"

They raised their goblets and drank, then lowered them as Baron DeGuerre rose from the table. They watched silently as he spoke a few quiet words to Josephine de Chaney, whose face betrayed no emotion, before he went to the tower stairs and disappeared from view.

"One of us is going to be satisfied tonight," Philippe said nastily.

"I think I'll go, too. You're getting drunk, and you're rather poor company when you're in that state."

Philippe took a large gulp of wine and watched George saunter away. He didn't care what they thought. They were all cowards, bowing and scraping before Baron DeGuerre.

He took a few more gulps. He didn't care what the baron thought, either. The man was mortal, like all the rest, and he lacked breeding, too.

Why didn't women see that? Why did they always pass over him, so much more deserving, and try to entice the baron? No matter what the others thought, he was sure that was what Gabriella Frechette was trying to do. She was a mere woman, after all.

A pretty, shapely woman with no male relative to protect her. God's wounds, what he wouldn't give to be in the baron's place at this particular moment.

Well, let the baron tame her first. He, Philippe, could wait.

Chapter Three

Gabriella wiped her sweating palms on the skirt of her gown as she paced the length of her parents' bed-chamber and struggled to stay calm. It was a losing battle, every moment seeming an hour while she waited for the baron to appear, trying desperately to convince herself that he would not dare to hurt her.

Her eyes caught sight of the narrow bed, the replacement she had provided for her parents' ornate one. Her gaze quickly returned to the marble beneath her feet.

Oh, if only Bryce were here! He would save her. He wouldn't shrink from fighting the baron himself, if he had to. He was always ready for an altercation, with his father, with Chalfront, with the reeve, the miller, the cloth merchants. How many times had she acted as mediator? Too many to count. She had come to pride herself on her diplomacy.

What had happened to her skill when she had con-fronted Baron DeGuerre? Had pride made her fool-ish? Had she felt so secure in her place and in the servants' regard that she had stupidly risked speaking without deference to Baron DeGuerre? Or had she been too upset to think with necessary clarity?

Whatever she had thought, she would never have guessed he would assert his authority by vile means.

She still could not quite believe it. She had never heard his reputation sullied with such an accusation, or any other abuse of women. He was said to be ruthless with his opponents in tournaments, but not vengeful. His ambition was considerable, yet many men wanted power and wealth. Women vied for his attention. Would they, if he was a rough and violent man?

Or was she desperately seeking succor where there could be none?

Once again she cursed herself for a stubborn fool. Would it have been so hard to bow her head, to act afraid, to cower before him? To at least remain silent in his presence?

Perhaps if she did so when he finally came here, he would let her go. She would kneel before him and beg forgiveness. Anything to let her retain her honor. After all, her personal honor was all she had left.

Yet what kind of honor was it that begged? If he harmed her, he would be in the wrong. She would know it, and the people would know it. Her family was not totally friendless. She could tell others what he had done. She would dishonor *him*.

What was she thinking? This was a man who lived openly with his mistress, and Josephine de Chaney was but one of a long line. He refused to give the proper tithes to the Church, and he was harsh in his punishment of those he perceived to have broken the law. It was said the only thing Baron DeGuerre respected was power, and she had none.

Gabriella pressed her frigid hands to her hot cheeks. Why did he not come? Was this part of her torture, this agony of waiting?

She went to the window and looked out in the faint light of the slender moon. Once this land had belonged to her family, until her father had let Chalfront take charge.

Chalfront! Her hands balled into fists. She hated the bailiff as much as the baron, with his talk of help and assistance, when she knew—knew!—that her father's financial difficulties were his fault.

What was Chalfront thinking now? Was he pleased to see her humbled and humiliated by Baron DeGuerre?

The door burst open and crashed against the wall as the baron strode in, looking like the very devil in his long black robe, his chestnut hair brushing his shoulders in that heathen fashion, his eyes gleaming demonically in the flickering light of the flambeaux he carried and set in a socket on the wall.

Gabriella stepped back into the shadows, trying somehow to hide.

Baron DeGuerre looked around until he saw her. With a leering smile made grotesque by the shadows cast by the torch's flame, he closed the door, shutting her inside the room with him. "Come here, Gabriella," he said, his deep voice low but the command clear.

Now was the time to beg for mercy, Gabriella thought desperately. She told herself she should throw herself on her knees. Implore. Plead.

Instead, all the proud heritage of her noble blood asserted itself within her, and she simply could not be the instrument of her own further humiliation.

The baron's brown brows lowered as his hands went to the lacing at the neck of his robe. With slow movements his long fingers untied the knot there, and as she watched, speechless, he drew the heavy garment over his head and let it fall in a heap on the floor.

His chest was muscular, covered with several small scars of battle, his broad shoulders powerful, his arms lean and sinewy beside his narrow waist. His hips, encased in taut chausses, were slender, but muscular, too.

Not taking his eyes from her, he went to the bed and sat on it. "Come here and take off my boots, Gabriella."

He had the strength to defeat her. She could fight all she wanted, and he would triumph at last. Struggling against him would be useless.

Slowly Gabriella raised her eyes to his face. What was he, really, but a man, and one completely in the wrong? She had righteousness on her side, and surely God would help her. She would not let this man defeat her. There must be some way, some weakness, if only she could find it....

"Take off my boots, Gabriella." He held up a booted foot and waited as if he had no expectation of refusal.

With watchful eyes, still searching for an opportunity, Gabriella moved slowly toward him. She reached out to take his boot in her hands—and then she thrust his leg up as far as she could and made a dash for the door.

Not fast enough. He was off the bed in an instant. He grabbed her arm before she could reach the latch, yanking her around and pulling her against him. His icy blue eyes stared down into hers as she struggled in his strong, encircling arms.

All her efforts to disengage herself from his grasp seemed to be no more than a petty inconvenience to him. Aware of his arms around her, his naked chest against her rapidly rising and falling breasts, the proximity of his mouth, she stopped struggling. "You can't do this!" she cried desperately.

"I can't prevent a servant from leaving my bedchamber before she has finished her work?" he asked coolly, not attempting to tighten his embrace.

"Work?" she gasped incredulously. "Is that what you call it? You have a mistress for that!"

"I don't need an unwilling wench to excite me," he said, letting go of her and stepping away toward a table bearing a goblet of wine, "although you might consider Josephine's example as a way of achieving your former level of prosperity. She, too, comes from an impoverished noble family."

Freed from his grasp and convinced that he did not mean to rape her, Gabriella frowned at his insult. "I will never be any man's whore!" she said, tossing her head.

The baron arched one eyebrow as he turned to look at her. "I would not be so quick to condemn Josephine de Chaney," he said as he picked up the goblet.

"What do you know of her life, or the choices *she* has been forced to make?"

"I would rather die than take such a course!"

He took a sip of the wine. "Really? I wonder." He sauntered toward the bed, then faced her, running his gaze over her in a way that brought a blush to her face. "Josephine needs a maidservant. I think you would do well in that capacity. Now take my tunic and wash it."

She tried to decide if he meant what he said, or if he was toying with her.

"I assume you know how to wash a simple tunic?" the baron asked sarcastically when she did not move at once.

She did not, but she nodded anyway.

"Then take it and go." His tone was dismissive, and she knew she was indeed free to leave.

She quickly gathered up the discarded garment in her arms. It smelled of leather and horse and smoke... and him.

As she started to rise, she realized a woman was standing on the threshold.

"Ah, Josephine," the baron drawled. "Why the delay, my dear?"

Josephine de Chaney's look was sweetly venomous as Gabriella hesitated, not wishing to push past the lady whose voluminous skirts filled the doorway, but anxious to be gone.

"You're not jealous of this serving wench, surely?" the baron said with a deep, throaty chuckle that contained no true joy. He came toward his mistress and pulled her into his arms, out of the doorway.

The way clear, a relieved Gabriella hurried out of the room. Once in the corridor, she glanced over her shoulder to see Josephine de Chaney bent back over the baron's powerful arm while he kissed her with fierce, unbridled lust. Before she could go on her way, Baron DeGuerre raised his eyes and looked at her over Josephine's head, his lips still upon his paramour's and the expression in his eyes mocking.

As Etienne continued to kiss Josephine, he subdued a smile that had nothing to do with the beautiful woman he held in his arms.

Now Gabriella Frechette should finally understand her place, he thought. It crossed his mind that he might have thought of a better means of education; however, he had not, and he never wasted time with useless regrets.

Not that he would ever have taken Gabriella against her will. He truly despised men who violated women of any status, and he would certainly never stoop to such a loathsome tactic.

How much better and easier it would have been if the wench had been born a servant in this castle. Then he would have given her a small present, she would have been thankful, he would have given her another and made a proposition, which she would surely have accepted, and then she would be in his arms, returning his kiss with passionate intensity....

"A moment!" Josephine protested softly as she reached up to grasp her stiffened crown and scarf that he had pushed askew. "You are going to strangle me, my love!" Josephine gently extricated herself from his embrace, watching him shrewdly as she walked past him, carefully folding the expensive scarf and placing the jeweled headdress on the table.

He realized she often looked at him thus, like a master attempting to gauge a pupil's response. When had he ever seen Josephine truly passionate, whether with desire or hate? Never before had it occurred to him how cool and remote she often was; or perhaps, if he had noticed, he would have considered that a blessing, for he had no wish to be tied to a woman in any way. His two marriages, both of them advantageous alliances, had not been pleasant experiences. When each of his wives had died, he had been more relieved than sorry. Fortunately, he no longer had any need to increase his personal wealth or power by such a method.

What was the matter with him? He had the most beautiful woman in the kingdom to share his bed. More than that, she was also a wise and perceptive woman. Even if she was desperate to know what had passed between himself and Gabriella, she would never ask.

He had the perfect arrangement with Josephine. He gave her gifts, fed and housed her and even allowed her to act as hostess in return for the pleasures of her body and the reward of her beauty. She was like a tournament prize, a living, breathing illustration to all men that he could have the most beautiful woman in the kingdom.

"What happened to your tunic?" Josephine asked as she sat down before her mirror.

It struck Etienne that since he had entered this room, he had not observed its state at all. His attention had been drawn to Gabriella immediately.

The chamber was distinctly barren, except for the items that had been unloaded immediately from the baggage carts. No tapestries, only one chair, Josephine's own table where she kept her perfumes, another bearing wine, the mirror, their chests of clothing and a bed that was much too narrow. He would have that remedied tomorrow. As for the rest, Josephine would see to it.

"I thought Gabriella needed to learn who was in command here," Etienne replied, answering her unspoken question.

Josephine's reflection revealed a mildly surprised and pensive reaction. "Half-naked?" she inquired. "Still, if you wished to impress her, I can think of no better way."

Etienne turned away to hide the sudden flush of a blush, something he had not felt since he was a youth. At that moment, Etienne DeGuerre would have died before admitting that Josephine, the wise, the shrewd, had guessed something even he had not dared to confess to himself. Deep in his heart, he had expected Gabriella to be overwhelmed by his physical presence, as so many women were. He had more than half expected her to fall into his arms, or at least respond to the sensation of his embrace. When she had not, only then had he concocted the excuse that she should wash his tunic.

"What is it?" Josephine asked, genuine distress in her voice.

"It is too cold in here." He went toward the battered chest he had used all his life. He opened the lid and drew out his fur-lined robe.

Josephine gave him a glorious smile, reminding him of her beauty. "This castle is a fine one, Etienne. A worthy gift from the king. With some proper furnishings, this room will be quite comfortable." She hesitated a moment. "I am not surprised she refused to leave it."

Etienne did not insult Josephine's intelligence by asking who she meant. "I didn't expect her to stay. She seems an overly proud woman." He wrapped himself in the robe, the fur soft against his naked skin.

"But one with limited alternatives," Josephine noted. "She is not unattractive. Perhaps someone will offer to marry her. Will you allow that?"

"Of course," he answered brusquely, then told himself he was simply annoyed as always when Josephine spoke of marriage. From the beginning, he had made it very clear that he had no intention of marrying again. For him, marriage had been terrible, his wives demanding his attention when he had more important business to attend to than what he would like on the table for the evening meal or if he liked her latest gown bought at great expense. And as for the alleged pleasures of the nuptial bed—he would rather spend ten hours in the saddle than make love to a woman raised only to be a nobleman's wife, taught that what took place in the marriage bed was merely a disagreeable duty to be endured.

"The bailiff seems most anxious about her," Josephine remarked with another smile.

"Why do you say that? He did little enough to defend her below."

"I saw his face when you ordered her to this room," Josephine said. "He was most upset and actually ran out of the hall."

"If he wants her, he can have her," Etienne replied. "For the present, I ordered her to wash my tunic."

Josephine's brow furrowed with a frown. "It is not her fault that her father was a wastrel," she said softly.

"I know, and that is why I gave her money to leave. She chose not to take it."

"But a laundress!" Josephine looked at him with mild reproof. Still, even that much condemnation was rare for her.

He went to Josephine and took hold of her slender shoulders. "I do not mean for her to be that permanently. You need a maid, and she will know what you need done."

Josephine did not meet his gaze. "Yes, I need a maid."

He pressed a kiss to her fingertips. "There is no need for you to be jealous," he assured her, and leaned down to kiss her lightly.

"She is a pretty creature."

"I had not noticed," Etienne lied. "Gabriella Frechette means nothing to me. You seem to be seeing jealousy everywhere."

An obviously relieved Josephine flashed him a brilliant smile. "Since I have no maid for the time being, Etienne," she murmured huskily, presenting her back to him, "will you help me with my gown?"

Etienne went to stand behind her, untying the laces below her pale, smooth neck, a thoughtful frown on his face.

He should be extremely happy. He was rich, powerful and respected, and he had done it all on his own, with no help from influential friends or family. He had achieved every one of his cherished ambitions: wealth, fame and power. More, he had fulfilled the destiny his mother had always claimed for him, the destiny the death of his father before he was born had seemed to circumvent. He *was* very happy.

"Thank you, Etienne," Josephine whispered. "I can finish by myself."

"As you wish." He went to the bed and began to pull off his boots, recalling for a moment the astounded look on Gabriella's face when he had requested her assistance. Clearly she had expected him to drag her onto the bed and overpower her, and he marveled at the defiant pride she maintained in the presence of such a belief.

She really was unlike any woman he had ever met. It was a pity the circumstances of their lives were as they were.

As he straightened and looked at Josephine while she brushed her hair, her body wrapped in a velvet robe, an overwhelming feeling of loneliness swamped him. Theirs was little more than a business arrangement. He did not love her, and he was quite certain she did not love him.

Which was of no consequence. They were pleased with each other, and understood the boundaries of their relationship. If he was lacking anything, it was only a son and heir, and that was not important. He had worked and fought not to acquire goods to bequeath to some unknown offspring who might squander them away, but for himself alone.

With renewed resolution to put the late earl's daughter from his thoughts, he went to stand behind Josephine. He took the brush from her hand and set it down, then ran his fingers through the golden cascade. She sighed and leaned back against him, the contact increasing his arousal.

His hands slipped down her slender neck to her shoulders, and into the bodice of her gown toward her breasts. Gently he caressed her, her nipples pebbling beneath his palms, until she moaned with unabashed pleasure.

He removed his hands and she rose without speaking, turning toward him, a gleam of unmistakable lust in her limpid green eyes as she brushed her fingers over his hardened manhood.

As he closed his eyes, he was determined to lose himself in the delight of Josephine's talent, to enjoy her exquisite body and to marvel at her particular skills.

Gabriella was surely a virgin.

Etienne pulled Josephine impatiently into his arms and pushed his tongue between her lips tinted with red wine while he gripped her buttocks and pressed her to him. This was the woman who shared his body and his bed. He would think of no other.

With a low moan, Josephine responded, her hips moving seductively and her expert fingers caressing the muscles of his back. Her tongue flicked against his nipples, adding to the exquisite sensations.

"I was indeed a fool to be jealous," she murmured as she arched against him.

"Yes, you were," Etienne replied, kissing her passionately and effectively stopping any additional discussion. He had no wish to further examine the state of his emotions, and he knew of one very good way to quiet his thoughts.

Chapter Four

Perched precariously on her haunches on the bank of the river where the townsfolk did their washing, Gabriella lifted the wet, heavy tunic and began to wring it out. It was an arduous process, complicated by the sheer size and weight of the garment, as well as the fact that her freezing hands ached with the unfamiliar task. Cold water ran down her arms, dampening her bodice and soaking her skirt so that it clung to her uncomfortably.

A group of women from the town were doing their laundry a short distance away, occasionally glancing at her so woefully that Gabriella wanted to scream that she had done nothing wrong, that the baron had not attacked her, that she did not need or want their pity or their sorrowful looks. What she wanted was their friendship, or some sense that she had not erred in doing whatever was necessary to remain here.

She let her gaze pass over them down the river toward the mill. A group of laborers were busy there, replacing the grindstone, or so Guido had said, and the huge wheel was still. The cook had been delighted to tell her about it, for apparently he had been complaining to her father for weeks about the quality of flour and blaming it on the old and worn grindstone. It seemed the baron, on his first full day as master of the estate, had seen that for himself, among other things, and given orders that it was to be replaced immediately. Several of the outbuildings were to be rethatched, more hay had been purchased for the livestock that would be allowed to overwinter, and the castle stores were to be replenished, albeit not with the luxurious foodstuffs the earl had preferred, but more common fare such as peas and lentils.

Word had also flown through the castle that the baron was asking about poaching. The baron possessed the right of *infangenethef,* to punish poachers caught within the bounds of his estate, and woe betide the man who would be judged by him!

Although her father had also been granted that right, he had turned a blind eye to poaching, claiming the peasants worked better with a full stomach. She didn't doubt his wisdom; however, in the case of a man like Osric, who had been brought before her father three times for the offense and who was yet the hayward, she wondered if he had been too kind.

Her father had also been indifferent when it came to collecting the *gersum,* which was the fee a man would pay for taking possession of a tenancy, as well as the tenants' tax, and the *heriot,* the payment to the lord of the best beast a villein possessed on his death.

The baron would certainly demand everything that was his due. He had even gone into tenants' byres and outbuildings personally, seeking livestock not registered on the estate lists.

Gabriella cursed softly as the hem of the weighty, wet tunic dragged in the mud. Whoever would have guessed simply washing one garment could be so difficult? She had not, and had refused Alda's offer of assistance. Now she felt an increased respect for the castle maidservants. Nevertheless, she had been given this job to do, and she would do it with the same thoroughness that the baron was giving to the running of his estate.

In truth, she welcomed the chance to wash the garment. All night, it had laid at the end of her bed, a constant reminder of her confrontation with the baron, and the frightening moment he had removed it. The sooner she washed it and returned it to the bedchamber, the better.

Getting a good grip on the tunic, she pressed her teeth together tightly as she wrung another portion with all her strength. If only this was the baron's neck she held and not his clothes . . .

"My lady!"

She looked over her shoulder as Chalfront approached. He ran his hand over his jowls nervously and looked about him as if he expected some disaster to befall him. However, he often wore that expression, and he had escaped unscathed thus far, so she turned back to her work. "What do you want?" she asked, hearing him stop behind her.

"I . . . I wanted to say that I'm glad he didn't hurt you," the man said.

"You've said it, so you may leave me alone."

"Gabriella!" he protested, squatting down beside her.

How much she wanted to tell him that he had no right to call her by her first name, except that she was now merely a servant and he outranked her. That realization was nearly as galling as anything the baron had said or done. "What are you doing here?" she demanded.

"I must speak with you!" he whined. "I've been looking for you since dawn."

She glanced at the curious women. She wanted nothing at all to do with Robert Chalfront and she writhed inwardly at the thought of being linked to him in any way.

"Why are you avoiding me?"

"I am too busy to take any notice of your whereabouts," she said, her tone cold and brusque in her desperation for him to be gone.

"I want to make sure the baron hasn't...doesn't... mistreat you."

"*What?*" she cried, disbelief in her voice and expression as she straightened with the wet tunic in her hands. "And what would you do if he had?" she asked. "Heaven forbid that you should criticize your new master, for *anything* he might do!"

"I would!"

"As you did last night when he ordered me to his bedchamber?" She raised her voice as much for the benefit of the listening women as to lend force to her words. "He did not harm me in any way. He only gave me this to wash." She thrust the black garment out like a dagger in the hands of an assassin. "And I have done so. Now go away, Robert, and let me finish my work. Won't the baron need you to wipe his lips or pull out his chair?"

He grabbed her arm. "You must and shall listen to me!" he cried, a flash of anger in his usually cowlike eyes.

"Take your hand off me," she said fiercely.

"You are not the mistress of this estate anymore, Gabriella," he proclaimed desperately, his grip tightening, "and you *will* listen to what I have to say. I want you to pay attention to me. *Me!* For once in your life!"

She had never seen Robert like this before, and he almost frightened her. Unsure what to do, she forced herself to remain calm. "You are hurting me."

He became instantly contrite, again the helpless child. "Why won't you marry me?" he asked mournfully. "I could pay your debt and you would never have to wash a thing!"

"I don't love you. I could *never* love you," she said firmly. She could not believe that he didn't understand. His unreasonable persistence was beyond annoying. She had certainly made her feelings, or lack thereof, known the first time he had proposed—and the second and the third and every time after that.

"But *why?*"

She clasped the wet tunic to her chest. "For the last time, Robert, I will never marry you. I would sooner marry the Baron DeGuerre than you!" she replied, citing the most outrageous example she could think of.

Which seemed to be the appropriate means to pierce Chalfront's self-delusion. The hopeful light went out of his eyes, and although she didn't enjoy seeing it, she couldn't help feeling relieved.

Then he sighed and said, "You needn't have put me in danger with your false accusations."

"*False* accusations?"

"The baron does not trust me, and there is no reason he should not."

"You led my father into ruin and worried him into an early grave!" she charged.

"Do you still believe that?" he asked incredulously." I did everything I could to help him—but he wouldn't listen! Why, I even used my own money to try to pay his final debts!"

He had told her that before, when he had first broached the subject of marriage to her. At the time, she had thought he was saying so only to make her consider his suit. Yet now, when he finally appeared to comprehend that he had nothing to gain, he still maintained what had seemed to her to be impossible, and there was a ring of truth in his words that she found hard to deny. "Why would you do that?" she demanded in a low voice, aware that the women's eyes were still upon them.

"For you," he said softly, looking at her with pleading eyes like a lonesome dog. "To know that I was helping you by doing so, so that I might have one kind word from you."

"You . . . you should have asked my father to raise the rents!" she said.

"I love you, Gabriella! I would do anything for you, for even one kind word from you. I had hoped you would be grateful—"

"Well, well, well, what touching scene is this?"

Gabriella and Robert moved quickly apart as Philippe de Varenne strolled toward them. With his sleek black hair, dark garments and narrow eyes, he reminded Gabriella of a hawk before the falconer let it fly after its prey. She clutched the damp tunic more tightly to her chest. Chalfront, pale and panting, looked as if he were seriously contemplating running away as fast as his legs would carry him.

"What business have you accosting the maidservants, Chalfront?" de Varenne demanded scornfully.

"Sir, I...I..." Chalfront stammered helplessly.

"None, I think, beyond trying to seduce her, eh?"

Gabriella had never wanted to slap a man's face so much in her life. No, not even the baron's, for he had not looked at her with such bold, lustful impertinence, even when he held her fast in his arms.

"My...lord! Sir! You misunderstand!" Chalfront spluttered.

"He was not trying to seduce me," Gabriella said firmly.

"No? It certainly looked as if he were up to something. I suggest you run along, Chalfront. I believe the baron is looking for you."

Chalfront's glance darted from Philippe de Varenne to Gabriella, then back to Philippe before he bobbed his head and hurried away.

"If he troubles you, you should let me know," Philippe said condescendingly.

In truth, this man troubled her far more than Chalfront ever would or could. "If you will excuse me, sir, I have work to do."

"So I see," Philippe replied, grabbing the tunic from her and holding it out. "He has made you a washerwoman?"

She didn't answer as she shivered from the dampness of her bodice.

He ran his gaze over her and suddenly she realized that her wet clothes clung to her skin and her nipples had puckered with the cold. She hugged herself, as much to shield her body from his lascivious stare as for warmth. "If you will excuse me, sir," she said again through clenched teeth.

"Of course, pretty Gabriella." He held out the garment so that she had to reach for it. She took hold of it, but he would not release it. Instead, he tugged hard, so that she was pulled against his chest. Before she could respond to his impertinent action, he stepped away and started to chuckle smugly. "I must have you do my laundry, too."

"Philippe!" The baron's voice rumbled toward them from the drawbridge. She had been so intent first on Chalfront and then Philippe de Varenne that she had not seen the baron approach. He was mounted on his black stallion and accompanied by Sir George, as well as a small armed troop. As always, the baron was dressed in black and wearing no jewelry. His cloak was thrown back over his shoulder, revealing his muscular chest, and his sword brushed against his thigh.

Sir George wore a bright cloak of robin's egg blue lined with scarlet. His tunic was also red, trimmed with gold, and his hose was blue. He gave her a warm and sympathetic smile, which did little to assuage her embarrassment.

"Adieu, Gabriella," Philippe said with a parting leer before he sauntered toward his lord, who watched them with an impassive face.

Gabriella, clutching the wet garment again to her chest, glared past Philippe to the man who was responsible for putting her in a position to have to endure Philippe de Varenne's rudeness, then turned on her heel and marched away.

Two days later, Etienne sat in the solar and rubbed his aching temples as he stared at the pile of documents spread out on the table before him. He was attempting to wade through the last of the lists, charters, receipts and records that pertained to his new estate. He would be a happy man when his steward was able to leave his other estate to come here and take charge of the accounts himself.

It was not just that the late earl had been an overgenerous, lax superintendent and that the bailiff had felt it necessary to record every ha'penny spent or received; reading itself taxed Etienne's patience, since he was far from skilled at it. He had learned to read when he was a grown man, out of necessity rather than desire, and he would far sooner spend his days in the lists facing the couched lances of aggressive knights than studying these cramped letters and figures.

He had spent several more hours in the past few days examining lists of tenants' goods and accounts, supervising the arrival and purchase of necessary food and furnishings, as well as riding through the estate looking for livestock conveniently left off such lists, and finding several, all obviously the best beasts their

masters owned. He had seen to the repair of the mill
and the granary, for it seemed that the late earl, so
particular about his castle, had been much less so
about other buildings on his estate. He had realized
that poaching was going to be a problem, for his men
had found several traps and snares in the estate woods.
They had no clue who had set them, or if they were the
work of one man or a gang. Whoever was breaking the
law, when they were caught, they would rue the day
they tried to do so on *his* estate.

Outside, a heavy rain fell, which meant all of his
men were cooped up inside instead of out in the woods
hunting or practicing their fighting skills in the nearby
meadow or the large courtyard. He could discern their
voices coming from the great hall. Philippe was teasing Seldon about a rather plump serving wench that
Seldon fancied. If Philippe wasn't careful, he would
wind up with a broken nose. It would serve him right,
Etienne thought coldly, and might cure the fellow of
some of his vanity.

Again Etienne remembered Gabriella and Philippe
on the riverbank. How angry she had been, and jus-
tifiably so, and how attractive, with her thick, curling
hair and blushing cheeks, her gleaming brown eyes
and defiant stance, holding his tunic against her perfect breasts. For a moment, he had envied his tunic.

He wondered what Philippe had said to her, although that wasn't so very difficult to guess. Her response was rather obvious, too. However, the baron
didn't doubt that he could control the young man for
some time yet, and hoped that de Varenne's ambition
would soon lead him elsewhere.

It was regrettable, perhaps, that Gabriella Frechette should be in such a tenuous position, but that could not be helped. He had done his best to compel her to leave, and she had refused. She would have to face the consequences.

He sighed, then reminded himself that he should be giving his attention to the documents before him.

Nevertheless, in another moment, Etienne was distracted by Philippe's scornful voice, Donald's serious tones and George's pleasant intercession, no doubt trying to solve a conflict. Before he could figure out what they were talking about, their voices dropped. Apparently George had managed to circumvent trouble again. One day George was going to make some lucky woman a fine husband, if the indifferent fellow could ever be persuaded to make such a decision.

A woman's laugh wafted into the solar, and he recognized it as Josephine's. She had found plenty of things to do since their arrival, and quite happily had seen to the decorating of the hall and bedchamber. He understood she was busily working on a new tapestry for their bedchamber, which was now as comfortably furnished as any man could wish, a delight for the eyes as well as the succor of the body.

He surveyed the solar, noting with pleasure the carved lintel and the rain splashing against the glass windows. To be sure, such decorative measures were extravagant, yet he was fast coming to believe that the pleasure was worth the price. Within reasonable limits, of course.

Chalfront, looking like a whipped dog, sidled into the solar, yet more parchment scrolls in his hands.

Etienne was beginning to understand why someone would dislike Robert Chalfront. He had all the personality of a limp rag, and was so obsequious, the baron was often tempted to shake him. He never ventured an opinion, but seemed to expect to be told everything. It was a wonder he could find it in his power to decide how to dress each day! On the other hand, he was responsible and meticulous, working as diligently as if this estate was his own.

Nevertheless, Etienne had to subdue the urge to scowl. Really, the fellow had no need to look so browbeaten. Perhaps had the bailiff possessed a more forceful personality, the late earl might not have been so exploited by his tenants.

With a slight sigh, Etienne reached out for his chalice of wine before glancing at the bailiff, who sat on the opposite side of the long trestle table at Etienne's gestured invitation.

Etienne drank deeply of the delicious wine, thinking that he would have been very pleased if the earl had laid in a larger store of the beverage before his death. "You have certainly documented everything thoroughly," he remarked, making his words a compliment instead of betraying any hint of his frustration. "Just tell me, how many villeins are *ad censum?*"

"There are twenty-two who pay rents in cash, my lord," Chalfront replied eagerly. "David Marchant the miller pays the most, fifty shillings a year, and John the Smith pays the least, two farthings. The rest are listed here." He indicated another closely but neatly written parchment.

"And these?" Etienne waved at the following group of names on the same parchment.

"Those are the villeins *ad opus*. Beside their names, you will see that I have noted what work is expected of them per week and per annum, my lord."

Etienne gave the bailiff a brief nod and the list an even briefer glance. "You seem to enjoy making lists, Robert."

"I enjoy having things neat and orderly, my lord," Chalfront replied respectfully. "I would draw your attention to my notes regarding the mill rate and pannage, my lord, and—"

"My head aches," the baron said truthfully, silencing the bailiff. He picked up a document with an elaborate seal, and another one with a smaller seal. "This is my Charter of Extent," he said, indicating the former, "detailing the lands, services and rents I am supposed to receive, and this is the Charter of Custumal, the obligations and rights of the tenants, that I found among the late earl's papers. I want you to examine them and tell me if everything is in order."

The bailiff's pale blue eyes widened. "You would trust me with this responsibility, my lord?" he marveled.

"Yes," Etienne replied, only then considering that perhaps he was not wise to give this fellow such a duty. "For the present. My steward, Jean Luc Ducette, will be arriving in a fortnight. He will examine the records when he arrives. He had better be able to confirm what you have to tell me."

The bailiff nodded enthusiastically.

"What are all these other lists?" Etienne asked, gesturing vaguely toward another pile of papers.

"I thought you would wish to have certain information before the tenants swear their oaths of loyalty. Here are three new men who have yet to pay their *gersum* for becoming your tenants," Chalfront said, pointing to a group of names on the topmost document. "This man needs to pay the *merchet* before his daughter weds next month. These two men have died since the earl, and no one has collected the *heriot*. And finally, my lord, I really think you should decide about the pannage."

"What did the earl usually ask for the privilege of letting pigs roam in his forest?"

Chalfront named sums that would have been appropriate in the last century, and Etienne said as much. "No wonder the earl found himself penniless," he added. The baron eyed Chalfront shrewdly. "Why did you not inform the earl that he was not demanding nearly enough?"

"I did, my lord," Chalfront said with great humility. "He refused to listen, even when I made it clear that he had set himself and his family on the road to ruin. He was a man who wanted very much to be liked by his tenants. Too much, perhaps, but it is certain that they all genuinely mourned at his death."

If Etienne needed any additional confirmation that the late earl was a man of misplaced priorities, Robert Chalfront just provided it. It was not important that one's tenants *liked* their lord; it was important that they respect him, obey him and make him a wealthy man. "I see." Etienne ran his gaze over the unprepossessing man sitting across from him. Would a man like that truly dare to upbraid his master? Would he have the courage to make the consequences of the earl's misplaced generosity apparent? Or would he mumble and stutter and try to follow the lord's instructions somehow?

"Forgive the intrusion, my lord."

Etienne recognized the rarely heard feminine voice immediately and looked toward the door. Gabriella wore the same simple, golden brown homespun garment she always did. Apparently it was none the worse for wear after its soaking the other day, when it had clung so tantalizingly to her body.

He noticed that she looked pale and tired; however, her eyes still gleamed with a defiant light to which he was becoming accustomed. Etienne was quite used to seeing contempt in a person's eyes when they spoke to him, and if seeing that in these particular eyes troubled him, he was well able to subdue the reaction.

Nevertheless, he would have given much to know what she was thinking as she stood there watching him dissect what had been her father's estate, although he thought he could make a good guess. She probably wished him at the bottom of the millpond with the new grindstone tied around his neck, and with the same intensity that he wished she was waiting for him in his bed.

God's wounds, such ruminations would avail him nothing! "What is it?"

"The reeve, the hayward and the woodward are here as you requested," she announced deferentially. Ob-

viously his little demonstration the other night had
partly achieved its goal: she had managed to modu-
late her tone to one of humility.

"Bring more wine for me, and ale for the reeve and
the others, Gabriella," he ordered.

She bobbed a curtsy in acknowledgment before
turning away. As he watched her lithesome figure pass
out the door and into the hall, he wondered where
Philippe was, and if he was watching her with the
greedy look in his eyes that Etienne had seen before.
"Take these things away, Chalfront," he ordered, then
rose and stretched his arms over his head, wishing his
head didn't throb so much. He very much wanted to
be alone, away from his men and Josephine and especially Gabriella Frechette.

Unfortunately, it was necessary that he meet these
men and have them swear their loyalty before the rest
of the tenants. He had put it off for three days as it
was, for what he considered a very good reason, especially after word had reached him of the disgrun-
tled reaction of the villagers to his treatment of the
former lord's daughter. He had decided to see if they
would do more than complain.

They had not.

Adjusting his garments and smoothing out the
folds, Etienne leaned back in his chair and waited, as-
suming his most imperious manner while Chalfront
scrambled to gather up the parchments. He finished
and bowed his way out of the solar as three men entered, pulling the soaking caps from their heads as
rivulets of water ran off their wet cloaks.

The tallest of the three was also the obvious leader, for he walked a pace ahead of the other two. He was a towheaded, square-jawed fellow, with massive forearms and broad shoulders. The other two men were both dark haired, and of smaller stature. There was a complacency about them that wisely disappeared as they approached the baron.

The tall man knelt on one knee. "I am William, the reeve, my lord," he said in a deep, gruff voice before tugging his forelock.

"I am Osric, the hayward," said the stockier of the two dark-haired men as they also knelt.

"And I am Brian, the woodward," said the last.

"Because you are leaders of the village, I have summoned you to give your oaths of loyalty first." How easy it was to flatter these rustics, he thought, as superior glances passed from one to the other. "I assume you are willing to do so."

Before the reeve could speak, Gabriella entered the solar with a tray bearing a chalice and three mugs. She made her way gracefully toward them as if she had been doing this all her life.

She set the tray upon the table and, keeping her eyes demurely lowered, handed the baron his wine first. She went to give the reeve his ale, but before he accepted the mug, he rose.

"My lord," William said with a distinct lack of respect that immediately angered Etienne, "I have no objection to swearing my oath of loyalty to you. One Norman is much like another, to my way of thinking. But this isn't right." He gestured at Gabriella, who shook her head slightly in a futile warning.

Etienne could not believe the effrontery of the peasant. Who did he think he was addressing, Robert Chalfront? Then to look to Gabriella Frechette—and for her to try to silence him! They all had best find out who was in command here.

And Gabriella needed to learn something more: that she had misplaced her allegiance by deciding to stay. These men, these fine leaders of the villagers she held in such apparent esteem, had had ample time to come to him about her plight and suggest a means to alleviate it. All they had to do was offer to pay her debt, which, considering how little they had paid the earl in rents, should not have been a difficult thing. However, they had not—and now they dared to imply that he was a despicable man!

Gabriella started to back away from the table, but he reached out and grabbed her arm. "No, Gabriella. I did not give you leave to go." Even as he spoke, he couldn't help noting the warmth of her flesh against his. "Are you presuming to question any of my decisions, reeve?" he asked calmly as he slowly ran his gaze up Gabriella's slender arm to her breasts straining against the fabric of her bodice before glancing sharply at the reeve.

William, who flushed an even deeper shade of red, swallowed hard and quickly averted his eyes, which had also been trained on Gabriella's breasts. "Well, my lord, we all think it isn't right that she should... suffer," William offered weakly.

"How, pray tell, is she suffering?"

The reeve looked taken aback. "Well, my lord, she's a noblewoman, isn't she, and, well—"

"And now she is doing the kind of work your mother, your wife or your daughter might be expected to do." Etienne lifted Gabriella's hand, deliberately not looking into her face, and turned it over. With his other hand, he stroked her palm, inadvertently noting the blisters there. "Are you concerned that she is unfit for such service? That this delicate hand will become callused and hard? She was the one who made the choice to become a servant. It was she who refused to go. If she suffers, it is her own fault. Besides, I see no reason to call honest labor 'suffering.'"

Again he glanced swiftly at the men, and again caught them staring at her. Judging by their expressions, they were imagining having Gabriella a servant in their own households.

They were men, after all, and she no longer had social position to protect her from their lustful thoughts. They wanted to think *him* evil, yet he did not doubt that each one of them was envisioning Gabriella in his bed. She must be made to see that, too; to realise that she should depend on no one for aid, and that she would have been wiser to leave when she had the chance.

He continued to hold her hand and smiled coldly. "Her virtue is quite safe, I assure you, at least from me and the men under my command."

The feel of her hand in his, the softness and heat of her flesh, moved him more than he would ever have suspected, especially with an audience, belying his words. He was suddenly aware that he lusted after this wench as he had not done in many a long year, for many a more beautiful maiden.

What kind of foolish weakness was this? He did not need her, and she clearly did not want him. It was not necessary for him to engage in a futile quest for this poor, landless, and not exceptionally beautiful wench.

The men glanced at each other uneasily. The hayward looked about to speak but apparently thought better of it.

"If anyone is to blame for the situation Gabriella Frechette finds herself in," the baron continued, meaning his words for her as much as the men, "it is not me. It is she herself, and it is *you* and the other tenants, for exploiting the generosity of the late earl."

He paused for effect, not because he was surprisingly reluctant to make his next offer. "However, there is a way you can help your former mistress. Perhaps one of you will offer to pay her debt and set her free?"

Chapter Five

With a hopeful smile, Gabriella turned to the reeve, who colored and stared at the stone floor, then the hayward, who suddenly found the table an object of fascination, then the woodward, who blushed and stammered, "My lady! I have no money to spare, as you well know and—"

With sudden horrible certainty, Gabriella realized they were not going to help her. Despite all her father had done for them and their families. After all her kind care and worry for them, they were not going to help her!

Her gaze went to the baron's unreadable face, down to his battle-hardened, slender fingers that had stroked her hand so gently—and as if she were only another of his whores. Couldn't William and the others see the precarious nature of her situation? Couldn't they find the money somehow?

"There is another way," the baron noted dispassionately in his cold, deep voice. "There may be someone among you who would be willing to make her his wife. I would be happy to demonstrate my generosity by excusing her debt under those circumstances. Then she will be able to stay in the village, as seems to be her fondest wish.''

''What?'' Gabriella gasped.

''My lord!'' Chalfront said, appearing immediately in the doorway as if he had been lingering outside listening all the while. ''My lord! I will marry her!''

That she should be offered up like some kind of baggage was the final insult. ''I would rather die!'' Gabriella snapped. Only the continuing awareness of Baron DeGuerre's scrutiny stopped her from fleeing the room. She would not give him the satisfaction of thinking he had successfully humiliated her again.

''Gabriella!'' Chalfront protested, spreading his hands in supplication, as if she were the one at fault here.

The baron held up his hand to silence him and there was the hint of a smile on his handsome face. ''It would seem, Chalfront, that the wench would rather be my servant.''

He laid a slight emphasis on ''my'' that made Gabriella turn her glare onto him. He appeared to be implying she would . . . she would . . . she would do what Josephine de Chaney had done! Is that what he believed beneath that impassive exterior? Had he let her leave his bedchamber unmolested only to toy with her more, convinced by his arrogant vanity that she would eventually submit? Never!

''Is there no one else?'' the baron inquired. Sweet mother of God, he made it sound as if he would auction her off to the highest bidder. "Since no one desires you for his wife—"

"There is no one here I would choose," she said between clenched teeth.

"You shall have to remain a servant here until all your family's debt is repaid," he said, her opinion obviously counting for nothing. "Now you may leave us, Gabriella."

She glared at him, then hesitating, looked at Osric, the poacher, who did not meet her eye. Perhaps if she hinted to the baron about what she knew concerning his previous illegal activities, Osric would find the necessary money. Then she thought of the penalties for poaching and decided not to speak. She would not purchase her freedom at the price of a man's fingers or eyes.

The baron ignored her and spoke to the reeve kneeling before him. "William, it is your right to refuse to swear an oath of loyalty to me, provided you are willing to leave my estate and try your luck elsewhere. What do you wish to do?"

William stared at the floor as he said, "I swear to be loyal to the Baron DeGuerre."

The baron turned his cold, impartial eye onto the others as Gabriella went to the door, her heart filled with bitterness and, beneath it all, dismay that no one had offered to help her. She moved slowly, hoping that William and the others would yet change their minds.

"And I, my lord," said the hayward. "I so swear."

"My lord, I so swear," said the woodward.

"I thought you might," Baron DeGuerre replied as Gabriella left the room. "You can inform the rest of the tenants that tomorrow, I raise the rents."

"Now, you understand this is not to be washed with soap," Josephine de Chaney said not unkindly to Gabriella a few days later, holding up a fine scarf of pale blue silk. Her voice was soft, gentle and melodious. "Nor is this." She indicated an embroidered brocade overtunic. "And this should not be wrung out, ever," she finished, pointing to a velvet gown lying upon the new bed.

It was a large, heavy piece of furniture built of age-darkened oak and made up with the thickest feather bed Gabriella had ever seen. On top was spread a finely embroidered coverlet, Josephine's handiwork perhaps. There were also several colorful cushions and pillows laid at the head. It looked, Gabriella thought, like something more befitting an Oriental potentate's harem than a Norman lord's bedchamber. Why, even her father would have considered it extravagant.

The marble floor had been covered with beautiful, thick carpets, woven with scarlet, green, indigo and blue wool. Additional furniture had been unloaded from the baggage carts by this time, and included a slender, delicate chair, a table strewn with bottles and jars that, by their scent, were perfumes, soaps and perhaps cosmetics, although Josephine de Chaney certainly had no need for artifice, a finely carved table, a multibranched candle stand, and a large mirror that was propped on the table. She wondered if the money she owed the baron and that being collected daily by Chalfront would be used to add more cushions, or provide another silver goblet. The baron had nearly doubled the rents, and sent along his soldiers to enforce the collection. When she heard of this, she did not begrudge William and the others their reaction to the baron's suggestion that they pay her debt. Of course she had been dismayed by their reaction before the baron, but he was an intimidating nobleman and they were only peasants. If they would not help her, surely it was because they dared not. It had been wrong of her to be upset with them.

Besides, the baron had asked his question before they had any idea what the increase in the rent was going to be, and later, when the amount was made known, she couldn't find it in her heart to blame them anymore. She would rather continue as a servant than see their families impoverished.

"I understand, my lady," Gabriella replied woodenly, for Josephine was clearly expecting her to say something.

Josephine sat on the delicate chair and pondered her reflection in the mirror, arranging the folds of her splendid gown of soft, dark green wool. A gold-colored silken shift showed at the neck of the bodice, beneath the hem of the gown, and where the long, pointed cuffs were rolled back. Around her slim waist was a girdle of gold links, and about her neck was a chain, also of gold. An emerald pendant hung from it, nestling above her breasts.

Gabriella instinctively avoided the mirror. She could guess how she looked compared to Josephine de Chaney, without visual evidence.

"I know this has not been easy for you, Gabriella."

"No, my lady," she answered, thinking it so obvious, what need was there to say so? She had no wish to discuss her situation with anyone, let alone a woman like Josephine de Chaney, who had used her body to achieve prosperity.

"I am not your enemy, Gabriella," Josephine said so kindly that Gabriella was immediately ashamed of her harshly condemning thought. "Indeed, I was once in a similar position myself."

"So Baron DeGuerre told me."

Josephine was obviously taken aback. "He did? When?"

"The night...the night you arrived, my lady," Gabriella replied, trying not to blush and not succeeding. The memory of her time alone with the baron was all too vivid as she stood in this particular room.

"When you were here alone together?" Josephine's lovely, large eyes widened. "You spoke of me?"

"Yes, my lady."

Josephine leaned toward Gabriella, an intent expression on her face. "What did Etienne say about me?"

"He said that you were from an impoverished family," Gabriella answered. "He said I could follow your example, and when I said I would rather d—not, he told me I should not be so swift to judge, since I did not know your circumstances."

"Really? Etienne said that?" Josephine remarked with a pleased and beautiful smile that displayed her perfect teeth.

Was it any wonder she used her beauty, Gabriella thought suddenly. It was a powerful commodity. "He said that, my lady."

Josephine reclined on the soft cushion against the back of the chair and her expression grew magnanimous. "He spoke the truth about my past, you know. My father lost all our money in drink, and when he died, I was left on my own. I had to make my way in the world, and the first thing I did was find a strong protector." She eyed Gabriella shrewdly. "There are worse fates, as I believe you are discovering. Tell me, now that you have sampled what it is like to be a servant, are you not tempted to do the same?"

"As I said to Baron DeGuerre, my lady, I could not."

Josephine adjusted one of her cuffs and laughed indulgently. "You are a woman of principle, are you?" She became more serious. "You cannot shame me with your words, Gabriella. I made my choice, and I am content with it, as you are with yours, for the present. I shall ask you again in a few months how you enjoy being a lady's maid. You may discover that it is much more pleasant to be waited upon than to do the waiting."

"If pleasantness was all I wanted, I would have taken the baron's money and gone to a convent."

Again Josephine de Chaney's melodious laughter rippled through the chamber. "I think that would be the most unpleasant place of all, with no men!" The courtesan became thoughtful again. "Is there no one who can rescue you from a life of servitude?" she asked solicitously. "No relative? No sweetheart?"

"If my brother knew what had happened, he would come at once."

"Ah, yes, this brother of yours. You truly have no idea where he is, then?"

Gabriella shook her head.

"How sad." Josephine surveyed Gabriella. "You're a pretty thing. I cannot believe there is no lover to save you."

"There is not, my lady."

Josephine gave her another shrewd and searching look. "Not Chalfront?"

"Definitely not."

"I confess I concur with your taste," Josephine said ruefully. "He is not much of a man to stir a maiden's heart."

"I do not wish to marry *anybody,* my lady."

"No, of course not," Josephine replied in a tone that implied she thought that would change soon enough. "I believe I shall go to the hall. Sir George is sure to be there, and he is a charming, amusing fellow. He shall keep me most pleasant company while Etienne is out trying to discover if any of the other tenants have thought to cheat him. Heaven help them if they have! Please tidy up here, and then you may do as you wish until the evening meal."

"Thank you, my lady," Gabriella replied as Josephine glided out of the room.

Gabriella began folding the heavy gown of gold velvet with quick, abrupt movements. Josephine de

Chaney's tone, words and attitude were absolutely insulting! She didn't want that woman's pity!

She grabbed the lovely scarf of pale blue silk as thin as a butterfly's wing, then gasped as her grip wrinkled the beautiful fabric. She would have to be more careful.

She grinned ruefully. She should not take her anger out on a piece of cloth, especially one like this.

Gabriella walked over to the large, surely expensive mirror. Now that Josephine was gone, she gazed at her reflection with frank curiosity.

She was rather pleasantly surprised, for she looked better than she thought she would. Her skin was a bit brown from being in the sun, but not overmuch. Her hair was rather unkempt, and after a guilty glance at the door, she picked up a brush and quickly smoothed her wavy locks.

Her face seemed a little thinner, yet that was not so bad. Indeed, it made her eyes look larger, and since she considered them her best feature, this was not displeasing.

Not that she had any intention of appearing attractive. That would only bring more unwanted attention.

A mixture of pleasant scents drifted to her nostrils and she picked up one of the crystal bottles. She closed her eyes and inhaled, catching the smell of roses, a light scent like the first blossoms to appear on a bush. She set it down, then, with another furtive glance at the door and a sigh of regret for her own lost clothing, draped the scarf about her head.

It was hard to give up such luxuries. If she had been as outstandingly beautiful as Josephine, might her choice not have been the same? She still had the hope of Bryce's return to make her strong; apparently Josephine had been left completely alone and friendless.

She had quite a friend now in Baron DeGuerre.

Who, she suddenly realized as she glanced at the mirror, was standing in the doorway, watching her. Gabriella snatched the scarf from her head with a gasp as she whirled to face him.

"This room is in complete disarray," the baron observed as he sauntered inside.

His cheeks were ruddy from the cold autumn air, and his hair looked windblown, as if he had just returned from a swift ride or dashed up the stairs. She wondered if he had expected to find her here, and what it meant if he did.

"Yes, my lord. I was to tidy it." Gabriella swallowed hard, not sure what to do. Josephine's clothes were scattered everywhere, but she no more wanted to be alone in this room with the baron than she wanted to be alone with Robert Chalfront or Philippe de Varenne.

"Then continue."

She nodded wordlessly before doing as she was told. She moved as quickly as she could, but her haste only made her clumsy, and even more aware of the baron's presence as he stood in the center of the now well appointed room.

"So, Chalfront wants you for his wife," the baron remarked. "Your refusal was rather... unequivocal, shall I say?"

"One of the last things my brother said to me before he went away was that I shouldn't trust Chalfront," she said as she arranged the bottles on the table, knocking one over and righting it quickly.

"And you believed him?"

"Of course," she answered without a moment's hesitation. "What happened after my father died proved that he was right. If Chalfront had been a completely honest, trustworthy, competent bailiff, I would not be indebted to someone like you," she said, her tone carefully matter-of-fact as she repeated aloud what she had so often told herself. She folded the pale blue scarf and took it to the large open chest, keeping as far away from Baron DeGuerre as possible.

"But before that," he said, his tone equally bland, "did you have any reason to suspect Chalfront?" He came toward her and she hurried over to pick up a gown laid upon another chest. "It is my understanding that your brother disliked Chalfront because the bailiff often cautioned your father against giving his son extravagant amounts of money," the baron continued.

Gabriella's hands slowed as she folded the gown. "During his final illness, my father continually spoke of something that was not right," she said quietly, her eyes on the gown. "He often mentioned Robert's name in the same breath. Then, when the state of my father's finances became known, it was clear to me that both Bryce and my father were right to suspect Chalfront.''

"Yet Chalfront maintains he tried to warn your father." The baron's voice sounded low and soft in her ear and she knew he was standing directly behind her. She tried to continue folding the heavy gown, as if his proximity were not disturbing her. "Chalfront maintains he even gave your father money of his own," he said. "Did he not tell you of this?"

Gabriella turned abruptly and glared at the baron's handsome face, frustrated by the strain of his presence and his questions. "Since you seem so fascinated by my relationship with Chalfront, I will tell you all about it," she said angrily, hurrying to the other side of the room before facing him. "First, you must try to understand that I loved my father very much, something I am sure a man like you probably cannot comprehend. When he died, I was devastated, but I was not given any time to grieve. There were so many creditors to appease, workmen to pay, and little money.

"Nevertheless, I did what I could to pay all his debts, obviously without complete success. Robert helped me, but he made his assistance sound so condescending! And then he intruded upon my sorrow and offered to marry me, this man who I believed could have—and should have—guided my father's finances better, if he had not actually stolen from him, for which I admit there is no evidence. I ask you, Baron DeGuerre, how would you feel about such a person?''

He regarded her steadily, apparently unmoved by her story or her question, and she took several deep breaths to calm herself.

"Do you still think he cheated your father?"

Gabriella clutched the velvet gown and tried to re-gard Baron DeGuerre with the same impartiality that he did her. She wanted to tell him, yes, Chalfront had cheated him. That her family's troubles were some-one else's fault. That her father had been deceived, lied to, tricked.

And yet her sense of honesty held her. Her father was an extremely generous man who enjoyed luxury, and it was not hard to believe that he had not been wise. Would Chalfront have stayed to face the wrath of a man like Baron DeGuerre if he had been dishon-est? Would he not have gone as far away as he could?

Her love and loyalty to her family might have made her blind to the truth, and honor demanded honesty. "I don't know, my lord," she said at last.

The baron's gaze went to her hands, then back to her face, his expression unchanging. "I saw the rent rolls. Your father was much too lenient with his ten-ants. The rents, the pannage, the *heriot* should have been higher. Poaching is completely out of hand. The mill rate was appallingly low."

"My father was beloved!" she protested, as much to remind herself of the parent she had loved as to give the baron an explanation.

"I'm sure he was." Baron DeGuerre eyed her coldly. Another man, one who valued seduction over honesty, might have told her that her father was merely too beneficent and too kind. Etienne, however, was not such a man. "Anyone who lets his underlings take advantage of him is a fool."

Gabriella's lower lip started to tremble and she stared down at the soft fabric in her slender, shapely hands. It was far too easy to imagine those hands on his body.

"Anyone," he repeated firmly, commanding himself to pay attention to his own words, "and I have no intention of being made a fool. My steward found no evidence of tampering in the accounts when he first examined them. Still, such a crime would be easy for a bailiff to hide. I will make sure Jean Luc checks them all again, carefully."

She nodded slowly and chewed her lip, her sudden vulnerability nearly overwhelming him. She had always been so strong before, and he had desired to partake of her passionate strength. Now, however, he wanted to take her in his arms and simply hold her, to offer her the comfort of his embrace.

This was a feeling so new to him that he suddenly felt hopelessly ignorant and alone, as he had all those years ago when he had entered his first tournament. He had been an untried youth, thrust into the world of arms and men, at once frightened and thrilled.

However, he had displayed nothing of his emotions then, and he wouldn't do so now. "If Jean Luc discovers that Chalfront spoke the truth, you will owe him an apology," he remarked calmly.

She raised her eyes to look at him, strong again. Thank God. "If I must, I will make him one," she said just as calmly.

"If you give your apology with that same lack of grace," he observed, "I think it would be better not done."

"I have my work to do, Baron DeGuerre."

And so did he, but he was strangely reluctant to leave her. "Look at me, Gabriella."

She glanced quickly at his face, then away.

"No, *look* at me," he commanded, approaching her. He took her chin in his hand, the contact as exciting as another woman's most passionate kiss would be. "I regret what happened in the solar with the reeve and the others." His voice was soft, almost gentle, and Gabriella thought she saw kindness in his eyes that was nearly as surprising as his comment about her apology.

She wished he would let go. Or leave the room. Or that Josephine de Chaney would appear. Anything, other than to be alone with him, too well aware of the hot heaviness in her limbs, the rapid beating of her heart and the unbidden blossoming desire in her breast.

"It is never easy to lose one's innocence, but the world is a harsh place, and we all must learn that lesson." He let go of her chin but didn't move away. "Nevertheless, I do not enjoy being the instrument of enlightenment."

"I was not aware I was being taught a lesson," she said, trying to sound angry or cold and failing miserably.

His piercing blue eyes seemed to lock onto hers. "We are all alone in this world and can count on no one's help."

"I . . . I have my brother!" she protested weakly.

"Who is nowhere to be found. And those others in the village, the ones you are so loath to leave, they would not help you."

"They would! If I were truly in danger—"

"They would save themselves first. It is the way of the world, Gabriella, and you have to learn that."

She shook her head as she lowered it. "No, I won't believe it!"

"Then you will be disappointed many times." His voice dropped to a deep whisper, like the low moan of the sea. "I would spare you that, Gabriella. I would help you."

Suddenly Gabriella had a clear vision of herself in the baron's arms. Kissing him. Caressing him and being caressed in turn. Lying in his bed and making love.

She emitted a little gasp and drew away, horrified by her own reaction. This man had taken her home, made her a servant—and she wanted him to love her?

"I don't want your help!" she wanted to say, but the words would not come as he put his muscular arms around her and drew her toward him. Her breasts pressed against his chest as she lifted her face to him, her gaze searching his face, seeking . . . what? The look of blatant desire in his eyes, or something more . . . ?

Then, when he bent his head to kiss her, it suddenly didn't matter what he had done, or why he was here with her. All that mattered was the overwhelming sensation of his lips upon hers and the burning desire that coursed through her body like flames in dry tinder.

Chapter Six

In all his years, Etienne had never known such a kiss. It was as if Gabriella were at once naive and awestruck, swept up in the delight of the sensations they shared, and at the same time knowing and sensuous, as well aware of her power as the most experienced courtesan. He had not meant to kiss her, but by God, he did not rue his decision as he pulled her closer, feeling the rapid heartbeat beneath her soft breasts.

With a low moan, she responded as his tongue sought to enter the confines of her mouth, arching back against the support of his arm. A surge of powerful desire jolted him when their tongues met with increasing pleasure. His hands stroked her slender, supple back, and beneath his palms he felt the tension flee her spine. As the kiss deepened, he had no thoughts of what he was doing beyond attempting to prolong the exquisite, growing excitement.

"Stop!" she cried, pulling away suddenly, her eyes wide and guilt stricken.

He was shocked by the abrupt sensation of complete abandonment that rushed over him, a feeling as intense as his surprise. "Why?" he asked, determined to ignore the emotions she aroused within him. There was no doubt in his mind that she had enjoyed their embrace at least as much as he. Even so, he tried to convince himself that it was mere lustful desire they felt, and nothing more. "You want me as much as I want you, Gabriella, or you would not kiss me so." His voice dropped to a husky whisper. "There is nothing wrong in a kiss."

Her gaze faltered for the briefest of moments, and her cheeks reddened. He moved to embrace her again, wanting more than anything to feel her in his arms, and telling himself her protest was no more than natural maiden modesty, but she stepped back, a look of such contrite guilt on her face that he felt as if he were the devil incarnate.

"Is this another lesson on the loss of innocence?" she demanded, a condemnation in her resolute eyes that struck him to the core of his lonely heart.

"Not unless you wish it," he said, achieving a flippant tone that belied the effort it took.

"I do not. For a moment, I . . . I forgot."

"Forgot what?"

"Who you are."

The contempt in her voice wounded him as deeply as the thrust of a dagger, but he would not betray this weakness he had not known he possessed. Instead he frowned darkly. "Gabriella, that your family has suffered is none of my doing," he said, his voice all the colder for the desire that he could not quite subdue.

Which was to be expected as she stood before him, with her amazing, shining, defiant brown eyes, and swiftly rising and falling breasts. He told himself it was only a physical attraction that compelled him to want her, not a fierce longing to partake of her incredible passion, or a sense that she could meet him strength for strength.

"And that you were the one chosen to take away my home is not yours," she answered. "But such is the way of things, Baron DeGuerre. You are who you are, and I am who I am. Please allow me to get on with my work and don't attempt to seduce me again."

"Is that what you thought I was doing?" Etienne asked with a scornful laugh to hide his frustration. "A kiss is hardly a seduction. Think of it as a lesson to beware being alone with a man."

"So many lessons, my lord. I suppose I should be grateful that you take such an interest in your servants. I thank you for all your concern that I learn what noblemen are truly like and that the world is a cold, heartless place." She gave him a curious, sidelong glance, as if he were some kind of monstrosity. "Tell me, Baron, who taught such a lesson to *you?*"

"My mother," he snapped, the honest answer bursting from his lips unbidden.

She lost that dismissive expression, gaining instead a pitying one.

By God, he would *not* be pitied, by her or anyone.

He grabbed her by the shoulders and glared into her face, happy—yes, happy!—that the pity was replaced with dread. "I know full well who I am, Gabriella. I am the master here."

"I am a free woman, Baron," she declared. She struggled in his arms with a desperate fierceness that brought him at once to his senses. He didn't want her pity, but he didn't want her to be terrified of him, either.

He let her go, and she moved swiftly behind the chair as if it were a shield. "If you take me against my will, you will be guilty of a crime," she warned.

"I have no intention of taking you against your will," he said truthfully, then another need that had been so vital for so long arose inside him. He must be in control, of himself, of her, of everyone around him. "You cannot deny that you want me, Gabriella," he continued. "I could taste your desire. I could feel the excitement in your body. When you come to my bed— and you will—it shall be of your own free will."

She stared at him with horrified disbelief. "The only way I shall go voluntarily to any man's bed will be when I am married, and I can assure you, Baron DeGuerre, that if you were the last man in the kingdom, I would not marry you! I know how you treated your wives!"

"*You* know how I treated my wives? How could you know?" he demanded.

"Everyone knows. You married them for their property, and then neglected them."

Of course it would have appeared so to the people around them, and her assessment was, in fact, partly true. He had not loved his wealthy wives, nor had they loved him. They had craved the dangerous excitement of his reputation and the passion of the marriage bed, lying there like limp fish for him to arouse. He had considered the wealth and prestige they gave him small recompense.

But it was not for this naive young woman to judge him, or Josephine, or anyone else.

"I have no intention of explaining myself to you." He raised one eyebrow. "Tell me again about your brother, the knave. A spoiled brat who quarreled with your father and left in a childish fit of pique."

"That's not true!"

"He did not quarrel, and then go, never to return, no matter how dire your family's straits?" he asked, apparently incredulous. "Can it be that common knowledge is not to be trusted?"

"You don't understand!" she cried fervently, slapping her hands onto the back of the chair. "If he only knew what has happened, Bryce would return at once!"

For a moment, Etienne wondered what it would be like to have such faith in a person that one would cling to a belief in their worthiness despite so much evidence to the contrary. However, he dismissed such thoughts as idle speculation and said, "So, common knowledge can be wrong."

He walked to his old and battered chest and opened it. "Here," he said, taking out the familiar purse of coins and holding it out to her. "Take the money and leave this castle, or if you stay, know that I will offer you only such protection as I give all my servants, neither more nor less."

After a long moment of nearly unbearable silence, Gabriella shook her head. "You cannot force me from here now!"

"You are an attractive woman, and attractive *servants*—" he laid a slight reminding emphasis on the word, both for her sake and his own "—make trouble among the men."

"Order them to leave me in peace, and there will be no trouble. This is my home, and I intend to stay." Her defiant gaze faltered for the briefest of moments, her dusky lashes brushing her silky cheeks and making him want to lay a kiss on each eyelid.

One moment, she was proud, defiant, as strong as the stoutest oak, the next, she was as delicately vulnerable as a rare and beautiful flower. And yet she was a woman, a desirable, fascinating woman whose kiss had melted away years of reserve.

Therefore, Etienne's mind cried out, *she is a dangerous woman. You have always been alone, apart from everyone around you. You will, you must, always be so. To forget that is to be weak. You must never be weak!*

"Get out!" he growled, raising his voice as he had not done in years, frustrated and angry.

She stared at him.

"Go!"

Although he did not see her depart, he knew Gabriella had run from the room as if pursued by a demon. And that demon was the Baron DeGuerre.

What did it matter? he told himself as he strode to the window and stared out unseeing. He didn't want Gabriella Frechette, except in his bed. He didn't want Josephine de Chaney, except that other men coveted her. He didn't need anyone, either, except those knights and soldiers necessary to maintain what he had won.

But sweet savior, he didn't want to be alone anymore! Was it too much to ask, to have one person to love him? Truly love him, for himself?

He had never had that. His wives and mistresses wanted him for his looks and his wealth. Men followed him because of his power. Even his mother had not wanted him because he was Etienne, her son. To her, he had been nothing more than a living image of his father.

He tried to recall all he had accomplished, and how far he had come. He was the rich, the powerful, the envied Baron DeGuerre.

Yet all he could remember was the moment he had lost control. And the sudden fear and dismay in a pair of shining brown eyes.

The baron was still standing at the window when Josephine entered the chamber sometime later, her thoughts on the best choice of color for the background of the tapestry she held in her hands—until she saw Etienne. She had never seen him stand thus, pensive and inert, and a shaft of fear struck her heart. If something happened to him, what would become of her?

"Are you ill, my love?" she asked solicitously, setting down the tapestry and going to him immediately. She wrapped her arms around him and leaned her head against his strong, rigid back. "Has it been a trying day? Sit, and I will pour you some wine and bathe your head with cool water."

"I am not sick," Etienne replied somewhat brusquely as he turned away from the window.

He didn't look indisposed, Josephine thought with relief, and she smiled before going toward a small table upon which sat a goblet and carafe of wine. As she proceeded to fill the goblet, she realized that the room had not been tidied completely. Either Gabriella had deliberately left before finishing her work out of laziness, or she had been interrupted. By Etienne? Had something happened between them to send Gabriella away before her work was finished and to make Etienne so thoughtful?

Her hand started to shake and she took a deep breath to calm herself. She was Josephine de Chaney, famous for her beauty and grace. John Delaney had killed himself when she refused him. Alfred de Morneux and Ralph Bordette had mortally wounded each other over her. Surely she had nothing to fear from a wench like Gabriella Frechette.

After all, it could very well be that Etienne had come here to think and sent Gabriella away to be alone. Or perhaps he had come here looking for *her*. "Do you wish me to stay, Etienne?" she asked in her gentlest tones as she handed him the wine. "Or would my presence disturb you?"

"Your presence would never disturb me," he said with a slight smile as he sat down.

"Does your head ache?"

"A little. You are getting to know me too well," he observed.

Josephine's brows furrowed slightly as she watched him drink. *What did he mean by that?* "Perhaps you would care to retire?" she asked innocently. If he wanted to go to bed but not rest, she would, of course, be willing.

"It's early yet," he said absently, and her heart sank. Was this the beginning of the end between them?

"I have decided to make a visit to Roger de Montmorency and then to Beaumare to fetch Jean Luc myself. I need his expertise," he announced.

He spoke to her as if she were one of his lesser knights, not his paramour, and she began to feel the trickle of perspiration down her sides. Nevertheless, she forced a smile onto her face. "When should I be ready to leave?"

"You?" he asked as if he had not even considered that she would accompany him. "You might as well remain here. I won't be gone that long." He smiled with as much genuine warmth as she had ever seen from him, and her heart started to beat again. "The journey would be too tiring," he continued. "Besides, you have made this room—indeed, this castle—such a place of comfort and beauty, you should be able to enjoy it for as long as possible."

Because he was planning to send her away? Because he had his lascivious eye on another woman, one with thick, wavy brown hair, defiant eyes and a shapely body?

"Very well, Etienne," she said, fighting to keep her tone even and noncommittal. "Will you take *anyone* with you?"

"Philippe de Varenne." He came toward her and gave her a light kiss and subtle caress. "I would not leave something I valued alone with that one. I can trust George with anything," he added significantly, "so I will leave him in command." He stepped away and surveyed her with approval. "Wear your new blue gown tonight. You look like a goddess in it."

She nodded and smiled and tried to feel relieved, but the smile turned to a worried frown as Etienne strode away.

Two days later, on a morning when the air was chill with the winds of autumn that sent bits of chaff from the stables swirling around the courtyard, Gabriella stood at the well that was between the hall and the stables. Carefully she hoisted the bucket and tipped it so that the clear, cold water flowed into one of the buckets she was to take to the kitchen. In what she was coming to think of as the "old days," she had never appreciated the work necessary to keep the kitchen supplied with water. Now, as she noticed the hardening calluses on her once-soft hands, she knew it all too well.

Perhaps this was another "lesson" she needed to learn, she thought bitterly, shivering in the cold and wishing she had thought to wear her shawl. The baron would surely think so. Fortunately, he had not yet returned and she had been spared seeing him again after that last, disastrous, unsettling encounter. His absence had given her time to think through what had happened, and she had come to the conclusion that she had been unready for his evident kindness and overwhelmed by his technique. After all, he had been seducing women for years, and she had been caught unprepared. No wonder his kiss had affected her as it had. That would not happen again, and if he so much as touched her, she would be ready!

She was also glad that Philippe de Varenne had gone away with him. The young knight had not spoken to her after that day by the river, but he had *looked* often, and his gaze was unwholesome and unwelcome. If he decided not to return, that would be a blessing.

There was something else to be thankful for, and that was the change in Robert Chalfront. He didn't exactly ignore her; instead, he acted as if she were just another person in the household, which was a great relief. Of course, he was kept very busy during the baron's absence, especially since Sir George was apparently much more interested in hunting and gaming than running an estate, even for a few days. It seemed the vast majority of the inhabitants of Castle Frechette were more cheerful because of the baron's absence, as if a dark shadow had been lifted from them.

Not that she was reconciled to her state. If anything, she was more determined than ever to pay her debt. She didn't want to leave her home any more than she ever had, but there could be no alternative.

She simply had to get away from the baron's overwhelming presence.

She sighed as she lowered the well bucket again and began to draw it up.

Nearby she could hear two stable hands teasing each other and laughing as they went about their work.

From one of the upstairs windows nearby, she caught the sound of Alda singing a ballad. The breeze carried Guido's bellowing orders all the way across the courtyard. He was still anxious, but considerably less so than he had been before the baron's arrival, for it was clear that the baron intended to allow him to remain as cook.

The only person who really seemed to miss the baron at all was Josephine de Chaney, and then only when she retired at night. During the day, she sewed and chatted with the knights, for she was always surrounded by a bevy of admiring swains. Even Chalfront lingered occasionally, displaying a capacity for idleness that quite surprised Gabriella the first few times she noticed it.

No doubt Josephine missed the baron's presence in her lonely bed. The masculine scent of him beside her. The feel of his strong and capable hands on her body. The insistent pressure of his lips . . .

With another sigh, Gabriella set the large bucket on the side of the well and lifted the filled smaller ones. As she staggered away, water from the heavy buckets sloshed onto the stones.

"My lady!"

Instinctively Gabriella glanced over her shoulder. Mary, one of the widows from the village who Gabriella had always liked, hurried toward her from the inner gate, her careworn, middle-aged face concerned and her doelike brown eyes full of dismay as she looked at Gabriella.

"It's true then, what I've heard?" Mary demanded, coming to a halt and putting her hands on her broad hips.

Her frowning scrutiny rekindled all of Gabriella's original embarrassment and renewed her determination to avoid any taint of pity.

"I've been visiting my sister over in Barton-by-Attley and just got back. I couldn't believe it." She shook her head, setting its linen covering swaying. "'It can't be true!' I said when Elsbeth told me. Elsbeth's such a gossip—it was her who put it about that my John used to drink more than he ought, so you know I didn't believe her right off. 'Swear on the name of Mary,' she said, and that gave me a turn, I will say."

"Yes, it's true," Gabriella admitted lightly, setting down the unwieldy buckets. "I didn't have much alternative."

"Has he . . . has he hurt you?" Mary whispered the question with genuine concern, not the intense speculation of gossip.

"No," Gabriella replied, although she reddened, thinking of the kiss they had shared. He had upset her, but he had not hurt her.

"What about that other fellow, that Philippe de Varenne? Elsbeth said she saw him talking to you at the river, and she thought—"

"Philippe de Varenne has gone on a journey with the baron."

"That's a relief, is it?"

"Yes," Gabriella said, and she could not suppress a shudder of distaste as she recalled the way Philippe had looked at her on the riverbank. "I would be happy never to see him again."

"And the baron, too, I daresay."

Gabriella didn't reply, because her own reaction startled her so completely. Never to see Baron De-Guerre again? She should have answered with the same speed and elation that she would if Philippe de Varenne disappeared from her life. Instead, the notion of Baron DeGuerre's permanent absence was disturbing, nearly as disturbing as...well, as Bryce's.

Mary glanced at Gabriella with shrewd eyes. "Elsbeth says the baron's terrible fierce, always in black like the devil himself. A good-looking man, but about as much expression as a grindstone, and about as much heart, too."

Gabriella thought of the look in Baron DeGuerre's eyes as he bent to kiss her. The baron had a heart, she believed, but he kept it very well hidden.

"Well, I'm glad you're not in any danger." Mary's smile stretched across her face as she bent to take hold of one of the buckets.

She straightened when George de Gramercie, Donald Bouchard and his friend Seldon came out of the stables, George and Donald involved in an animated discussion. It was obvious from their words, the game they carried, their ruddy cheeks and windblown hair that they had been hunting.

Despite the nature of their recent activity, Sir George wore a fine cloak of brilliant red wool. His black boots shone and his hose had not a wrinkle. Indeed, no matter what Sir George was about, his clothes were always perfectly clean.

Donald Bouchard, who clearly had not the money to spend on clothing that Sir George had, was dressed with his customary simplicity, which also seemed an extension of his character.

Seldon apparently threw on whatever was handy. His dark brown cloak was askew and his boots were thickly covered with mud.

On the other hand, Gabriella noted, while Sir George looked good, he held but one dead duck. Donald and Seldon both held the corpses of several pheasants.

"If you wish to work yourself into a sweat over a couple of birds, I see no reason to condemn the rest of us," she heard Sir George say jovially as the men strolled toward them. "After all, we can only consume so much. Any more would be wasteful and a sin."

"*Some* of us did not take time to rest on the riverbank, napping beneath a broad oak," Donald replied with his usual gravity.

"There's a lot of us to feed, too, eh?" Seldon noted in his deep, slow voice.

"And some of us eat much more than others, Seldon, eh?" Sir George grinned, then caught sight of the two women by the well. He bowed graciously and smiled as he went past.

"What a bunch of stout fellows!" Mary exclaimed softly when the men were out of earshot. "Is the baron expecting an attack?"

"Not that I'm aware of," Gabriella replied. As she looked at the three knights, she wondered if there was indeed some unknown reason that the baron kept such a force about him. Or perhaps it was simply the trappings of wealth and power, and she should attach no particular significance to it. She bent down to pick up the buckets.

"Here, my lady, let me take those for you," Mary said.

"I can manage, Mary," Gabriella said, grabbing the rope handle of the other bucket and reaching out to grasp the one already in Mary's hand. She was quite capable of doing her work. Mary didn't have to treat her like a child.

"I've got it," Mary said firmly, not letting go. The bucket started to swing precariously.

"You'd better let me have the bucket," Gabriella insisted. She nodded toward the retreating figures of Sir George and the others, who were nearly at the door of the hall. "I don't want anyone telling Baron De-Guerre I'm not doing my share of chores."

Mary did not release her grip. "They're not looking at us. Besides, two's too heavy for you, my lady."

"No, I can do it!" Gabriella said urgently. "Mary, please!" She gripped the handle harder and pulled.

With an equally determined expression, Mary still held on and for a moment, the bucket swung wildly between them. When the rope began to cut her hand, Gabriella had to let go. Unfortunately, at that precise instant and in midswing, so did Mary. The bucket sailed through the air, spinning and dispersing water as it went, before it landed and broke right behind the startled Sir George. The remaining water splashed everywhere, including all over Sir George, then disappeared in rivulets between the courtyard stones.

Chapter Seven

"Sir George, I'm so sorry!" Gabriella cried, setting down her intact bucket and running up to him. "Forgive me! It was all my fault."

"As long as this isn't some kind of a hint that I need to bathe," Sir George remarked mildly, looking down at his wet clothes. He began to wring out the bottom of his soaking tunic.

Behind Sir George, Donald Bouchard actually smiled and Seldon's loud guffaws echoed off the stone walls. Grooms and stable hands came rushing out, Guido appeared at the kitchen door, dripping ladle in hand, and Alda stuck her head out of one of the narrow windows of the upper apartments.

Gabriella stood awkwardly, wondering what she should do next and biting her lip in embarrassed agitation.

"Calm yourself, my dear," Sir George said with his sincere and charming smile. "I've been drenched before, but rarely by anyone as pretty as yourself."

The onlookers smiled and Gabriella sensed many suppressed chortles, giggles and guffaws.

"It was me done it," Mary said staunchly, coming to stand beside Gabriella.

"Really, ladies, it matters not to me just how I came to be in this condition. However, I think I should change before I take a chill. That would be a rather ignominious cause of death, don't you think?" He made a polite little bow. "If you will excuse me."

Gabriella had to smile as Sir George sauntered off as calmly as if he spent every morning in wet garments. Donald and Seldon, who were still chuckling, followed him to the hall without a word to the women. Guido went back into the kitchen, the stable hands returned to work, and Alda, after a tense moment of obvious panic, succeeded in getting her head inside the window.

Gabriella wondered what Baron DeGuerre would make of this incident, should Sir George, Bouchard and Seldon or any of the servants tell him of this additional embarrassment. She dearly hoped no one would mention it.

"It's a pity *he* didn't get the castle," Mary said thoughtfully. "He's a nice fellow."

"He's a charming man," Gabriella agreed. *And that's all*. She couldn't imagine Sir George ever actually leading a battle, or even a skirmish. If it came to defending this castle, she wasn't sure he would be up to the task.

Gabriella had never seen Sir George de Gramercie fight, or she wouldn't have doubted his abilities. It was simply that, compared to the Baron DeGuerre, most men seemed to be lacking.

"I suppose I'll owe the baron even more now," Gabriella said regretfully, beginning to retrieve bits of broken bucket.

Mary grew grave as she helped Gabriella. "I wanted to ask you something else. Is it true that the baron would have let William and the others pay the debt for you but they refused?"

"Yes, it is," Gabriella answered as she straightened, pieces of bucket in her hands.

Mary let fly a colorful epithet, then reddened when she saw Gabriella's shocked visage. "Why, everybody knows they could pay that sum! That's why I didn't believe that they hadn't. Men! Bunch of selfish oafs, if you ask me." She stomped toward the remaining bucket.

"You haven't seen the baron." Gabriella felt bound to point this out as she hurried after the irate Mary. "And he *did* raise the rents afterward."

"But they didn't offer *anything?*" Mary demanded as she picked up the bucket. "To think that after all your good father did for them, they'd pay you back like this! I'm ashamed of the whole lot of them!"

"My servitude won't last forever," Gabriella said.

"It still isn't right!" Mary grabbed Gabriella's arm and pulled her to the other side of the well, where they would be shielded from prying eyes. "I've got some money put by," Mary whispered, looking about furtively. "So have a few of the other women." She reached into her bodice, her hand snaking down nearly to her waist, and pulled out a cloth tightly wrapped and tied in a knot. She held it out. "It's not much, but it's a start. You can give it to the baron, to help pay the debt.''

Gabriella looked at the sincere offering. Her faith in her father's people, seriously shaken despite her justifications, began to renew. If only the baron were here to see this! Then she thought of the raised rents and shook her head. ''I can't take it, Mary. You may have need of it.''

Mary frowned and did not lower her outstretched hand. ''My lady—and you will always be that to me, so no use to tell me to stop—your father gave us all a lot more than this, in his way, and I cannot stand by and see you brought low.'' Her face assumed the desperate expression of one of the holy martyrs depicted in the stained-glass window in the chapel. ''If you don't take it from me, I'll... I'll give it to the baron myself!''

Gabriella guessed that Mary would rather trade places with the holy martyr, but she also knew Mary well enough to guess that if she didn't take the offering, Mary would screw up her courage and go directly to the baron. She clasped the woman's work-hardened hand and collection of coins in hers. ''I thank you with all my heart, Mary,'' she said with sincerity and humility. ''I would be honored to accept your gift.''

Mary's face broke out into a wide smile. ''There are others who want to help, too. Jhane, for one, but she's afraid that ninny William will find out. I told her it was *her* money—she's the one who does the brewing, isn't she?''

''Mary,'' Gabriella said as she tucked the coins into the belt around her waist, ''as much as I appreciate everyone's kindness, I don't wish to be the cause of trouble. Let Jhane keep her money."

"Well . . ." Mary hesitated, as if she were far from convinced that Jhane's funds were not necessary.

"Thank you, Mary, truly. This is more than I ever expected," she said. She gestured toward the remaining bucket. "Now I had better get to work, although thanks to you, my days as a servant should be somewhat shorter."

"And then you must promise to come and live with me. My cottage isn't much, but it's mine."

Gabriella smiled a tremulous thanks and nodded. She knew she should be grateful for Mary's offer. The debt would be repaid, and she would have a place to go. She would be beholden to no one. She would be free.

If she did not feel completely elated at such thoughts, surely it was simply that she would not be staying in the castle, which had been her home.

Robert Chalfront hurried toward the hall, wanting to speak with Sir George, since that knight was temporarily in charge. Surely the baron must have left more orders for tasks to be done in his absence. Unfortunately, Sir George seemed to have forgotten most of them if he had, recalling one or two at a time as the mood apparently fell on him. Robert dearly hoped that the baron would not find fault with *him* for Sir George's poor memory.

Once inside the door, he glanced around nervously, hoping that Gabriella would be in the kitchen or assisting Lady de Chaney. He had no wish to see Gabriella and be reminded of his foolishness. He had asked her to marry him with the best of intentions, only to be rebuffed. That was the thanks he had gotten for trying to help her immoderate father and prodigal brother. Then, like a dolt, he had kept hoping against hope. The knowledge that she would prefer to crouch on the riverbank and wash another man's clothes rather than be his wife finally destroyed his delusion.

He had been infatuated with her, that was all. Besides, he had never loved her enough to risk his life for her, which every minstrel's ballad maintained was the true test. He must have been mad to ask her to marry him. Well, he was an older and a wiser man. He would beware being trapped by a woman ever again.

Unfortunately, there was no sign of Sir George, or the other men in the hall, either. A few servants were sweeping up old rushes and trimming flambeaux, but otherwise, the large room was empty.

The hall had undergone a noticeable improvement, he thought as he looked about him. It was a well-proportioned room, and the wall paintings were generally excellent, if somewhat overwhelmingly bright in spots. Lady Josephine had added to the decor in a most delightful and subdued manner. Some of the more garish parts of the wall had been covered by simpler tapestries. The linen for the tables suggested wealth without the rather overdone opulence that had been the earl's style.

Robert had heard, of course, about the baron's bed and the lavish coverings. He could only be relieved that the lady expended her need for such bold extravagance in the privacy of the bedchamber.

Suddenly he caught sight of the lovely Lady de Chaney standing on the tower stairs.

She *had* to be the most beautiful woman in England, he thought admiringly, and never had she looked more so than at the present. She wore a lovely gown of soft wool dyed in a deep, dark rich blue. A cap of similar fabric sat on the golden mane of her hair, and a filmy scarf of blue served for her wimple. A thin girdle of supple leather painted red sat low on her hips and emphasized her slim waist.

And her smile! It was a glorious thing to behold, and Robert could only wonder that any man, even the baron, would leave her behind.

She beckoned to him.

Robert gulped and furtively surveyed the hall, which was now empty. Incredulous, he pointed to his chest and was nearly paralyzed with shock when she nodded her head.

By all the saints! What could the baron's mistress want with *him?*

Then it occurred to him that perhaps she had a task for him. Maybe the baron had imparted some orders to her to pass on to the bailiff.

Yes, that might be it, he thought as he approached her. Undoubtedly the baron knew that Sir George might forget something, and so had told Lady Josephine instead.

"Come with me to the solar," Lady Josephine said quietly when he was close by.

Still feeling rather like a conspirator, Robert glanced back over his shoulder to see if anybody observed them together.

He was being foolish. This beautiful woman belonged to Baron DeGuerre; there was no reason for anyone to believe that anything other than the business of the estate would be cause for a conversation between them.

Despite this firm and reassuring belief, when Josephine de Chaney closed the door of the solar behind him, Robert began to sweat. "How may I help you, my lady?" he asked nervously.

She sat down behind the baron's immense table and smiled. "Please, sit," she said, her soft voice reassuring and kind.

He did, or rather, he perched on the very edge of the chair she indicated.

"Tell me, Chalfront, what do you think of the baron?"

His eyes widened and he cleared his throat. What kind of question was this? Was it some kind of test? Did she expect an honest answer? "It is not for me to think anything," he demurred. "He is my lord."

"A very proper answer." Again, Josephine de Chaney smiled, but this time, he noticed a different expression in her eyes. Sadness, perhaps. Or wistfulness. Yes, wistfulness. She looked at her slender hands resting on the table. "I was surprised that he decided to go on this journey, when Jean Luc was to be here so soon anyway."

"He said he had necessary business."

"Yes," she replied slowly, raising her eyelashes to look at him in a way that took his very breath away. "Business."

For a moment, Chalfront actually bristled with anger at Baron DeGuerre. The man seemed to have a positive genius for upsetting women! First Gabriella and now Lady de Chaney, who sounded on the verge of tears! "Surely it must be important business, to take him away from you," he said sincerely.

"How kind of you to say so." Josephine de Chaney smiled again. Holy heaven, she was the most beautiful woman in the world! "Where are you from, Chalfront—or may I call you Robert?" she asked, her manner neither pompous nor condescending.

"Please, my lady, I would be honored!" He smiled happily. "I am from Oxfordshire."

"I guessed as much!" she cried with pleasure. "My family's home was not far from that town." Robert wondered how it was he had not seen Lady de Chaney in Oxfordshire, until he recalled that he would hardly have moved in the same social circle, which seemed a great yet unfortunately unavoidable pity. "Tell me, did you know Douglas, the carpenter?" she asked.

"Know him? He was my uncle, my lady."

"Ah!"

"He died this past winter, my lady, I am sorry to say. He was immensely old, you know. Nearly sixty."

"Yes, I remember," she replied with genuine sadness that touched his heart. "He had gray hair when I was just a little child. He was a very fine man."

"Always joking, and making people laugh. I thought he should have been a jester."

"And what about the abbot there?" she asked. "*He* was as grim as a sepulcher."

"Father Harold? Alive and well yet, and just as grim," Robert acknowledged with a grin. "It may be sacrilege, but I fear he will live forever. Surely even the angels have no wish to see him in heaven. Of course, he may be more pleasant once he is dead."

Lady de Chaney laughed, and her laugh was like honey, warm and sweet, as well as full of the friendship of shared memories. Robert felt all his worries slipping away under the spell of it.

"Perhaps someday I will travel there again. I have so many happy memories of childhood wrapped about the old town."

"As do I, my lady."

Josephine de Chaney sighed and they sat in companionable silence for a moment before she suddenly regarded him with a directness he found disconcerting and said, "There is something else we share, Robert, besides our memories of Oxfordshire. We are both dependent on the baron. A knowledge of his...how shall I put this?" She thought a moment. "His *state of mind* is essential to us both."

"Yes, my lady," Robert agreed.

"I will be direct about my fears, Robert." She leaned forward and fixed her surprisingly shrewd eyes upon him. "Do you believe Gabriella Frechette wants the baron?"

"For what?" Robert replied, momentarily stunned by her question. When the answer came to him without any help from Lady de Chaney, he gasped aloud. "No! Never! I believe she hates the man! He took away her home, you know."

She nodded but still looked unconvinced.

"You don't think the baron wants her, do you?" he asked, shocked to the marrow of his bones. "Only a fool would want Gabriella when he could have you! Whatever else the baron is, he is not a fool."

"No, he's not a fool," Josephine conceded. "Nor is he in love with me. If he truly wants Gabriella, he will have her. No woman could resist Etienne for long."

"I still say he hasn't got a hope of succeeding," Robert said firmly. "She would never give herself to a man as if she were..."

"A whore?" Lady de Chaney asked with startling frankness.

Robert reddened with shame that he had forced the comparison, but she didn't seem particularly troubled by it. She was a most intelligent, practical woman. "No, she makes that very clear," Josephine de Chaney continued. "But Etienne is... well, he is a very attractive man. She might be swayed—"

"No, my lady. Not her," Robert interrupted. "Besides, she clings to the hope of her brother's return."

"Do you think that likely?"

"No, my lady."

"I am truly sorry to hear you say so," Lady de Chaney said, and Robert knew she meant it. How kind she was, to think of Gabriella's plight with so much sympathy! "You think I have nothing to fear?" she asked. "That the baron doesn't desire her?"

"Why would he want her when he has *you?*" Robert repeated, truly mystified by her apparent insecurity. Why, she was without question the most desirable woman in the whole world.

"Because he knows I do not love him, either," she answered simply and honestly.

"You don't?" Robert's heart started to beat with a wild, unfamiliar rhythm.

"I do not. I have never *loved* any man."

Robert didn't know what to say. Indeed, he didn't believe he *could* speak, even if he had found the appropriate words, after her unexpected admission. He was too excitedly dumbfounded.

"I suppose *you* would leave here if he did make Gabriella his mistress?" she asked wistfully.

That was *not* something Robert had expected her to ask and he wasn't quite sure what to make of it. Then, suddenly, a vision rose up before him of his home with this lovely woman at his hearthside. *Impossible!* Even to think such a thing was madness at best, traitorous at worse. She belonged to Baron DeGuerre. Why, despite their pleasant conversation moments ago, she would surely never see him as anything more than a peasant. And—horrible thought!—perhaps the baron had told her of Gabriella's accusations concerning his honesty.

Nevertheless, despite his thoughts and fears, at that moment, Josephine de Chaney completely, totally and irrevocably captured Robert Chalfront's lonely heart.

She rose gracefully. "You have given me much to think about, Robert," she murmured, holding out her hand to him. "I'm sure you have much to do, and I will not keep you from your work any longer."

She will stay with the baron. She belongs to the baron. He was a simpleton, a dunderhead, a fool, he silently chided as he bent forward to kiss her incredibly soft fingers.

But that was not what Josephine de Chaney was thinking as she watched Robert Chalfront hurry away. She was thinking that it had been many years since she had enjoyed a conversation as she had this one. Robert Chalfront had not tried to seduce her or impress her or flatter her. She had not felt compelled to constantly wonder if she had said the right thing, or what she should say next, or to try to gauge her companion's mood. He was not as physically attractive as some, but there was a sincerity and kindness to him that more than made up for that lack.

All in all, it had been a very refreshing and enjoyable time.

She went to the glass window, where she could see the round-faced young man—for he was young, a fact somewhat hidden by his constantly worried expression—hurrying across the courtyard. He was also dutiful, clever and, she was sure, honest. He would make some woman a good and loyal husband. Some virginal young woman who had not sold herself to a nobleman.

With a ragged sigh, Josephine straightened her shoulders. What she had done could not be changed. Now she had to think of her future.

Chapter Eight

"My lady?" Gabriella asked softly as she knocked on the bedchamber door seeking Josephine, who had gone to change her gown after the noon meal. "A cloth merchant has arrived. He would like to speak with you. His wife is a milliner."

"Indeed?" Josephine answered, coming to the door. "I shall be there directly. Oh, wait one moment." She turned back inside the room and was gone a short time. She opened the door and Gabriella saw a bundle of cloth in her hands. "Is there someone in the village who could make use of these old clothes?"

"I think so, my lady," Gabriella answered, her gaze drawn to a plain black garment she did not think had ever belonged to Josephine.

"Good. Here." She gave them to Gabriella. "You may go to the village now, if you wish. I daresay I will be quite some time with the merchants." With that, Josephine passed her and went down the stairs.

Gabriella followed and watched her greet the fawning merchant and his less obsequious wife, who had arrived with bundles and baskets of goods to try to sell.

Robert Chalfront entered the hall. He gave Gabriella a curt nod of greeting before his attention went directly to Josephine de Chaney.

Not that there was anything so unusual in that. All men watched Josephine, especially when she smiled and wore a lovely gown of sumptuous velvet that emphasized her shapely body. Today her dress was made of burgundy fabric trimmed with gold thread, and cut low in the bodice to expose both her dark green shift and soft white flesh, while accentuating her swanlike neck.

Gabriella was about to hurry away on her errand, but there was something about Chalfront's expression that made her hesitate.

He was looking at Josephine de Chaney in the same way he had regarded Gabriella in the days before he had asked to marry her. Was it possible that he no longer pursued her because he had transferred his affection to the baron's mistress? Quite possible, she surmised, and extremely dangerous if the baron suspected him of—what? Trying to seduce Josephine de Chaney?

Gabriella chided herself for a fool as she went on her way. What woman would consider another man when she had Baron DeGuerre for a lover? She flushed at the turn her thoughts had taken and told herself the baron's relationship with anyone was none of her business.

Nevertheless, she waited near the door as Robert spoke to Josephine, watching the woman's reaction carefully. It was polite and friendly, but that was all, which was to be expected.

Determined to keep her mind on her errand, she left the hall quickly. Mary would see that those who had need of the clothing would receive it.

She enjoyed her walk to Mary's cottage, after a fashion. The air was damp and cold and threatened rain, but at least she was away from the castle and its inhabitants.

A group of peasant children were busily gathering the dark, ripe elderberries that dotted several of the hedges. Among them were the orange-red berries of bittersweet. Many of the leaves of the taller trees on the outskirts of the village had already turned brown and different shades of yellow, from the lighter yellow of the elm through the gold of the chestnuts and maples, to the deeper red-gold of the beech, heralding the approach of winter.

Gabriella arrived at Mary's cottage on the far side of the village to find Mary busy dying her wool. The process was messy, complicated by Mary's penchant for trying new combinations of tints. It was the woman's hope that one day she would hit upon a new color that everyone would want, and she would become rich producing the dye, which naturally she would keep as her own, closely guarded secret.

Therefore, Gabriella felt rather like an unwelcome intruder in an alchemist's shop, which Mary's cottage resembled with its collection of plants, herbs and clay vessels stained in a range of colors. Mary, witchlike, bent over the pot boiling on the hearth, and the smell of damp wool was nearly overpowering.

Gabriella had no wish to linger there, so she set down the clothes and briefly told Mary where they had come from and what they were intended for, all of which was received with a distracted nod.

Gabriella tried not to feel insulted by Mary's inattention, even though she had never had such a rude reception from the woman before. Well, she reasoned as she left the cottage, she had never interrupted Mary at her dying before.

She shouldn't tarry in the village, either. Josephine might have need of her maid if she purchased new clothes or accoutrements.

As she walked back toward the village, Gabriella sighed wistfully. It would be a long time before *she* had a new gown, or even a ribbon for her hair.

Then she spotted Osric, the hayward, hurrying toward his cottage by the river. He should have been supervising the sowing of the winter wheat in the far pastures. He looked red faced and anxious, and she thought she saw blood on his clothes. Perhaps he had injured himself.

She decided to follow him, for his aged mother might need assistance if his injury was a serious one.

She hurried toward his cottage, his reluctance to help her momentarily forgotten in her concern. She paused outside the slatted door to knock when she heard Osric's harsh voice. "He nearly saw me," the hayward gasped.

"Who?" his mother demanded querulously, and Gabriella was too stunned to move, either to knock or go away. She had never heard grandmotherly Alice speak in any but a gentle, humble voice. Now she sounded like the most brusque, shrewish alewife in England.

"The baron—and then I would have been as good as dead," Osric said in an unpleasant whine. "Maybe it's time to move on."

"And leave these woods?" Alice replied after an astoundingly obscene curse. "Don't be daft, Osric. The rabbits hereabouts have the best fur I've ever seen. You'll just have to watch yourself, that's all."

"I tell you, it's too dangerous now," her son complained. "The baron's a different kettle of fish from the stupid old earl. The easy days are over!"

"They are if you act like a fool!" his mother barked. "We'll just lay low for a while, that's all. These bones are too old to be jostled about the countryside. Get me some ale and stop your moaning. Then hide them clothes."

Gabriella moved away from the cottage like one in a dream. Her poor dear father had indeed been exploited. Who else had thought him stupid and made sport of him? Who else among the villagers had stolen from him?

She had tried so hard to justify their reluctance to help her, only to discover that the baron was right, or at least partly.

She didn't know what to do. Should she tell Baron DeGuerre what she had learned? Or go to William, who had looked at her with barely disguised lust the last time she had seen him in the baron's solar?

Just where did her loyalty lie now? she thought mournfully as the first heavy drops of rain fell on her while she made her way back to the castle.

The cold rain pelted against the barren branches of the trees that crowded the road leading to Castle Frechette and turned it into a muddy morass. The gray and cloudy sky seemed like the smoke-stained ceiling in the vault of an old and mildewed tomb. No bird song disturbed the silence, only the raindrops and the slow, heavy thud of the horses in the baron's cortege as they reached the ridge that overlooked the river valley.

Nevertheless, Etienne was pleased to be returning. It had taken the contrast with his other, lesser estates to enable him to truly appreciate the astonishing beauty of Castle Frechette, even on this damp and dreary October day.

He also told himself he was pleased because the decision he had reached on his journey was a wise one.

Gabriella Frechette had to leave his estate. Her mere presence encouraged disrespect among his servants and impertinence in the tenants. It must have been taking over the estate that had temporarily blinded him to the obvious.

So, go she must. He had thought of granting Gabriella her freedom immediately upon his return, until he realized that might look like weakness to the other tenants. Spring would be better. He had not specified her term of servitude to the day, so he would be magnanimous at Easter.

He shifted in his saddle and glanced around. Jean Luc Ducette, tall and lean as a cadaver, rode stiffly beside him. Philippe was riding behind, probably scowling because he was not in the favored position, but his mood was of little concern to Etienne. They would soon be in his hall, with a good meal and a warm hearth—and Josephine, too, of course.

God's wounds, he should be more content. He had a beautiful mistress, ten prosperous estates, a fine castle. Jean Luc had told him that his manors had made even more money than expected and there was a sense of peace in the land, so no need to dread that he might be called upon to go to war during the harsh winter months. Indeed, he should be very happy.

Perhaps it was the petulant presence of Philippe that lessened his joy. Philippe was born to be discontented and always blaming someone else for it. If only the scoundrel would feel indignant enough to leave his service, but there seemed small hope of that easy solution.

Philippe had only himself to blame if he felt neglected lately. It was not the baron's task to seek out Philippe, but for Philippe to be at his lord's disposal. Instead, the few times the baron had gone hunting, Philippe had been otherwise occupied, usually getting drunk at the nearest tavern or the baron's own kitchen.

In the spring, Etienne decided, he would send Philippe away, too, if the man was not already gone.

Then Etienne spotted something off to the side of the road and pulled his mount to an abrupt halt. He jumped from his horse, twisting his ankle in the process, but he straightened without a sound and ignored the pain as he strode toward the dead animal.

It was a deer, a large female, and it had been in the process of being butchered when the poacher had obviously heard the approaching men and run off.

Etienne frowned grimly and muttered a quiet curse. So, someone had dared to ignore his warning.

If he had not found it necessary to remove himself from the temptation of Gabriella Frechette, he might have been able to enforce his edicts more effectively. It had been a mistake leaving the more careless George in command.

By now Philippe, Jean Luc and most of the foot soldiers had joined their lord, staring silently at the bloody carcass.

"Have it brought to the hall," Etienne ordered. "I will give ten gold coins to any man who brings me a poacher, with his catch for proof."

Etienne marched back to his horse, his teeth clenched tightly together in frustration and to subdue the pain from his ankle. When he mounted and his foot hit the side of the horse, he was very glad no one was nearby to hear him gasp at the agonizing contact.

He couldn't afford to let anyone know he was hurt. He despised weakness in others, although not as much as in himself. With luck, he would be able to hide any sign of injury until he could be alone.

He punched the side of his stallion with his good heel and rode ahead, leaving the others behind.

Etienne tried not to grimace as he went up the few steps to the entrance of the hall, although his ankle was swollen and painful. He had managed to hide his condition from the grooms and stable boys, but he would be relieved to get to his bedchamber, where he could be alone. He would have to think of something to send Josephine out of the room, of course . . . and then it occurred to him that she had not been in the courtyard to greet him. Usually she left strict orders with the watchmen to summon her immediately when he was seen from the battlements. It was raining; perhaps that was why she was not there.

He shoved open the door and entered, pausing on the threshold as he removed his dripping cloak and trying not to wonder where Gabriella might be.

No wonder Josephine had not come to the door. She was enthroned on a chair near the blazing hearth, surrounded by the wares of a cloth merchant and milliner as if she had been transported to an Eastern bazaar. The merchant, a man of sturdy build and anxious mien, hovered nearby, holding out a bolt of what even Etienne recognized as very costly cloth of gold. The female milliner, more patient perhaps, stood silently amid an array of caps, crowns, coronets, scarves, snoods, netting, dried flowers and feathers, blocking the way to the stairs. Chalfront was there, too, his back against the wall and watching with a comical mixture of awe and worry. No doubt the fellow was upset by the amount of money Josephine was spending.

The baron put a pleasant expression on his face and strode forward. "What is this, Josephine?" he asked. "Another opportunity to give away my money?"

Chalfront started as if the baron had sent an arrow whizzing toward him, while Josephine smiled calmly. She well knew that he didn't begrudge her buying fine clothes. So attired, she only increased her value to him.

The merchant blanched. "Oh, my lord!" he cried, bowing so low his bulbous nose almost touched the rushes. "Greetings! Welcome to our village! We are fortunate to have you here!"

"You mean you are fortunate to have my *money* here," Etienne replied, crossing his arms and casually leaning his weight on his uninjured foot.

"Baron DeGuerre!" the merchant said, aghast. "Naturally, I welcome your patronage, but as I was just telling Lady de Chaney, I would be most gratified and delighted if she would accept this cloth as a gift."

"A gift?" Etienne exchanged a knowing look with Josephine. "You expect nothing in return?"

"Well, my lord, no. Not really. Of course, should a visitor wish to know where Lady de Chaney obtained the fabric, I would hope she would recall my name."

"Of course," Etienne replied. This had happened many times, yet it never ceased to please him. Cloth merchants, jewelers, furniture makers—all gave Josephine gifts of their wares with the hope that others, perhaps trying to imitate her and her exquisite taste, would seek to purchase similar goods.

As much as he enjoyed watching Josephine deal with such fawning, flattering tradesmen, his foot was too painful for him to stay. "I'm going to change my clothes," he announced. "Jean Luc and the rest should be here soon." He spoke directly to Chalfront. "We'll be going over the accounts tomorrow." Etienne scrutinized the man carefully to gauge his reaction, and was pleased to detect only keen interest, not guilt.

He must be honest, Etienne thought, or he would have discerned *some* sign of culpability.

"Would you like some assistance?" Josephine asked, half-rising, a worried expression creasing her alabaster brow.

Etienne's attention was still focused on Chalfront, and that was the reason Etienne saw something flash in the man's eyes. Envy, perhaps? Or jealousy?

"No, I can manage quite well," he answered coolly, surveying the group. "You stay and buy yourself whatever you like. Chalfront will fetch the necessary coins."

The merchant's grinning, greedy reaction would have amused Etienne another time; now, he had more serious things to consider.

Something had happened to Chalfront during his absence. Apparently he no longer pined for Gabriella Frechette and it seemed he may have transferred his affections to Josephine. Etienne's first reaction was a temptation to laugh. Chalfront and Josephine de Chaney? It would be like the pairing of a purebred mare with a farmer's draft horse. On the other hand, he recalled one draft horse that had sired an astounding number of offspring. He had reason to be concerned, though, for an alliance between a man's bailiff and his mistress could spell disaster.

But Chalfront and Josephine! It was ludicrous. Besides, Josephine was far too intelligent to try to deceive him. Ever practical, she would know that she would gain more by pleasing him than by betraying him.

Josephine seemed to enjoy the man's attendance, for she certainly glanced his way often enough.

Etienne paused on his progress toward the stairs and glanced over his shoulder. At that moment, Gabriella came through the door from the kitchen bearing a chalice and two goblets, and he forgot about everyone else in the hall. Despite his resolve not to feel anything for her, need and desire rushed through him.

She looked pale and drawn. Was she ill? If she were unwell, he would absolve her from further duties until she recovered.

Gabriella's gaze met his for a short moment, and he thought she blushed. With pleasure that he had returned? She looked quickly away, and her mouth turned down into an unmistakable frown.

God's wounds, she would not even look at him, and he had been so concerned for her health. He should have found the strength to stay here, and ignore the passion she stirred in him.

His absence had been a mistake on many fronts. Worse, it had been an act of weakness, unworthy of him. He must, and would, reassert his command over his emotions, and over everyone under his rule.

''Bring me some hot water,'' he ordered Gabriella, not bothering to gauge her reaction before pushing his way through the remainder of the milliner's goods.

Josephine rose with an anxious face. "I will bring the water."

"No, the merchants are not finished. Gabriella can do it." If his order disturbed Josephine, so much the better. It would remind her where her priorities should be.

With a stony, impassive expression, Etienne mounted the stairs to the bedchamber.

Chapter Nine

It was only a matter of moments before Gabriella stood outside the bedchamber with a basin of warm water in her hands. Fortuitously, Guido had some ready to be used for soup that he had reluctantly relinquished when she had hurried to the kitchen.

She had returned to the castle almost by instinct after hearing Osric and his mother, too preoccupied to notice anything until she reached the kitchen. There she had gone about her tasks mechanically, until she saw the baron's stallion being led into the stable. At once she had been determined to tell him about Osric, her sense of betrayal overpowering everything else.

She had realized the moment she saw the baron that something was different about him. He looked ill, or in pain. Perhaps it was only that she had forgotten how grim his usual expression was. She had tried to ignore her curiosity and told herself that if something was wrong, it was none of her concern.

Then the baron had stared at her with those cold, impartial eyes, and ordered her to do his bidding as if she were the meanest of servants, and she had decided she would say nothing about Osric. The baron didn't deserve her help, and Osric would probably convince his mother to flee, after his close call in the forest today.

Now, since the door was ajar, she, anxious to be gone, her hands encumbered, the water cooling and the baron expecting her, didn't bother to announce her presence, but shoved the door open with her shoulder. The first thing she saw was the bed, with its sinfully rich coverings.

Then she realized that Baron DeGuerre stood beside the old chest that she had noticed in the corner before, leaning his weight on his splayed hands. When he heard her enter, he spun around, winced and uttered a vehement curse that Gabriella had never heard before. His face was extremely pale and he favored his left leg.

"Do you need any help?" she asked, everything else momentarily forgotten by her surprise that he could be hurt, like any other mortal.

"I can manage," he growled.

"I...I brought the water you wanted," she murmured, moving hastily toward the table, which was unfortunately covered in jewelry, brushes, small fragrant jars, a needle and spool of thick thread. She set the basin down on the stool beside it, then she turned to face him. She was sure he was in some kind of physical pain, or was ill.

He limped toward the bed and sat on the end of it. "Bring the basin here."

"You *are* hurt," she charged as she obeyed, concerned to see him in pain, as she would be for anyone. As she had been for Osric, she recalled bitterly. "Is it your foot? When did it happen, on the journey or at your other castle?"

"It doesn't matter. You've brought the water. Now you can go."

"Perhaps you need some assistance—?"

"Have you come to enjoy your servitude so much you want to help me disrobe?" His sarcastic tone surprised her, for she had rarely detected any emotion in his voice. He was always so controlled.

The notion that he possessed human frailties gave her a strange sense of excitement, and diluted the aura of unnatural self-possession that set him so apart from other men. "You are injured," she said firmly, ignoring his scowl, "and from the way you moved just now, I think you might have broken your foot. I know a little about broken bones, enough to tell if a bone *is* broken, anyway. Let me examine your foot, my lord."

He raised one dark brow. "Are you willing to remove my boots at last?" he asked with an attempt at frivolity.

She looked at him sternly, like a mother facing a recalcitrant child. "I have to feel the wound."

"As much as I would enjoy having you at my feet, it is nothing serious."

"It pains you, does it not? It could grow worse, especially if the bone has broken the skin." She crossed her arms and frowned. "Of course, I could do as you wish and do nothing, but if the wound festers . . ."

"I understand your point, but I assure you, it is not serious," he said as he waved his hand dismissively. "My ankle barely hurts."

She gave him a skeptical look, then crouched in front of him to remove his boot. She pushed up the mud-spattered hem of his robe, then stared. "There is blood here."

"From a dead deer," he explained matter-of-factly.

Of course. He would have been hunting while he was gone. She took hold of his foot and he winced. His face quickly resumed its usual inscrutability. "Liar," she muttered.

"What did you say?"

"Nothing, my lord." Then she grasped his boot and tugged it off, trying to be gentle now that she was sure he was in pain.

Despite her care, he shot back on the bed and let out a subdued yelp when the boot came free.

"I thought you said it didn't hurt," she remarked before taking his foot in her hand and tenderly feeling the swollen area through his woollen stockings. "I don't think anything is broken," she said.

"I told you it was not serious."

With somewhat less gentle care, she let go of his foot, which struck the ground, making the baron wince again. "What the devil did you do that for?" he demanded.

She sat back on her haunches. "I thought you could endure the pain, my lord," she said innocently.

"God's teeth, yes, but I did not expect to be tortured!" His eyes narrowed. "You seem rather confident, for a *servant*," he noted dryly, setting his foot down cautiously.

She recalled the coins Mary had given her, and reminded herself that they indicated a loyalty far more important than Osric's betrayal. "I will not be a servant for very much longer," she replied.

"That is quite a sum you owe me. It will take many days' labor to repay it."

"If I were dependent on my work alone, perhaps. But you see, Baron DeGuerre, the world is not quite the terrible place you believe it to be, not when one has friends, and I have friends in the village."

"Who?" he demanded.

His angry reaction surprised her. Why should he be so upset to discover that she was not completely alone and friendless? He would get his money. Or was it that she would not be at his mercy if she had friends?

If he were Philippe de Varenne, perhaps. But not Baron DeGuerre, for he had possessed the opportunity before and had not taken advantage of it, or her. He was an honorable man.

Yes, honorable. In the days since her arrival, she had discovered that he was not the cold, cruel monster he was reputed to be. He was ambitious and expected his tenants to work, but that was not unreasonable. He wanted the law upheld and was ready to see it enforced. She could understand now that her father's methods were not perfect; indeed, she was slowly beginning to appreciate the trouble misplaced charity could cause.

"The men of the village may not be overly generous," she replied, "but I am pleased to tell you that such a thing cannot also be said of the women. One has offered me a home, when I am free."

He rose slowly. "You are willing to take their money? I should think the peasant women can ill afford to lose any."

"Especially since you have raised the rents so high," she said, keeping her tone matter-of-fact despite the sudden pounding of her heart as he came close to her. "It was offered to me out of kindness, and with thankfulness, I took it. It will be repaid."

"You must enjoy being in debt," he noted wryly as he passed her and went to pour himself some wine.

"It will not be so terrible to be in debt to *them,*" she said with a hint of defiance. "Provided their generosity does not make their lives any more difficult."

"And I suppose you think yourself able to decide the point when they are giving you more than they can afford?"

She didn't answer, because her doubts were returning at his question. Was Mary going to suffer for helping her? Perhaps she should have refused, after all.

"How will you judge?" he went on coldly. "You have never been poor."

"Neither have you," she retorted defensively.

"Haven't I?" he queried, looking at her with his inscrutable blue eyes over the rim of his goblet.

Suddenly she knew he had been, and this unexpected knowledge forced her to admit how little she knew of the man before her. She had seen the outer man, the unemotional commander. But the inner man, the one who had mentioned his mother with such bitterness, the one who would not allow himself to appear anything but strong—what did she know of him?

What did she wish to know of him?

Before her heart could answer, her pride arose to remind her that she had not made a completely selfish decision by taking Mary's money. She would not feel badly for accepting it, and she would not give way to her curiosity concerning his past. Besides, who was the baron to stand here and try to make her feel guilty? It was *his* fault she needed Mary's help. "You should stay off your foot, my lord," she said dispassionately, turning toward the door.

In immediate defiance of her words, he strode in front of her. "I can't do that, and you must tell no one I am hurt."

"It is no sin to be injured," she proclaimed, straightening her shoulders, raising her chin and wondering why she was not angrier. "Nor is it a sin to accept help when it is offered."

"It is no great honor, either," he said as he walked toward the chest again, and she marveled that he could move with such agility, despite his injury.

"You are determined to appear invincible, aren't you?" she demanded.

"A man in power must always appear invincible," he said quietly, glancing at her over his shoulder, "for power can be as fleeting as a summer's breeze, a man's span of rule as short as a winter's day. For every man who admires Baron DeGuerre, there are as many who would gladly see him weakened."

"Men like Philippe de Varenne?"

He sat on the battered chest and regarded her steadily. "Yes, men like Philippe."

"Why do you keep him near you, then?"

He gave her a ghost of a smile. "So I know what he's up to, of course." Etienne turned away and fumbled at the side of the chest, shielding the secret drawer from her sight. The pain was getting worse and it was getting more difficult to hide it from her shrewd gaze. "You may go," he ordered brusquely, his fingers seeking the hidden latch.

He found it and the drawer sprang open. Then he realized she was still standing there. "You seem rather reluctant to leave me, Gabriella. Is there anything else you would care to ask, or is it that you cannot bear to leave my company?"

She remained motionless, watching him.

By all the saints in Christendom, could it be that she *did* desire his company? He had asked the question flippantly, without really expecting her to answer. He had thought she would flee the room. If she did want to be with him, that would explain her reluctance to leave his bedchamber, her persistent questions, her tenderness . . .

No, it couldn't be, he told himself as his hand tightly gripped the vial inside the drawer. Her apparent concern for his injury was perhaps a ruse to discover how seriously he was hurt. The strangely sorrowful look in her eyes when she had entered the hall was probably regret that he had returned. The sensation of her gentle fingers probing his ankle didn't matter except to remind him to ignore her.

Finally she curtsied and left the room.

Well, what else did he expect? That she would admit to a passionate love for him?

God's wounds, the ache in his foot was making him foolish! Soon he would be imagining that his mother had doted on him.

With careful movements Etienne removed his stocking and set his foot in the basin of warm water. Then he pulled the stopper from the vial and put a few drops of the liquid into the water. A pungent aroma greeted his nostrils as he set his foot in the basin and leaned back on his elbows.

The preparation he had added to the water, a secret elixir of his mother's concoction that he had hoarded since her death, would numb the pain enough to enable him to walk normally at the meal tonight. His foot would ache and be tender for days, but no one need know how painful it might be.

No one except Gabriella. He was thankful she hadn't tried to mother him. Not that he knew what it was truly like to be mothered. His mother had rarely nursed him, telling him it was better to suffer in silence. To be a man.

Nevertheless, he should have ordered Gabriella from the room at once, instead of letting her stay and revealing his injury. What if she told others of his state? What if that ambitious puppy Philippe de Varenne found out?

Philippe would never challenge the baron's authority directly. He wouldn't have the stomach for it.

Nevertheless, any sign of weakness might pave the way for a lessening of respect, and a sense that the once powerful Baron DeGuerre had grown vulnerable. Philippe had many equally ambitious friends, and Etienne DeGuerre had made some enemies on his climb from the gutter. There would be several who would be only too happy to see him brought low.

He would have to trust to Gabriella's discretion, and he hoped that he could.

As for those vultures who would one day come circling around him, let them come. They would find that Etienne DeGuerre was still more than a match for any of them.

"Did anything interesting happen while I was away?" Philippe asked nonchalantly as he joined Sir George and the others in the hall that night before the evening meal.

"No," George replied with a shrug of his slim shoulders.

"Gabriella Frechette gave George a bath, though," Seldon said, a grin on his face.

Philippe turned to stare at the usually self-possessed· George, whose blushing face was nearly as red as his tunic.

Donald frowned and Seldon gave him a befuddled look. "Well, she soaked him, didn't she?"

"A bucket of water escaped her slender fingers and happened to land on the ground near me," George explained.

"She was very upset about it," Donald remarked gravely.

"And she apologized very nicely," George said as if to end all talk of her.

Philippe was not in a mood to be dissuaded, especially when he remembered what he had learned about Gabriella's brother while the baron chose to ignore him on their recent journey. He had not wasted all his abundant leisure time at the Montmorencys. "How *is* the pretty Gabriella?" he inquired. "Does Chalfront continue to harbor hopes?"

The young knights exchanged furtive glances, increasing Philippe's curiosity. Despite his newfound knowledge, he wondered if he would have done better to refuse to accompany the baron. Obviously he had missed an important development at Castle Frechette. "What is it? Has he absconded?"

"No," George said immediately. "He's still here."

"Then what's happened?" Philippe demanded in hushed tones, aware that whatever it was, George and the others wanted it kept secret, something significant in itself.

"It's nothing," George said with surprising and unexpected sternness, confirming Philippe's suspicions.

"He's done something to anger the baron?"

"No," Donald said slowly.

"Then *what?*" Philippe asked with irritation. "It's my sworn duty to protect the baron, too. Or is it that you seek to use your information to your own ends?"

"I don't think I like what you're implying," George replied. Then he shrugged his shoulders. "But no matter. There's nothing to get excited about. Chalfront's done nothing wrong."

"So far," Seldon added significantly.

Philippe's gaze darted to the man's face, then back to George. "Don't attempt to divert me. I am not the village idiot, George. What do you think he's planning?"

George gave an exasperated sigh and looked daggers at Seldon. "I told you, it's nothing. Lady de Chaney seems to enjoy the bailiff's company, that's all."

Philippe's suspicious mind jumped to a fascinating conclusion. "Do you think they're conspiring against the baron?" he whispered eagerly.

George looked at him with mild distaste. "No, I do not. They are never alone together. We, um, made sure of this."

"You've been spying on Lady de Chaney?"

"No!" Donald was quick to deny. Rather too quick, Philippe thought. "They've done nothing wrong except spend some time together."

"A lot of time," Seldon added, obviously not nearly so sanguine as the others. "Well, they *have*," he protested when Donald shot him another angry glance.

"George just thought to make certain. I wouldn't say anything to the baron," Donald warned.

"Of course," Philippe said agreeably. "I mean, the idea of Josephine de Chaney having improper relations—oh, I meant conversations—with a little toad like Chalfront is ridiculous. So is the notion that she would work against the baron."

"Yes, it is *quite* ridiculous," George confirmed, obviously choosing to overlook Philippe's purposeful slip of the tongue. Donald and Seldon nodded their heads.

But perhaps the baron wouldn't think so, Philippe thought smugly. He scratched his nose so that the others wouldn't see his satisfied smile. Now he had two very interesting pieces of information that he could use, and use them he would.

The baron marched down the stairs, his black tunic swinging from the speed of his steps and the length of his strides. "Well, George, you have managed well in my absence," the baron remarked as he came toward them.

"In truth, there was little enough for me to do."

"Chalfront was helpful?"

Philippe watched George intently, wondering if the man was going to keep his suspicions to himself.

"Yes, indeed he was." George grinned ruefully. "He seemed to think I was rather...how shall I put this? Useless, as the lord of an estate. Wanted me to tax my brain and come up with all kinds of work, I gather." George sighed heavily, as if Chalfront's expectations had been completely and utterly unreasonable. "You set too high a standard, Baron."

"And you enjoy hunting too much," the baron replied as he sat on the bench beside the nobleman. It was not a condemnation. It was simply a statement of fact.

George was not going to tell the baron his suspicions, Philippe thought gleefully. If the man's implications about Chalfront and Lady de Chaney were true, and the baron found out that George had known before, the nobleman would suffer for keeping the secret.

On the other hand, if George could offer no proof, perhaps he was wise to keep silent. A false accusation would cause certain enmity between the baron and the accuser. That was not something a wise man would seek.

Philippe decided to leave Chalfront's fate in George's hands. He didn't particularly care about Chalfront, or the baron's mistress, either. Gabriella was by far the easier prey, and Philippe always chose the simpler course.

"You look fatigued, my lord," George noted.

"I did not sleep well last night."

"You work yourself too hard, my lord," Philippe said sympathetically.

"Running several estates is not a simple matter," Etienne replied, "although it has its rewards." He was disgusted by the man's overt flattery nearly as much as the fellow's inability to hide his greedy curiosity. Nevertheless, it was to Etienne's advantage that Philippe's thoughts were so obviously displayed, so it might be best that Philippe never learn the ability to mask them. As *he* had, so long ago.

"Such as Josephine de Chaney," Philippe said with a smile rather too much like a leer. "No wonder you did not sleep well, far from her. We should all enjoy such rewards!"

He made Josephine sound like some kind of furnishing, say a feather bed or a cushion, and as if any man could expect such a prize.

While Etienne did not love Josephine, he esteemed her as a woman and a friend, and he would not allow her to be disparaged by anyone. "I would take care you speak of her with respect for, of course, I will in-

terpret any disrespect for her as disrespect for me,"
Etienne said, his voice quiet—so quiet that George
grew a little paler, Seldon a little redder and Donald
even more immobile. A few of the other knights who
had entered the hall also fell silent. Even the ubiqui-
tous hounds seemed to be listening.

Philippe scowled. "I meant no disrespect, my lord,"
he said sullenly.

"Good. Otherwise, I would have to kill you."
Etienne rose slowly and ambled toward the high table.

After a short and heavy silence, George and the
others began to talk of hunting and the upcoming fall
slaughter. The dogs resumed their constant prowl for
scraps of food. The other men returned to their interrupted conversations, albeit with several wary glances
at the baron.

Philippe didn't pay attention to anyone save the
tired Baron DeGuerre. Let him threaten as he would,
Philippe told himself. The man had better take care of
more important things than whether or not his whore
had been insulted. He should beware insulting a man
from a wealthier family, one that could afford to pay
well for a man's death.

He should beware conspiracies, too, between a
beautiful, neglected woman and the man who had
control of even a small portion of his purse.

A very interesting situation was developing here.
Better perhaps, Philippe thought, to save his own
money and let others destroy Baron DeGuerre.

The famous, the powerful Baron Etienne De-Guerre brought low by a woman. That would be something to witness.

A few nights later, Gabriella lay awake on her cot in the long, narrow room above the storerooms where all the maidservants slept. Around her, others stirred and murmured in their sleep, but rest would not come to Gabriella Frechette.

To watch the baron during the first meal after his return and during the past few days, one would never guess he was in any pain, unless you happened to catch a fleeting expression in his blue eyes when he moved suddenly. She saw it, of course, because she knew to look for it.

Apparently, however, she was the only one who did. Josephine de Chaney carried on as if nothing were amiss, and made no effort to persuade the baron to retire early or to lessen his work. Neither did Sir George, or any of his other men.

Once more she told herself that it should not please her that *she* seemed to possess knowledge that Etienne DeGuerre had not shared with his mistress, or George, or his steward, or anyone else. After all, he would not have told her had she not surprised him.

What kind of life had the baron had, what kind of childhood, to make him so determined to keep even a relatively minor injury so secret? Certainly nothing like her own. She had been loved and had lacked for nothing, whether affection or material possessions. In fact, she had to admit, she had been somewhat spoiled.

Apparently Etienne DeGuerre had been raised in a bleak and hostile world, a world of mistrust and loneliness, of poverty and need. Perhaps, for him, happiness and an end to loneliness had come only recently, and he was not yet used to the security of his wealth and power, or such security as wealth and power could provide, which he seemed to think was very little indeed. He was not as confident as he pretended to be, nor did she believe that he was happy, or even content. She guessed that it was loneliness she had seen in him that first day when he stood in the courtyard, alone and apart.

He was right, too, that she truly knew nothing about being poor. Even now, she had food and warmth. And he had been correct, at least partly, about the tenants' relationship with her father. Perhaps he was also right that she had erred taking Mary's money, if he knew far better than she how Mary's gift might cause her to suffer.

The feelings of guilt she had managed to subdue suddenly seemed overwhelming. Surely she could endure the work better than Mary could spare any extra coins she might have saved. She was far younger than Mary and the other women who were willing to help pay her debt. She should give the money back.

But Mary had been so keen to offer it! To refuse it would have been an insult to the widow's good intentions, wouldn't it? And she would pay Mary and the others back just as soon as she could.

On the other hand, the baron had raised the rents. He had increased the pannage, too, and who knew what else? Mary and the rest of the peasants would have to pay more if *they* were to remain in their homes.

She had been proud of her father's concern for his people, and she still was, despite what she had heard pass between Osric and his mother. She could not put her own needs before theirs.

She would work the extra days. Being Josephine de Chaney's maid wasn't taxing. She would have to endure the baron's presence, but she thought she could manage. He was a better man than rumor reported. A little more leniency on his part would even guarantee that everybody saw his good qualities. His manner could be improved upon, certainly. He was always so cool and calm, so distant.

Except when he had kissed her. Then he had been hot rather than frigid, his passion setting her afire within.

Her attraction for the baron could prove far more dangerous than anything else, including Philippe de Varenne. Only now, as she lay alone in the dark, did she dare to acknowledge its potency. The true danger was not the baron, but her own yearning weakness. The sooner she could get away from the baron, the sooner she would once again be in control of her wayward emotions.

But must Mary, or anyone else, pay the price of her vulnerability?

No. She must find a way to be strong. To ignore her growing desire, and his rare moments of revelation, until she could be free.

She must, and so she would.

Her decision irreversibly made, Gabriella reached beneath her pillow and pulled out the cloth-wrapped coins. She would return them immediately, while her resolve was at its height, and when there would be few others awake to see her go to the village.

What if the watchmen at the gate tried to stop her?

She remembered the secret tunnel her father had planned beneath the altar in the chapel. She had never used it herself, but she knew that she had only to push aside the altar to find the trapdoor entrance.

Gabriella slipped quietly out of the bed and hurried from the room. Cautiously she made her way toward the steps leading to the storeroom below. She paused near the bottom and listened carefully. Something was making a rustling noise below.

One of the castle cats, she guessed, after a mouse who was trying to get into the food. There were several cats. Guido was always complaining about them, although he couldn't deny that without them, mice would be a problem.

Once, when she was a very small child, Bryce had enticed her to go on a midnight raid to the storeroom for some leftover sweetmeats, and while sneaking through the room, she had stepped on a live mouse. She remembered her terror vividly, so now she moved very slowly, feeling her way with her toes as she went around the corner.

She halted and blinked in the unexpected light of a tallow candle, for it was not a cat making that noise, and certainly not a mouse.

Chapter Ten

Philippe de Varenne turned to face Gabriella, his lips twisting into a pleased smile. "Well, well, well," he said softly, the candle he held tipping precariously as he swayed slightly.

He was drunk, Gabriella thought, anxious to return to the upper chamber. Mary's restitution would have to wait, for her way was blocked by Philippe as effectively as if he were a stone wall.

Then she saw the burlap bags, brooms and kindling behind him. If the candle fell on them, the room would be on fire in an instant.

She started forward, determined to snatch the candle from Philippe, but he straightened and gripped it tighter, lifting the candle higher so that the flickering flame cast sharp shadows over his angular face.

"What have we here?" he slurred with a feral grin, yet not so drunkenly that she didn't realize her danger. Even intoxicated, he could do her serious harm. "Is it a watch wench? Are you going to demand a password? What, speechless, pretty Gabriella? Not *you*, who can find plenty to say to Baron DeGuerre."

She began to back away. "I heard a noise and came to see if a rat had gotten into the food," she said with seeming deference.

"Ah," he breathed. "How commendable."

"Apparently I was quite wrong, so if you will excuse me, sir, I shall go—"

"There is no rush, my dear." Philippe sat on a pile of flour bags and blew out the candle.

Gabriella gasped as the room plunged into complete darkness. She couldn't see anything. She could only hear the sound of breathing, her own short pants and Philippe de Varenne's deeper exhalations. Keeping her lips tightly together to still even that small sound, she continued to inch backward.

Then it occurred to her that if she couldn't see Philippe, he couldn't see her, and she moved with more confidence, anticipating the feel of the wall against her back. Once she found the wall, she could find the stairs.

Philippe spoke, and it was as if he were a disembodied spirit. "Your brother's name is Bryce, is it not?"

"Yes, sir," she replied, all her energy focused on finding the stairs leading upward.

"I met him once, in France, you know. Not so very long ago."

She hesitated. "When?" she asked, curiosity mingling with her dread. Then she began moving again. Anyone in the castle could have told him her brother's name, and France would have been a logical destination. That was where she had sent her messengers first.

"So many questions—and you forgot to say 'sir.' That's no way to talk to someone who knows where your brother is."

Gabriella peered across the room. Her eyes were more accustomed to the darkness now, and she could see the shape of the man sitting on the bags. She felt an instinctive urge to flee, but what if Philippe de Varenne did know something about Bryce? If she left, he might never tell her. "Where exactly did you see my brother, sir, and when?"

"What will you give me for the answer?"

"I . . . I beg your pardon?"

"How much is my knowledge worth, pretty Gabriella?"

She chewed her lip and wondered if he had indeed seen Bryce, or if this was some ploy. "I have some coins here, sir."

Philippe de Varenne put both hands on the bags and hoisted himself upright. "Oh, but it is not cold coins I want, my dear." He took a few tentative steps in her direction, and he seemed less than steady on his feet. "Just a kiss—that's all I ask. Not much, is it, when I can tell you how to find your brother?"

She didn't want Philippe to touch her in any way, let alone kiss her. "How do I know you're speaking the truth?" she demanded suspiciously as she continued to retreat, her back finally contacting the frigid stone wall.

"Because I am a knight. Besides, I would hardly dishonor myself by lying for a kiss," he replied, and she heard the tinge of anger in his voice. "However, since you do not give your favors easily, I will give you proof. Your brother has a small scar above his right eye. He told me that you gave it to him when you pushed him into a water trough.''

''That is common knowledge hereabouts,'' she replied, her hand feeling for the gap that would indicate the stairway.

''You pushed him in the water because he said you were fat.''

Gabriella sucked in her breath sharply, for that was perfectly true. She had been rather plump as a girl, and sensitive about it. Bryce teased her continuously and unmercifully, despite their parents' admonitions, until the day she exploded with rage and indignation and shoved him into the trough with all her might.

Her action precipitated quite a scene. She was wailing, the servants came running, Bryce's head bled copiously all over his new tunic, and then her parents arrived and demanded to know the cause of the uproar.

Bryce had been lightly punished before for teasing her. Nevertheless, he saw—as did she—that their father, usually loath to physically discipline his children, looked angry enough this time to seriously contemplate it.

Gabriella, immediately contrite, swiftly decided that Bryce had been punished enough. She told her parents they had been playing a game and she had accidentally tripped Bryce, sending him headlong into the trough. Bryce hadn't said a word then, but the grateful look in his eyes was her reward. Later he promised he would never tease her again, and they both solemnly vowed to keep the cause of his dunking a secret between them. To the best of her knowledge, he had kept his word.

A part of her told her to remain skeptical. It had been a long time. It was possible Bryce had talked about the incident. Nevertheless, she couldn't quite subdue the hope that Philippe might be able to help her find her brother. "If you *do* know where Bryce is, won't you help me? Can you tell me if he is well—sir?"

Philippe came closer. "Give me a kiss, and you shall have your answer."

Was he asking so much when she might finally discover where Bryce was? Once she had that information, she could send for her brother, and all would soon be made right. "Very well," she said, steeling herself for Philippe's touch and closing her eyes. "One kiss."

Philippe de Varenne *had* been drinking, as she realized when he put his lips upon hers. His sour breath and sloppy, wet kiss filled her with disgust and seemed to last an eternity before he drew back.

"Where is my brother?" she asked, anxious to wipe her mouth and remove any evidence of his kiss. She did not, because Philippe might see her action as an insult and refuse to divulge his information.

Philippe frowned. "That was hardly what I would call a kiss, my dear. You might have been dead, for all your enthusiasm."

"You did not specify that I had to make a pretence of enjoying it, sir," she said with a deferential tone distinctly at odds with the revulsion she was feeling. "Please, where did you see Bryce?"

"One more kiss—and one with some passion—and I will tell you what part of France he was in."

"Then he is in France?"

"No fair guessing," Philippe chided. "Now, with an attempt at ardor, if you please."

Gabriella hesitated. His kiss was unwelcome and his touch made her feel soiled, but France was large, and she had to know more if she was to find Bryce. "Very well," she muttered.

She put her hands on Philippe's shoulders and pulled him close, moving her lips over his with all the pretence of passion she could muster.

Philippe's grip tightened and, when she tried to pull away, he put his hand on the back of her head so that she could not move. His other hand snaked around her waist as he pinned her against the wall and shoved his knee between her legs. With increasing panic, she pushed against his chest with all her might, to no avail. "It's not so terrible, is it?" he said, his mouth trailing across her cheek. "I knew you would enjoy it if you would give me a chance."

She forced herself not to react as his hand slid up her arm and his lips traveled lower. *"Where is my brother?"* she demanded fiercely.

"I'm afraid, my dear, that the answer has momentarily slipped my mind," he mumbled.

"I kissed you!" she charged, once again trying to push him away. "I knew I couldn't trust your word! I shall tell the baron what you've done!"

He put one hand on the wall on either side of her, trapping her between his muscular arms. "Aren't you forgetting something, my fiery Gabriella?" Philippe asked, shoving his face uncomfortably close. "I am a knight, and you are a servant, because of Baron DeGuerre. Who will the baron listen to, eh? Or have I made a terrible mistake? Perhaps you are closer to the baron than any of us knows. Has the little serving wench become something rather more?"

"You are despicable!" She shoved him with all her strength, knocking him off balance. He stumbled backward and she darted past him, colliding with a pile of flour bags. She scrambled over them and ran to the door. With a thankful gasp, she yanked it open and fled into the courtyard.

Philippe did not follow her. For one thing, he was too tired and too dizzy from drink, or perhaps the feel of that delectable body in his arms. For another, he was quite satisfied that the baron had not yet bedded her. Therefore, even if she did complain that he had reneged on their little bargain, no nobleman—not even the upstart Baron DeGuerre—would dare to take her side against Philippe de Varenne.

The castle's small chapel was as silent as a cata-comb in the middle of the night watch, and dim as a mystic's cave. The long, narrow nave was lit only by the small flickering flames of votive candles, for the moonlight was not strong enough to penetrate the stained-glass window. The ornately carved altar was barely visible. The narrow bench upon which the lone occupant sat was cold and hard, like the stone floor beneath his feet.

Etienne bowed his head and sighed heavily. He had not come here to commune with God or the saints. He was here because the numbing effects of his mother's potion had worn off and the ache in his ankle was so bad that he couldn't sleep. There was only a small amount of the medicine left, so rather than use any more, he had come here where he could endure alone.

He had managed to leave the bedchamber without disturbing Josephine, who had seemed rather distant during the days since his return. Perhaps she was upset that he had gone on a journey without her. Maybe she was annoyed that he had been too tired, and in too much secret pain, to make love with her recently. It could be that she realized he was losing interest in her, which was surely only because they had been together for several months. Such a lessening of desire was only natural.

Whatever it was, he could be sure that Josephine would never ask him. Nor would she complain, or criticize him in any way. She understood the precarious nature of her position too well. He could not imagine Josephine de Chaney upbraiding him in a castle courtyard in front of his men and the servants, as Gabriella had that first day.

Gabriella. What was it about her that penetrated the defenses of his heart, to reach the tenderness he had forgotten he possessed?

He let himself remember kissing Gabriella. The emotions her touch aroused in him were so startling in their strength!

Strength? That was amusing. What he felt was a weakness. Gabriella Frechette, with her big brown eyes and pale pink cheeks, was more of a danger to him than Philippe de Varenne or a hundred others ever would or could be. Had he not learned the folly of misplaced love at his mother's knee?

Suddenly a noise interrupted his bitter reverie. His hand went swiftly to the ever-present dagger in his belt and he rose cautiously, turning to peer into the moonlit dimness, glad as always that his black garment would make it that much more difficult for anyone to see him when he had no wish to be seen.

Someone was just inside the door, motionless, waiting expectantly. Who—an assassin? Why wait? For an accomplice? God's blood, he should, for it would take more than one man to kill Etienne De-Guerre!

Keeping in the shadowed recesses of the frigid and uneven stone walls, Etienne made his way toward the unwelcome intruder, his sore ankle completely forgotten, his tread silent as a cat's.

The shape had sidled closer to the basin of holy water. Etienne was soon there and he reached out to grab the intruder around the neck. A very slender, soft neck, Etienne noticed as the intruder let out a strangled cry of pain and surprise.

Almost immediately, Etienne realized he had a woman by the throat and relaxed his grip.

"Who...who is it?" the woman gasped, rubbing where his hand had grabbed her.

"Baron DeGuerre. Gabriella?" Given the train of his previous thoughts, her appearance seemed like a supernatural visitation.

"Yes, my lord."

At the sound of her husky voice there in the dark, he felt a remarkable sensation of pleasure and desire run through him, vibrating like the chords of a harp.

He was in danger of becoming as sentimental as a minstrel. "I thought you were an assassin," he explained matter-of-factly as he tucked his dagger back into his belt. "It is not wise to come upon me in such a manner."

There was something obviously wrong, he realized, as he surveyed her in the dim light. Her clothes were askew and torn, her hair unkempt, and her eyes puffy, as if she had been crying. "Are you hurt?"

"I thought no one was here, Baron DeGuerre," she said, a tremor in her voice that alarmed him. He caught the slight scent of stale wine. It mingled with the waxy smell of the candles, the damp air of the chapel and the lingering incense of the mass. But she was not drunk, despite her appearance.

"What is it?" he asked quietly. "What has happened to send you here in the chapel at this hour?" He took hold of her cold hand and drew her farther inside the nave. Her fingers tightened around his hand like the clasp of a child who has been frightened, and comes to seek help. Her apparent trust pleased him greatly and made his distress at her state all the more intense.

"I...I couldn't sleep. On my way here, I tripped and fell."

"I am not a stupid man, Gabriella," he said, a hint of frustration in his voice. "Even in this light, I can see that your hair is untidy, your garments are in disarray and you are upset. Something or someone has frightened you, or perhaps tried to do you harm. Since it is my duty to ensure the orderly running of my household and the safety of everyone in it, I demand to know what has happened."

"I can't tell you," she whispered, tugging her hand from his and glancing at his face with a defiant look.

"You will if I order you to."

"How can I be sure you will believe me?"

"Why would I not?"

"Because I am nothing but a servant."

"Am I to infer from this that someone of higher rank is responsible?" He struggled to keep any sign of his mounting anger from his voice, lest it silence her further. "Was it Chalfront again?"

"No, my lord. It…it doesn't matter now," she said wearily. She began to straighten her bodice self-consciously.

"Gabriella, look at me." She hesitated as if she meant to disobey and he spoke sternly. "Gabriella, if someone has harmed or frightened you in any way, I want to know. A man who treats a woman in such a fashion—any woman, whether highborn or not—is not welcome here."

"You would be a most exceptional lord if you meant that," she said skeptically as she tilted her head to look at him.

"I *am* an exceptional lord," he replied calmly.

"You won't understand. You can't."

"Because I am a nobleman?"

"Yes, and because you are a man."

"Therefore you think that I have been spared humiliation and pain, that I have always been accorded the respect I command now?"

She looked at him doubtfully.

"I was not born a nobleman, Gabriella. I am the bastard son of a minor lord who deserted my mother before I was born. If I have power and respect, it is because I have earned it. It took me a very long time, and for much of that time, I was *not* treated with deference, kindness or even courtesy."

Suddenly extremely aware of the baron's proximity in the dark confines of the chapel, Gabriella heard the bitterness in his voice. She had felt as taut as a fur stretched out to dry at a tannery after the horror of Philippe's attack and the shock of the baron's defensive grip around her throat. Yet now, the tension had changed; it was part excitement, part dread of her own weakness and part desire to feel his protective arms around her again. Every sense alive to the situation, her mind urged caution. She moved further inside the room, wanting to think and unable to do so close by him.

"I thought everyone had heard the rumors about me," he continued, his tone once more cool and impartial. "My particular favorite is that I'm the spawn of the devil and was suckled by witches."

His apparent attempt to make light of his past touched her deeply, because she heard the pain beneath. What a lonely life he must have led! How much she wanted to put *her* protective arms around him, and tell him how she admired him.

"Sit and tell me what happened," he ordered, gesturing toward the bench.

She obeyed, perching on the edge of the hard wooden seat. He joined her, sitting beside her but not touching any part of her.

"I was going to return Mary's money to her," she began, then hesitated, embarrassed and ashamed to continue, especially in light of his unexpected solicitousness. Here and now, he was so different from the coldhearted, aloof nobleman. He seemed kind and gentle, and genuinely concerned for her well-being. And so undeniably attractive, his body so close to hers...

"I am flattered to think I have swayed a woman of your conviction. However, that does not explain your current circumstances," he observed, abruptly drawing her back to the here and now. "Or why you chose to go to the village in the middle of the night."

"I wanted to go to the village when my absence wouldn't cause any inconvenience to Lady de Chaney," she replied, her mind conjuring up unbidden and unwanted the image of the baron's beautiful mistress.

"So, you left your quarters. Then what?"

"I heard a noise in the storeroom," she continued, determined to keep her thoughts focused on what she had to say. "I thought perhaps it was a rat. It was Philippe de Varenne."

"A rat, indeed. I should have known," the baron said, and she shivered at the harsh undertone in the baron's voice. "Did he hurt you?"

"No, not really," she admitted. "He implied that he knew where my brother was. He said he had met Bryce in France."

"I would not put much faith in anything Philippe de Varenne has to say."

"I didn't, but there was a chance he was speaking the truth, and I had to know." She took a deep breath. "He told me about Bryce's scar, which I was responsible for. I pushed Bryce into the water trough when we were children. It was a secret between us."

"So perhaps you were not completely foolish to speak with him, I grant you. Your brother means a great deal to you."

"He is the only member of my family left to me, my lord."

"Ah, yes. Family." He fell silent for a moment, and she didn't speak, not sure what to respond to his softly spoken words.

His reverie lasted only a moment. "Then what happened?"

"Philippe wouldn't tell me any more unless I . . ." She paused. If she told him everything Philippe had done, perhaps Philippe would keep the rest of his knowledge about Bryce to himself, if he truly possessed any.

"Unless you what?" the baron demanded, and she knew he would not accept her refusal to answer.

"Unless I kissed him."

"Did you?"

"It didn't seem so very much, not if I was going to find out about Bryce."

"I take it that was not enough for Philippe?"

"No," she whispered.

"Did he rape you?" the baron demanded coldly.

"No! No, he did not."

"Not this time," the baron said with complete certainty, "but one day..." He let his words trail off suggestively. "I will not have such a man in my retinue. He will be gone tomorrow."

"Please, Baron, don't send him away!" Impetuously she grabbed hold of his arm.

He turned a somewhat incredulous gaze upon her. "What do you mean, don't send him away? I should think you would be happy to have the fellow gone."

"I don't want to cause any trouble."

"You have been nothing but trouble since I arrived," he noted dispassionately.

"But there is a chance that he might truly know *something* of my brother's whereabouts, and if you send him away, he will never tell me what he knows."

"Yes, I suppose it is possible, *if* he did." The baron began caressing her hand absently, and she could not be sure he even knew he did so. Nevertheless, her throat went dry and she could not look at his face, wanting to hide the hot flush she felt coloring her face. "Unfortunately, I must tell you that Philippe de Varenne has never been to France."

Gabriella pulled her hand away as she sucked in her breath. "I knew I should not have trusted him!"

"No, you should not," the baron said, gazing at her with his customary intensity. "I certainly do not. Still,

he might have some information about your brother.
I will ask him. Rest assured, Gabriella, before he
leaves, he will tell me everything he knows about your
missing brother.''

She knew it would be so, and hearing the inexor-
able tone of his voice, she could almost find it in her
heart to pity Philippe de Varenne. Almost.

"Thank you, Baron DeGuerre," she murmured.
"Philippe de Varenne is a contemptible man.''

"People say the same of me," the baron noted quietly.

"You are not like *him*," Gabriella answered, her
mind screaming that she should leave his presence, her
body begging her to stay.

He placed the tip of his right index finger against the
seam at the shoulder of her gown. "Your dress is
torn.''

"Is it?" She looked not at her shoulder, but at his
face, so close to hers. His blue eyes seemed to glow in
the darkness, bidding her come closer, and she
obeyed.

His arms went around her, pulling her into an embrace she did not resist. "Let me kiss you, Gabriella," he whispered.

Chapter Eleven

Gabriella wanted to kiss him, so she did nothing to stop him. Indeed, she leaned toward him like a flower seeking the sun. When his lips met hers, she gave herself over to the rapture he inspired. Her arms instinctively encircled him while their mouths moved in a slow, sensuous dance of desire.

She felt his chest rise and fall against hers, and realized his hands were stroking her, their motion eliciting a pleasure-filled moan that broke from her lips without conscious thought. His mouth left hers and he licked the lobe of her ear, nearly tickling, this touch so exciting. Then his mouth was on her neck as he pushed her downward, his arm cushioning her against the hard wood of the bench.

When his other hand reached into her bodice and stroked her breast, she gasped with surprise and at the sudden intense pleasure he aroused.

She had never guessed a man could wield this kind of power over her. It was as if she were intoxicated with sensation. Heady with delight. Drunk with desire.

Sobriety returned with sudden impact when she felt the weight of his body upon her and his hips moving against her, the physical evidence of his arousal unmistakable.

He was seducing her, here in the chapel and she was acting no better than a whore! "Stop, stop!" she gasped, pushing against him and trying to rise.

He moved away at once. "What is it?" he asked, sounding genuinely confused.

She got to her feet and tugged together her loosened bodice. "This is wrong! You think you can seduce me! And in the chapel, too. You are a *wicked* man! You think only of your own pleasure—worse than Philippe de Varenne!"

Raising his eyebrows as if he truly didn't understand, the baron said, "Actually, I was thinking of your pleasure, too. As for wicked, I have often been called that. But to say I am worse than Philippe de Varenne is a very serious charge."

"You are!" she cried, nearly sick with shame and dismay and shock at her own weakness. "You have Josephine de Chaney with whom to assuage your lust!"

"That is very true." The baron folded his hands in his lap. "I would like to know why I am worse than Philippe."

She went to move past him, but he grabbed her arm. "Why am I worse than Philippe?" he demanded sternly.

"Because you...because you made me feel safe with you! Because I thought I could trust you," she cried defiantly. "I can't trust *anybody!* Now let me go!"

His grip did not loosen as he smiled slowly, with absolutely no vestige of joy. "You have just accused me of being a wicked man," he said so coolly that she felt like an idiot for being under his spell moments ago. "Do you think I will let you go to your quarters as easily as that if I am a wicked man?"

Her heart filled with fear that she had been completely wrong about him, but her doubt lasted only a moment, for he calmly remarked, "To prove that I am *not* worse than Philippe, I will let you leave. Not only that, but I will see you safely back to your quarters, lest Philippe be lurking outside."

He stood up, then cursed vehemently, reminding her of his injury. Well, she would not have any concern for him, not after tonight. Even if he wasn't a wicked man, he was still a cold and heartless one. "I don't want...I don't need an escort!" she said firmly. "I want to go to the village."

"Not tonight. Another day will do."

"But—"

"I told you, *not tonight,*" he ordered harshly. "I require your assistance," he continued, the words seemingly wrenched out of him. "I've twisted my damn ankle again. Give me your arm and help me to the hall. Then Philippe won't come near you." He gave her a scornful look. "I won't kiss you again, if that's what you fear. As I told you before, I have no need to force myself upon unwilling wenches."

As if she had to be reminded that she had been so willing a short time before! Nevertheless, he was right about Philippe, and it was very late, so she reluctantly put her shoulder beneath his arm. Conscious of the heat of his body next to hers and trying not to be, she helped him limp out of the chapel and across the courtyard, maintaining a stony silence all the way.

"What did you mean, you can't trust anybody?" he asked as they entered the hall.

"I meant I can't trust you or your men," she said between clenched teeth. He didn't need to hear what she had discovered about Osric. She didn't owe Baron DeGuerre anything except money.

"So, you have finally found out it is better not to trust other people."

She did not bother to respond. He so obviously believed he was right, he did not need her confirmation.

As they crossed the threshold of the hall, he grimaced with pain. "Be that as it may, I believe I will trust your advice and stay off my foot," he said quietly. "This once. Fortunately, I have a mistress of such renown that no one will be suspicious if we choose to pass most of the day in bed."

Gabriella pressed her lips together, and it took all her fortitude not to slam her foot down on his injured one.

Josephine shifted in the bed, drowsily aware of a most uncomfortable chill along her back. With a sleepy smile on her face, she reached around to pull more coverings away from Etienne, who tended to commandeer linens with the same authority with which he ruled his estates.

He was not in the bed.

She opened her eyes and sat up, looking at the luxurious coverings stupidly for a moment, then around the room. Where could he be? She had not felt him leave the bed, nor had she heard anything, such as a servant or soldier come to summon him away or tell them of an emergency.

Perhaps Etienne was making a surprise patrol of the sentries. Sometimes he did that, seeking any who were sleeping at their post, or who did not know the proper password.

Her repose destroyed nonetheless, Josephine climbed out of bed, drew her heavy velvet robe over her nakedness, slipped her feet into her cloth slippers and went to the window, peering at the courtyard, the gate house and the wall walks.

The sentries were clearly visible, but there was no sign of Etienne. Mind, he could be in a part not visible from the window, around a corner or in the shadows.

Then she gasped and her chest tightened as if a fist had struck her hard upon it, for there was Etienne in the courtyard, his arm around Gabriella Frechette in an intimate embrace. Thus entwined, they walked slowly toward the hall.

Tightly clutching her robe together with trembling hands, Josephine's incredulous expression was replaced by a grim one as she stepped away from the window. What need to wonder what was between them, when she had the evidence of her own eyes?

Josephine silently cursed herself, and her own complacent laziness. She had grown remiss in her attentions to Etienne. Although she had been dismayed by her exclusion from his recent journey, the separation should have sounded more of an alarm to her. She should have remembered that they had been together long enough for his desire for her to wane, and should have trusted less to the power of her beauty.

And she should have paid more heed to the way he treated Gabriella. She never should have relied on Gabriella's forcefully stated morals to prevent Etienne's seduction. Etienne was more than capable of gently wooing away all such protestations.

Josephine wandered toward the bed, rubbing her arms to give them warmth, then disrobed, climbed into bed and lay down to think, if not to sleep. In another moment, she heard steps outside the bedchamber. Etienne entered, moving silently and cautiously, clearly believing that she still slept.

She did not disillusion him, and kept up the ruse when he joined her beneath the coverings.

It was not easy to lie beside him, listening to him breathe, aware of his muscular body that had given her so much pleasure. But ignore him she must, for she had plans to make, and she had to make them quickly.

Etienne was pleased that Josephine slumbered undisturbed. He had no desire to make any explanations for his absence when he got into the bed beside his mistress.

It was warm under the covers, and certainly more comfortable than the chapel. He should be able to get to sleep now.

Provided he could stop thinking about Gabriella and what had just happened between them. He had, without a doubt, made one of the stupidest blunders of his life.

It was true that he had needed to know what had happened to her. The behavior of his men was his responsibility. Once he had heard, though, he should have sent her away. He should have listened to his logical, rational mind and never given in to the temptation to kiss her. Or to continue kissing her, even though he understood why he had done so.

He cared for Gabriella Frechette as he had never cared for any other woman, and he had foolishly given in to the impulse to demonstrate his feelings in the only way he knew how.

His mouth drew into a grim line as he lay motionless. For him, there could be no other way to express love, or at least what he understood by that word. What did he know of tender emotions? Who had been his teachers?

His mother had not loved him. He had been but a poor substitute for the man to whom she had given her whole heart. When he died, there had been no love left to give to her son. With him she could only share a sense of dreams unfulfilled, a need for power and glory, and of someday, perhaps, being worthy of a dead man.

Women had desired him, and some had claimed to love him, but there had always been that look, deep in their eyes, a hungry, greedy look that seemed to say, "What is my love worth to you?" There was not a one of them who would have made an unselfish sacrifice for his sake.

He recalled how Gabriella spoke of her brother. Her undying faith in his return. Her wistful tone, the look in her eyes.

What would it be like, he wondered, to have such a love? Or to possess a family?

Not a family like the de Varennes, who were as quarrelsome and vicious to each other as they were to their enemies, but a family such as the Frechettes. He had heard enough about them to know that they were admired and well loved; even the knavish Bryce was thought of kindly, his temper and imprudence put down to high spirits and an adventurous nature.

Undoubtedly he would never know.

He tried to tell himself that none of this was important. An ability to express a tender sentiment could not be expected, given his upbringing, and hadn't mattered to countless women.

Etienne continued to attempt to convince himself of the futility of yearning for something he could never have all the rest of the night.

The next day, Gabriella kept waiting for Baron DeGuerre to summon Philippe de Varenne, as he had said he would. However, the day passed, and the baron remained in his solar, closeted with his steward, Jean Luc Ducette.

She tried not to be disappointed that he didn't immediately see Philippe. She reminded herself that the baron was a busy man, with many things to consider during the harvest time.

Nonetheless, as the day progressed and it became clear that neither she, nor his vow to speak with de Varenne, were more important than talking of estate business with his steward, a sense of hopelessness pervaded her. Whatever else she thought of Baron DeGuerre, she thought him a man of his word.

Another, more disturbing notion came to her. What if Philippe had already been summoned, and he had told the baron his undoubtedly different version of what had passed in the storeroom? What if Philippe had been right, and she wrong, as to how the baron would react? What if Baron DeGuerre believed Philippe? Maybe, when all was said and done, she was nothing but a fool where Baron DeGuerre was concerned, and to trust him to help find her brother was the greatest folly of all.

At last the time came to help Josephine decide which gown to wear at the evening meal. She had to pass the solar, and hurried by the door, when it suddenly swung open and Baron DeGuerre stepped out. She halted so abruptly she almost collided with him. His arms grasped hers to steady her, and she looked at his face, startled, embarrassed and dismayed by the unexpected thrill the contact with his body caused.

As if to confirm her suspicions, he would not even meet her eye. Her surprise turned to scorn. He was a lying, dishonorable rogue who had promised to find out about Bryce and to send Philippe away, and he had done nothing.

She twisted away from him, glad she had not made love to him. To have given herself to one so unworthy would have been a complete humiliation.

Gabriella straightened her shoulders and proudly lifted her chin. Then she majestically marched away from the baron.

* * *

Etienne watched Gabriella stalk up the stairs toward the bedchamber and thought of the bitter reproach he had seen in her face.

He could understand why she would think he deserved it. She would know that he had not summoned de Varenne as the first order of the day, or as had been his intention until he realized that he would probably wind up killing the impertinent miscreant if he did so. He had no wish to lose his self-control twice within the space of a single day, and whereas what had passed with Gabriella would have no consequence, the killing of Philippe de Varenne, however justified, surely would.

"Who was that, my lord?" Jean Luc asked in his low, pleasant voice, which was a distinct contrast to his somber face.

"*That* was Gabriella Frechette," Etienne replied, walking down the stairs toward the hall, commanding himself to remain calm, although the feel of her body against his had aroused him instantly. In that brief moment, he had felt truly alive for the first time all day.

"The disinherited woman?"

"Yes."

"She is a spirited creature. I would hate to have her accusing me of a crime. A man sitting in judgment would surely be swayed by the righteous passion in her eyes."

Etienne paused and glanced at his steward. "She means nothing to me."

Jean Luc's thin lips smiled slightly. "No, my lord, I didn't mean to imply otherwise. Everyone knows you are immune to the simple attraction of a pretty face."

Etienne thought it would be wise to change the subject. "You are quite certain, then, that there had been no misappropriation of funds?" he asked, continuing toward the hall.

"None that I can see. The earl made several bad decisions, but it could have been much worse much sooner. I think we must accept that the bailiff did the best he could under the circumstances, and in fact, I suspect he did rather more than most men would have. Have you any idea why, my lord?"

They were nearly at the bottom of the stairs. Etienne paused and turned to Jean Luc once again. "Josephine believes he cares for the earl's daughter."

"Ah!" Jean Luc nodded understandingly.

"She, however, was quite convinced he was robbing the family."

"Far be it from me to contradict a young lady," Jean Luc said gravely, "but the evidence of the earl's spendthrift ways are all about us." He gestured at the fine stone walls and the carved lintel of the doorway leading to the great hall. "He would have needed a much larger estate to pay for such a castle without difficulty."

"Yes. I will tell her so tomorrow."

"Would you like me to be there, my lord? To show her the books?"

"No. I will do it myself. Now you must be very hungry. I think we have done nearly a week's worth of work today. Let us forget talk of money, rents and pannage and enjoy our meal."

"I agree, my lord," Jean Luc replied. "I look forward to dining with Lady de Chaney. She grows more beautiful with every passing day."

"Are you thinking of becoming a minstrel, Jean Luc?" Etienne asked lightly.

The steward chuckled noiselessly. "Not I, my lord, not I."

A dim shaft of early-morning sunlight that escaped the thick clouds illuminated Gabriella as she stood in the nearly barren solar, once again waiting for Baron DeGuerre. She had been told to come here after mass, by order of the baron. Alda had no idea why.

Gabriella did. Philippe must have convinced the baron she had lied about their encounter in the storeroom and the baron was going to confront her, perhaps even chastise or punish her.

As long as he did not try to seduce her again! However, this time she would be more on her guard than she had been in the chapel. She would remember he was nothing but a lustful, arrogant upstart, undeserving of her respect.

To take her mind away from contemplating the baron or his deeds and his motives, she let her gaze rove over the room. There was some new furniture, of course, to replace what had been sold, but apparently, Josephine de Chaney had not been permitted to utilize her decorative skills here. The table was large and plain, made of solid oak. The two chairs were identical and similarly plain. A single large candle was placed on the bare table, and she wondered what had become of the lists and papers Chalfront had provided to enable Baron DeGuerre to take command of her family's estate. They had laid on the top of that table like dead leaves of autumn, or pieces of a brittle shroud.

She could remember so clearly her father sitting in this very room! If he were here now, he would have at least three dogs sleeping at his feet, a brazier lit with coal, a carpet on the floor, a tray of delicious sweetmeats at his elbow, a goblet of wine in his hand and several candles illuminating the room. He would be wearing a warm, colorful robe and a large ornate brooch. His smile would have warmed her more than the brazier, and she would have been happy.

With the shock of an unexpected gust of wind on a mild summer's day, the baron strode into the room and passed her without a word before he sat in the chair behind the table.

He took possession of the solar like some kind of evil spirit, his face looming above his black tunic in the weak sunlight and his expression was as inscrutable as it had ever been.

"You sent for me, my lord?" she inquired stiffly when he continued to stare at her wordlessly.

"Sit down." He indicated the chair on the opposite side of the table.

"Servants should remain standing in the presence of their betters, my lord," she replied, wondering what kind of delaying tactic this was. She could well believe—indeed, she knew!—that he enjoyed making people wait until he deigned to reveal his aim, increasing their anxiety to a fever pitch. As he had done the night of her arrival. As he was doing now.

"Suit yourself, wench," he said with a shrug of his broad shoulders, the movement as graceful as a cat stretching. "I have summoned you here to tell you what my steward has discovered about Chalfront's handling of your father's affairs."

"Yes, my lord?" she responded, trying not to betray any eagerness.

"Jean Luc has told me, and more, shown me, that not only did Chalfront act properly, he went beyond his duties. Your family would have been bankrupt long before your brother left if it were not for the bailiff's management."

Gabriella stared at the baron's handsome, impassive face. She had been trying to maintain her faith in her brother's final admonition, despite Chalfront's continuous assertions of his innocence. Could it be that she had been as wrong about Bryce as she had been about Osric, and Baron DeGuerre?

No, it had not been right to think the best of the baron and villagers who she did not know well, but she could trust Bryce, or at least trust that he truly believed what he had told her. If only he had explained why he distrusted Chalfront before he had gone away! "Bryce must have had his reasons," she said, voicing her troubled thoughts.

"While it is commendable that you have faith in your brother's estimation of Chalfront's character," the baron said, his voice as cold as the room, "I regret that I must confirm that your father, and your father alone, was responsible for your family's penury. He spent far more than he could afford on this castle, on the food, on your brother's horses and armor—on everything, apparently."

"And you consider the money wasted?" she demanded, unwilling even now to hear her father criticized.

"I consider any man a fool who spends beyond his income."

"You did not know him!" she replied swiftly. "He was kind, generous, beloved—everything you will *never* be!"

The baron said not a word and moved not a muscle, but she saw a brief flicker of pain in his eyes.

Even in the midst of her anger and dismay, she knew that she had wounded him as surely as if she had taken the gold-hilted dagger from his belt and plunged it into his heart.

She did not regret her defense of her father, but she would have given much to understand why her angry charge disturbed him so.

Chalfront appeared in the doorway, his expression tentative and his eyes wide as he looked from the baron to Gabriella and back again. "You wanted me, my lord?" he asked.

The baron turned to face the bailiff. "Yes, I did."

How could he sound so calm? she marveled. He *did* have feelings. Deep currents of emotion roiled below that imperturbable face.

She realized that the baron had not spoken after the first, and that he was regarding her steadily. When her gaze met his, he shifted his attention to Chalfront.

"You will be pleased to hear, I'm sure, that Jean Luc has exonerated you from any wrongdoing."

The man's face broke into a wide smile. Gabriella, watching carefully, saw no triumph there, as if he were proud to have fooled anyone, only a happy and sincere joy.

"I believe Gabriella has something she wishes to say to you."

Gabriella remembered the baron's warning that she would have to apologize if Chalfront had been unjustly accused.

She had to decide, here and now, whether to accept the word of the baron and his steward over that of her own beloved brother, who had gone away in a fit of anger like a spoiled child. Who had made an accusation with no proof of any kind. Who was nowhere to be found. Who had abandoned her father, and her.

She rose and faced Chalfront. "It appears I have maligned you unjustly, Robert. I ask your forgiveness."

"You have it!" Chalfront replied enthusiastically.

"Have I your leave to go, my lord?" she asked, needing to get out of the solar and away from this man she kept trying fruitlessly to comprehend.

"Yes," he said, his inscrutable gaze on the bailiff.

She went toward the door, then leaned on the frame. She glanced back at him. "I know the villagers exploited my father," she admitted wearily. "I hope it pleases you, my lord, to be always right."

She disappeared before he could respond, if Etienne had had a response to make.

Damn the woman! he thought angrily, his body as tense as it had been when he had faced his fiercest opponent. He *was* right, about Chalfront, about the villagers, about her father, too, and he would make no apologies for that. She had been led astray by her love for her family, and that was not *his* fault. Chalfront had done his utmost to help her, and she had responded with accusations of duplicity.

The world was a harsh place, and that was not *his* doing, either. She had to find it out eventually. She should bless her good fortune that she had not been forced to learn the lesson earlier.

Chalfront hovered near the table, his face now returned to its customary anxious, humble expression, and said, "Is there anything else you want of me, my lord?"

"Yes," Etienne said, locking away his emotions as he had so many times before. "Find Philippe de Varenne and tell him I want to speak with him at once."

Chapter Twelve

As Philippe approached the solar, he told himself he had nothing to fear from Baron DeGuerre. When he had woken with an incredibly aching head and remembered his confrontation with Gabriella, he had been afraid that the baron would demand an explanation; however, nothing had happened all day. He could not be absolutely certain that Gabriella had not spoken to the baron about their meeting in the storeroom, yet it would seem that if she had, his assumption regarding the baron's reaction had been correct.

Philippe told himself it didn't matter if the baron didn't approve of what he had done. The de Varennes had come to England with the Conqueror, and were wealthy, too. Although he and his father had never seen eye to eye on anything, his father would surely back his son against a man like the Baron DeGuerre.

"I want to speak with you, de Varenne," the baron said when Philippe entered the room, his deep voice calm and his face as frustratingly inscrutable as always. Sitting behind his huge table in the near-darkness, wearing his habitual black, the baron reminded

Philippe of a huge and patient spider waiting for an insect to fly into his web.

"I am at your service, Baron," Philippe said, trying to rid his mind of that image and affect a nonchalant air in spite of his trembling hands and faint heart. "What do you wish? I have done nothing wrong."

"I have not said you did," the baron replied with one eyebrow very slightly elevated. "Tell me what you know about Bryce Frechette."

Philippe's eyes widened. The wench *had* told the baron about the confrontation in the storeroom, or at least part of it. Which parts? And how did she embellish her tale? What would be the best response? From everything he knew about the baron, it would perhaps be better to be truthful for as long as he could. "I know something of his looks, my lord," he answered.

"So she said. You described his scar, I understand. When did you meet him?"

"I never said I met him myself, Baron," Philippe lied. "I asked about him at Montmorency Castle, since I had nothing else with which to occupy my time, and discovered a groom who had met him."

"You did not encounter him in France?"

Philippe forced a genial laugh. "I have never been to France, my lord, as I'm sure you will recall. The groom said *he* saw Bryce Frechette in France."

"Where, precisely?"

"Anjou, my lord. About two years ago."

"And you thought this paltry information worthy of a kiss?"

How calm and how terrible was the baron's voice!

"It was *just* a kiss, my lord," Philippe protested. "You make it sound as if I raped her."

"Weren't you going to?"

Philippe knew quite well how the baron felt about men who abused women, so he quickly answered, "No! Never! I . . . I wanted to kiss her. She's a pretty girl." Then he grew bold in his desperation. "I think I am not alone in that opinion."

The baron's hand went to his dagger and he toyed with the handle, but it was the brief flicker of cold anger in the baron's eyes that truly frightened Philippe. "I know you want her, too!" Philippe blurted, torn between fear, pride and dismay. "Yes, even the great Baron DeGuerre, with his beautiful mistress, wants to have her!" He stabbed his finger at the baron, who did not move, or even blink. "You cannot deny it!"

"Pack your things and leave this castle."

"*What?*"

"I will not have you in my retinue any longer. I absolve you from your oath of loyalty and I order you to leave this place at once."

Philippe stared at him, aghast. "You will disgrace me because of a dispossessed noblewoman?" he cried. "Are you forgetting who I am? I will not permit it!"

The baron remained unperturbed. "It is not a question of what *you* will permit. I have decided, and so it will be." The baron drew out his dagger, his voice still calm and terrible. "I will be merciful with you, Philippe," he said, "because I should have sent you away much sooner. The reason for your going need only be known by you and me." Then the baron smiled his cold, distant smile. "If you wish to tell people it was your choice to leave my service, I will not say otherwise."

"I know you want her yourself!" Philippe screeched impetuously. "You are sending me away so that no one stands in your way!"

The baron rose slowly, the dagger shining dully. "Shut your mouth, Philippe, and leave before I kill you."

"You wouldn't *dare* kill me, Etienne DeGuerre!" Philippe shouted as he backed toward the door. "Or should I say, Etienne the bastard?"

The baron came around the table.

"I know all about you, my fine lord," Philippe cried. "I know your mother was a whore and your father a worthless, landless knight! You will not touch me, bastard!"

"Say another word, Philippe, and I will gladly slit your disgusting throat."

"I *will* say another word, you blind, arrogant fool!" Philippe's back struck the door and he fumbled for the latch. "I will go and gladly! Why should I stay with a man whose mistress and bailiff are in league together, plotting his downfall? Ah, now you stop!" he cried triumphantly as Etienne halted, watching. "Now you wait to hear me speak." Philippe turned and finally succeeded in lifting the latch. "It's too late! I'm going!"

"Then go!" the baron said. With one sudden, fluid motion, he threw his dagger with so much force that it vibrated visibly when it stuck into the wooden door.

An expression of naked terror on his face, Philippe twisted to look at the baron over his shoulder before stumbling from the room.

Etienne took several deep breaths to calm himself as he listened to Philippe clatter down the stairs. God's wounds, he had come so close to killing him! More, he knew he would have enjoyed it.

But slitting the arrogant fool's throat would have been a mistake, and Etienne DeGuerre had not achieved his current position by making mistakes.

Nor had he come so far to have his life destroyed by underlings, whether a defiant maidservant with passionate brown eyes or a mistress in league with a bailiff. It could be that Philippe had lied about Josephine and Chalfront; it would be just like the miscreant to blurt out an accusation when he was cornered like the rat he was. On the other hand, Philippe was not an imaginative man, so perhaps he had seen or heard something to create the lie. If that were so, Etienne vowed, he would find it out.

Indeed, it occurred to him as he stood alone in his solar, that he might have missed many things because of his weakness over a woman.

No more. Not when she hated him, as she had made abundantly clear.

Donald and Seldon could hear Philippe preparing to depart well before they actually arrived in the barracks. He was muttering angrily and shoving articles of his clothing into a large leather pouch without much care. Obviously he was departing the castle permanently, and it was not Philippe's idea.

"Leaving?" Donald inquired unnecessarily as they ambled closer. He gave Seldon a rather smug, secretive look.

"Yes," Philippe replied brusquely.

Donald rarely felt the need to be petty, but Philippe had caused him so much aggravation over the past year that he had an overwhelming urge to embarrass him. Therefore, he nonchalantly asked, "On an errand for Baron DeGuerre?"

"No," Philippe snarled, looking at them with blatant hostility. His gaze returned to the boots he was trying to force into the leather bag without much success. "I've had enough of him. I'm going to my father's."

This time, the glances Donald and Seldon exchanged were surprised, and not a little suspicious. "I thought you were never going to speak to your father again," Seldon observed.

"I don't *have* to speak to him if I go home," Philippe replied, "but even if I did, I would far rather have to answer his idiotic questions, bear with his stupid advice and listen to his interminable babblings than stay in this place another minute." He straightened and fixed his angry eyes upon them. "The baron's getting soft, if you ask me. I *thought* he was a man to admire and emulate, but I assure you both, I was *quite* wrong."

George sauntered into the barracks at that point, and regarded the scene before him with tolerant amusement. "Upset, are we?" he asked calmly.

"I have been falsely accused," Philippe announced. "That stupid wench has lied about me. I won't stay where justice is not done!"

"What wench?" George inquired.

Philippe didn't answer as George came closer. "Let me guess," George said, his usually jovial manner replaced by one far more serious. "Gabriella Frechette."

"It doesn't matter," Philippe muttered. "I think the baron's getting weak and foolish in his old age."

"Because the baron doesn't approve of men who take advantage of women?"

"I never did."

"I confess, my dear Philippe, that I am inclined to believe that if you did not, it was not for lack of trying. Otherwise, why go?"

Donald crossed his slender arms. "Yes, Philippe," he said. "I find it easier to believe that you tried to hurt her than to believe Baron DeGuerre is getting soft."

"I barely touched the wench!" Philippe snarled. "God's blood, if I had wanted to take her, I would have!"

"Yes," George said slowly. "That's the point. You would have."

"I'm leaving of my own free will. Baron DeGuerre isn't worthy of my loyalty." Philippe tugged on the lacing of the leather pouch, pulling it closed. "I don't have to explain myself to a bunch of fools!" He slung the bag over his shoulder and stomped toward the door.

"Farewell," Donald said quietly.

"Goodbye," Seldon said.

"I hope you all rot in hell!" Philippe snapped his final farewell as he went out the door, slamming it behind him with so much force the frame splintered.

"Good riddance," George muttered with unusual vehemence.

Donald grew pensive. "I must confess that although I'm quite sure the baron has his reasons for compelling Philippe to leave his service, I do not see the wisdom of enraging him. Who knows what mischief he might do in his present state? Do you suppose we've seen the last of him, after all?"

"Oh, who cares?" Seldon said jovially. "Let him try to make trouble. We're more than a match for him!"

"And his family?" Donald asked gravely.

That made Seldon's face fall. "Well... let's not borrow trouble, eh? Philippe doesn't get along with most of *them,* either, does he?"

"True enough," George said. "I don't recall the baron ever making an error of judgment before. I think we can assume he hasn't in this case, either."

George grinned, yet his eyes looked anything but merry.

Her head lowered to avoid meeting anybody's gaze, Gabriella hurried along the main road leading through the village. She didn't care that Josephine didn't know she was gone, or that she might soon be missed. Confused, upset, uncertain after what had passed in the solar, she simply wanted, and needed, to be alone.

She was almost through the village when she heard Mary call out, "My lady!"

Gabriella hesitated. She was in no mood to talk to anyone. On the other hand, she had not been in the village since she had made her decision to return Mary's money. She could do so now, and then she would go into the woods.

She put her hand to her belt, feeling the coins there as she turned to meet the woman walking toward her. "I'm glad to see you, Mary," she said. "I want to return your money."

"But my lady—" Mary stopped, surprised.

"Please, I've had some time to think, and I cannot take it," Gabriella said firmly. "I was going to give it back to you before but . . . something prevented me." She produced the coins. "Here, please take it."

"My lady!" Mary cried in genuine distress. "I won't have it back! You have to get your freedom."

"You need it more than I do," Gabriella insisted. "The baron may raise the rents again," she continued grimly, thinking of him sitting in the solar like a cold, unfeeling effigy of a man, rather than one of flesh and blood. Always right. Always so inscrutable, even when he was trying to destroy the cherished memory of her family. "The winter may be long and hard, too." She clasped Mary's hand, pressing the coins into her palm. "I truly appreciate your gift, Mary, but I simply cannot rest easy knowing I have taken what little you possess."

Mary did not look convinced. Fortunately, at that moment a biting east wind blew along the road and seemed to remind the woman that worse was yet to come. "All right," she said grudgingly, shoving the coins into her bodice. "But if I don't need it come spring, you'll get it back, and I won't take no for an answer."

"Very well," Gabriella said, knowing that might be the only condition under which Mary would agree. "Now if you'll excuse me, I'm ... I'm going to find some late-blooming wildflowers. Lady de Chaney wants some for her chamber."

Mary sniffed derisively. "That's the nobility for you! What a waste of time!"

"Well, waste of time or not," Gabriella said, "I had better not linger." With that, she continued quickly on her way.

The cold wind made her shiver and wish she had brought a warmer shawl. Her skirt blew against her bare legs and she hugged herself for warmth, her head low against the wind.

Once she was beyond the village, the road was more sheltered by the trees. Although they were nearly bare, she was a little warmer. Her brisk pace soon relieved the bite of the cold.

She avoided the fields where boys watched the cattle feeding on the stubble left after the haymaking. In other fields, she could see a few men planting their winter crops.

She spied a path leading into the woods and took it. It was even warmer here, and quieter. Nothing disturbed the solitude as she hurried along.

When she reached the edge of a clear, babbling stream, she sat down and wrapped her arms around her knees, then laid her head upon them.

Had everything in her past been based upon a misconception? Was her father a spendthrift who had let the tenants exploit him? Was her brother a quarrelsome wastrel who had acted like a child and abandoned her? Had love blinded her?

Perhaps love was making her blind now. What else would make her yearn to be in the baron's arms and to offer him comfort?

She couldn't decide what to believe, and she couldn't decide what to do. Maybe it would be better for her to leave this place and get away from the baron, even if it meant leaving her home.

"How delightful!" drawled a languid and unfortunately familiar male voice.

Gabriella jumped to her feet, turning to see Philippe de Varenne toss his horse's reins over a low bush. He wore his long cloak and heavy boots, and there were bundles tied onto his horse, as if he were going on a long journey.

"What do you want?" she demanded.

"I saw you come into the woods and thought I would take my leave of you," he said, strolling toward her with a singularly cruel smile, "since it's because of you I have to leave."

The baron *had* believed her and had ordered Philippe to go! That was her first thought; her second was that she was in very great danger, worse than that night in the storeroom, for now no one would hear her if she called for help.

No doubt Philippe de Varenne realized that, too, for he said, "All alone, are we? What a fortunate thing for me!"

"Sir, I have to go back to the castle," Gabriella said with all the dignity she could muster as she went to go past him, hoping he would let her go if she did not act afraid.

He grabbed her arm roughly and pulled her to him. "Do you think I'm going to let you have the better of me, Gabriella?" he demanded. "I assure you, I will have the victory—over you and Baron DeGuerre."

"Please, sir—"

"Oh, yes," he hissed. "Now you beg. Now you give me respect." His arms went around her, enclosing her in his grasp. "We all want respect, don't we? You, me, the great Baron DeGuerre. That's why he won't touch you, as much as he would like to. Do I surprise you? Come now, Gabriella, you're not *that* foolish." He took hold of her hair, tugging her head back so that she had to look up at his evil face. "Do you think he will respect you after I'm done with you?"

"Don't!" she gasped before he threw her to the ground.

"It's too late to expect kindness from me," Philippe snarled.

She began scrambling to her feet desperately, but he pushed her down with his foot. The cold mud oozed around her, the smell of the earth and dead leaves strong in her nostrils, as if she were already in her grave.

"That's where you should be," he said. "Groveling in the mud at my feet."

"Philippe!" The baron's voice boomed through the forest and the man himself appeared on the path, his dagger drawn and his expression so sternly fierce he looked like an avenging angel.

Or a demon risen from the depths of hell.

Chapter Thirteen

Philippe cursed and started to run, splashing away from them through the stream. Etienne scrutinized Gabriella quickly. Seeing no sign of injury or rape, he blessed the urge he had felt to follow Philippe.

His fortuitous decision did not decrease the rage that took hold of Etienne as he gave chase, his long tunic no more an encumbrance than the wind as he pursued Philippe on foot, for he had left his stallion tied near the road to lessen the chance that Philippe would realize he was being watched.

Philippe ran fast, but his cloak was a hindrance and he kept looking back over his shoulder to see his pursuer. Under such circumstances—indeed, even with the best of conditions—he could not outrace an infuriated Etienne DeGuerre. Etienne nearly caught him in a small clearing; unfortunately, Philippe managed to elude his grasp. Desperate to catch the villain, the baron threw his dagger, which struck his prey in the leg.

With a cry of pain, Philippe stumbled and fell. "Mercy!" he cried, his hands over his head, when Etienne reached him and turned him over with a kick.

"Mercy?" Etienne asked quietly as Philippe lay whimpering. "Do you think you can expect mercy from the bastard son of a whore?"

Philippe curled into a protective ball at the baron's feet, one hand clutching the protruding handle of the dagger as his body shook with sobs. "Please, please don't kill me!" he begged. "Please let me go!"

"As you were going to let Gabriella go?"

"Oh, God save me!" Philippe groaned.

Etienne reached down and tugged Philippe to his feet. "What . . . what are you doing?" Philippe spluttered, a froth of saliva at the corners of his mouth, and tears running down his cheeks.

"Taking you back to your horse," Etienne growled. Ignoring Philippe's whimpers and moans, he put one shoulder under Philippe's arm and dragged him along the path, not taking any particular care to be gentle, or to avoid the sharp branches and thorns of the bushes and trees.

Soon Etienne saw Gabriella standing where he had left her, her arms crossed over her chest. Her eyes widened when she saw them, and she stepped off the path to let them pass. Tired from the effort of running, determined to get rid of Philippe and, more importantly, not certain what to say, Etienne did not address her.

"Gabriella!" Philippe moaned pathetically. "Tell him! Tell him I never hurt you! He's going to kill me!"

Etienne threw Philippe's arm off and the young man staggered, nearly falling. "Baron DeGuerre, I—"

"Don't say a word or I'll get angry," Etienne muttered.

Philippe's eyes widened in distress and he nodded his head.

"Get on your horse."

Philippe hurried to obey as best he could. When he was mounted, Etienne stepped forward and yanked his dagger from Philippe's leg. "I could not allow you to take this with you. It's worth far more than your miserable life," he said coolly. "I suggest you bandage your wound as soon as possible, before you bleed to death."

Philippe nodded rapidly and pressed his hand over the bloody tear in his chausses. Then Etienne slapped the horse's flank, and it broke into a startled canter. Philippe clutched the reins and emitted a squeal of pain and alarm as the horse disappeared down the path.

Etienne turned to Gabriella. Her face was streaked with tears, but she smiled wanly at him, her bottom lip trembling. "How did you know?" she asked softly.

"I wanted to make sure he had not taken one of my horses," Etienne admitted. "Then I decided to make sure he left my land entirely. It was only by chance that I saw him disappear into the woods and wondered what mischief he was making."

"I am glad you did," Gabriella said.

"As I am," he replied, going toward her slowly. "You are not hurt?"

"No, my lord."

"This is my fault. I should have sent him away long ago."

She didn't reply, but simply stood there, alone and vulnerable—because he had made her so. As he looked at her, tenderness and concern overtook him. How much he wanted to embrace her and hold her safe in his arms! Yet he was too afraid she would misinterpret his action. He wondered if there was some way he could show her his contrition, something that she could not construe as an attempt to seduce her.

"I...I had better go," she said softly. "Lady de Chaney will be looking for me."

"Yes," he replied.

"I should go alone," she continued.

"Very well." He watched her walk slowly away, her head bowed as if lost in thought.

Then he realized a way to demonstrate his regard for her, as well as rid himself of his growing weakness where she was concerned.

He would forgive her debt. He would set her free.

There was yet more, to show the depth of his feeling. He would do his best to find her brother.

And then, when she owed him no more money, and she had a brother to provide the love and protection of a family, she would leave him. And he would be unloved and alone, as he had always been.

Once out of the baron's sight, Gabriella ran as fast and as far as she could, only stopping when her legs were too tired and she was close to the village. In her mind, she knew it was a fruitless flight, because she was not running from Philippe de Varenne, or even Baron DeGuerre. She was trying to run away from her own wild, intense emotions.

The moment he had appeared, she had been thrilled and relieved, certain that she would be safe. When he had gone after Philippe, she had not known what to do, except that she wanted to thank him.

Then he had returned, Philippe in his custody, and she had been shocked at the intense desire that filled her as she watched him send away her enemy. It was almost uncontainable, the need she felt to be in his arms, with no thought of whether it was right or wrong, the only necessity being to act upon her desire.

She must try to subdue these primitive, impossible feelings. He was Baron Etienne DeGuerre, whom she should hate.

If only Bryce would come back. Or if only she could find the strength to leave.

Although he knew he had made the right decision, Etienne was certainly not in a pleasant frame of mind for the next few days. He immediately dispatched Donald and Seldon to try to find Bryce Frechette, after cautioning them that it was a secret task, not to be discussed except between themselves.

Jean Luc Ducette left Castle Frechette to attend to matters concerning the baron's other property. Etienne busied himself with estate business, for it was nearly time to begin the fall slaughter. The beasts had to be counted and the decision made which ones to winter. He did not have the greatest of faith in the honesty of the reeve or any of the other tenants, and so thought his presence would be needed.

He also kept a careful eye on Robert Chalfront, in case Philippe's accusation and his own already stifled suspicions were not without merit. However, he saw nothing to justify any allegation that the bailiff was in collusion with Josephine. Indeed, he was beginning to think it was Chalfront's fate to continue to be unjustly accused.

As for his nights, Etienne could not remember a time when he had found it so difficult to sleep. He was often physically tired, yet could not find the necessary peace to drift into slumber. During the day, he could keep his mind occupied and nearly ignore Gabriella; at night, Gabriella was all he could think about, and he recalled the day's torturous glimpses of her, in every tantalizing detail.

He wasn't sure if Josephine noticed anything. He feigned sleep the moment his head rested upon the pillow. He felt absolutely no desire for her now, and had no wish to concoct excuses. He also didn't want her to blame herself for his lack of libidinous appetite, or the alteration in their relationship. It was all his fault.

Nevertheless, the situation between his mistress and himself was rapidly growing intolerable. He knew he should end it, yet he wished to avoid a confrontation, for then he would have to give her an explanation. He feared that the perceptive Josephine would see through any lies and, worse, realize that he was a slave to his own emotions.

Only one week later, however, he found Josephine in his solar waiting for him with a serious expression on her beautiful face.

When he saw how she started and flushed guiltily, he realized he had left several estate documents spread out upon the table. With sudden dread he wondered if the distance he felt growing between Josephine and himself was not totally his doing. Perhaps there had been truth behind Philippe's words. Had he been too involved in his personal troubles to see what was happening under his very nose?.

"Etienne," Josephine began softly, but with unmistakable rectitude, "I am leaving you."

Although this was unexpected, he felt relief that she was the one starting this conversation. She would be on the defensive; he need not make any explanations. "Why?" he inquired calmly.

A simple enough question, he thought, but she hesitated a long time before answering it with another question. "Does it matter?"

Did it? he asked himself, and the answer was immediate. No, unless she was engaged in some kind of sabotage.

He regarded her steadily, this woman who had shared his bed and his body if not his love, and saw no deceit in her beautiful green eyes. He had never had a cause to doubt Josephine's loyalty, and he would not do so until he had incontrovertible evidence to the contrary. "If you wish to go, so be it. Where?"

"To my uncle's."

"I will send an escort with you. And I will see that you do not lack for money."

"Thank you, Etienne," she said with a smile and no attempt at dissembling, which reminded him of the reason he had always liked Josephine. She was a practical woman, and took no pains to hide it. "You are a good man, Etienne." Her expression clouded. "I am going to be honest with you," she said with a tremulous smile. "I am leaving you to be married."

Whatever reason he might have considered for Josephine's departure, he would never have guessed this one. Holy heaven, where had his eyes been these past several days, that something like this should happen and he be so ignorant?

When he was sure he could maintain a calm tone, he asked, "To whom?"

"Robert Chalfront."

"Chalfront?" he repeated, too surprised to mask his incredulity. "He is only a bailiff." *And not a particularly good-looking one, at that.*

She laughed softly. "He loves me, and he wants to marry me. I will be a lawful wife, and—" she blushed, something Etienne had never seen her do before "—I love him with all my heart."

Etienne believed her, for her love was shining in her eyes, and he had never seen that before, either. "Are you not troubled by the fact that you will be marrying beneath you, Josephine?" he asked when he had recovered from his surprise enough to be pragmatic.

"I don't care about that, Etienne."

"Philippe de Varenne tried to give me a warning before I sent him away," he said slowly. "He thought you two intended to do me mischief."

"Etienne!" Josephine gasped, genuinely distressed, and Etienne knew he had been right to trust her. "I would not repay your kindness that way! Robert and I are planning to leave here and live elsewhere."

"I know I can trust you," he said with a smile, going to her and taking her soft, slender hands in his. "And I have no wish to find another bailiff. Jean Luc was quite effusive in his praise of Chalfront, or at least as effusive as he ever gets. I see no reason why he could not continue as bailiff here. Do you?"

"He is loath to leave here, although he said he would do so, for my sake," Josephine said, pressing a gentle kiss on his cheek. "Oh, Etienne, you are a good man!"

Rather than make a response to her statement, he said, "If Philippe suspected you, he may not be the only one. And people may think I am brokenhearted over losing you. While I am sure I will miss you, I think I had best prevent any such rumors by providing the wedding feast." He held up his hand to silence her happy exclamation. "Shall we say in a fortnight's time?"

"Etienne, you are wonderful!" She embraced him briefly.

"Am I?" he mused. "I fear others would not agree. Be that as it may, I will see about the feast. Now you had better start your packing, for you should go to your uncle until your wedding."

She hesitated, momentarily uncertain. "There will be rumors anyway."

"If I cared what others thought of me, I would not be the Baron DeGuerre."

"Etienne." Josephine embraced him gently. He made no response. "Etienne, I will see little of you after this. I want you to know I admire and respect you. You never made me feel...purchased." She went to the door slowly, then turned back to face him. "Is there anyone...?"

He knew what she meant. "No."

She sighed. "I wish there was, Etienne. You deserve happiness."

Then she left him. Alone.

With apathetic steps, Gabriella climbed the stairs to the baron's bedchamber to assist Josephine in her dressing for the evening meal. Helping Josephine de Chaney select and put on gowns and headdresses that emphasized her outstanding beauty was not a task she looked forward to, for it forced her to remember that the baron had a woman in his life; he did not need or want *her* beyond the pride of adding another woman to the list of those he had seduced.

Ever since that day in the forest seven days ago when the baron had made certain Philippe de Varenne was gone and she had come to know the true state of her feelings for Etienne DeGuerre, she had been powerless to subdue them, try as she might. She even dreamed of being in his arms, the images so vivid that, when she awoke, she was ashamed of herself.

What could it avail her to yearn for him? She should not crave even the sight of him the way she did. She should remember what he had done—taken her home and made her a servant. He had tried to seduce her, and she should be glad—*glad!*—he had not succeeded.

"Ah, Gabriella!" Josephine cried softly as she entered the baron's bedchamber. "There you are! You are late."

The room was tumultuously messy, as if Josephine had tried on several garments before selecting one. She had evidently managed to choose a gown on her own, for she wore a beautiful brocade creation of rich, deep forest green. The color highlighted the purity of her complexion and the brilliancy of her green eyes.

"Forgive me, my lady," Gabriella said listlessly. What kind of simpleton would think she could compete with this woman's beauty? If it seemed that Etienne DeGuerre revealed some of his feelings to her, what did that mean? Perhaps that was simply another weapon in his arsenal of seduction.

Then she realized that Josephine's eyes glowed with extraordinary excitement and her manner seemed curiously elated.

"Hand me that green scarf, will you?" Josephine asked gaily. "No, not that one. The one with the silver border. Isn't it lovely? There was a silk merchant traveling through the village and he sent this to me for a present. It should be just the thing to go with this gown, don't you think?" Josephine slid gracefully onto the stool in front of the mirror.

"Yes, my lady," Gabriella agreed, all the while wondering what accounted for the lady's present state.

Josephine stopped adjusting the scarf on her bountiful golden hair. "Are you ill, Gabriella?" she asked solicitously. "You look pale. Have you eaten enough today?"

Guido and the others in the kitchen had asked her that same thing many times recently, and Gabriella was finding it most annoying. Wasn't she allowed to feel unhappy, given the circumstances of her…whole life? Nevertheless, she fought to keep her frustration from her voice. "I am well," she replied as she started to pick up some of the garments scattered about the room.

Josephine hummed to herself as she adjusted her scarf a little more, the tune so gay and lilting that, in Gabriella's current state of mind, it seemed calculated to upset her. "You seem very happy, my lady," she noted as she bent to lay a thin shift in one of Josephine's large chests.

"I am," Josephine responded. She glanced at Gabriella over her shoulder. "I want you to come here first thing in the morning tomorrow. There is a lot of packing to be done."

Gabriella turned around very slowly, as if she had been given a sleeping potion. All her limbs seemed unnaturally heavy. Indeed, her mind seemed affected, for she said stupidly, "Packing? Are you…are you leaving?"

"Yes. I will miss this splendid castle." Josephine sighed, but it held only the smallest hint of regret.

"You are not coming back?" Gabriella asked.

"No." Josephine eyed her sympathetically. "There is no need to look so upset. I will see to it that you are not given heavier tasks than you have had as my maid. I'm sure Etienne will agree."

Why had she stayed here? Gabriella thought wildly. She should have taken the money the baron had offered her and gone away. She never should have remained after her father's death, never should have met the baron, never should have kissed him.

Never should have allowed herself to... yes, to fall in love with him, because he didn't care for her, and now he was leaving. "Thank you, my lady," she said, sensing that Josephine was waiting for a response. The words came with an effort, but they came.

Josephine shifted on her chair and faced Gabriella, a kind, sincere expression on her face. "I'm sorry we didn't meet under other circumstances, Gabriella," she said. "If we had known each other before... well, when we were girls, I'm sure we could have been friends."

"Yes, my lady," Gabriella replied woodenly. What else was there to say, after all?

Josephine looked at her shrewdly. "You *are* tired," she said firmly. "You need not come back to help me later. Go early to bed."

Gabriella bristled at the woman's pity. She had been a fool and weak, but she would not be pitied. "I can do my work."

Josephine smiled, and Gabriella saw friendship there, and respect, not pity. "I know. Nevertheless, we have much to do tomorrow. Come before mass to help me."

Gabriella nodded, reflecting that she had better do as Josephine suggested, for if she came back to the bedchamber after the evening meal, might not the baron be here, too? To see him now would be more than she could tolerate. "Very well, my lady."

"You do not have to serve in the hall tonight, either, if you would rather not. Eat a good supper and retire."

"Thank you, my lady."

Josephine rose and faced her maidservant. "Be of good cheer, Gabriella," she said kindly, and with fervor. "Never think things cannot become better than they are. For a long time, I thought...but I was so wrong...." She clasped her hands together and smiled brilliantly. "I...I have to tell someone my good news. I am so happy, I could fly. Or burst trying to stay silent. Can I trust to your discretion?"

With a sick premonition of what Josephine was about to say, Gabriella nodded.

"I am to be married!"

For a moment Gabriella felt a very real pain, then her pride sealed the break that had appeared in her heart.

It could be worse. She might have succumbed to the baron's lust at the very time he was considering marriage with another. Thank God she had not!

"My best wishes for your happiness," she said softly, wondering when and where the marriage ceremony would be. Not here, obviously, if Josephine was preparing to leave. She said a prayer of thanks for not having to be a witness to that.

"You may go, Gabriella. I can finish here myself," Josephine said happily. "Tell no one of my secret just yet. It will be common knowledge soon enough, and will make for much gossip, too, I suppose. Well, I don't care. I simply *had* to share my good fortune with someone.

"And you see, Gabriella, many things are possible. Even things we think are inconceivable may come to pass. You must never give up hope!"

"Yes, my lady," Gabriella said dully, wanting to be gone. She hurried to the door and with swift steps she left the room and Josephine de Chaney, who had just taken away a hope Gabriella hadn't even known she had harbored until it was gone.

The next morning, the hall was quite empty as Gabriella rushed through it on her way to the baron's bedchamber. She had to pack for Josephine de Chaney and wanted to accomplish her task as quickly as possible. It would be much easier if she was alone. She knew Josephine had gone to speak with Robert, probably about the transportation of her goods, so the lady would not interfere.

Most of all, Gabriella didn't want to see Baron DeGuerre. She could not bear to be near him, knowing he would soon be gone, and would find his impartial scrutiny torture. She had a fervent hope that the empty hall meant the knights, with their lord, had gone out hunting.

Her feet made no noise as she ran up the stairs, and a quick peek in the solar showed that room unoccupied, too.

She sighed with genuine relief. If the baron wasn't in the hall or the solar, he was surely out of the castle; therefore, she didn't bother to knock when she arrived at the bedchamber.

The room was not empty. Baron DeGuerre was there, standing by the window.

Chapter Fourteen

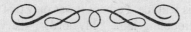

Before Gabriella could leave as swiftly and silently as she had entered, she realized how dejected he looked. His usually squared shoulders slumped unnaturally, and he hung his head. Her mind told her to go; her heart ordered her to stay.

He seemed to grow aware of her presence and, as he turned, he straightened, displaying to her his inscrutable visage, and her first thought was actually relief. Perhaps what she had witnessed was nothing more than a pensive attitude.

"Gabriella," he said, "what do you want?"

"Baron," Gabriella acknowledged awkwardly, bobbing a curtsy. She hadn't been this close to him since he had saved her in the woods. Her cheeks started to tingle with the remembrance, and her legs seemed turned to jelly.

"Well?" he asked softly.

"Excuse me, my lord, I've...I've come to pack Lady Josephine's things."

"Ah, yes, I would prefer it if you would do so later." He turned back to the window, apparently contemplating the scenery outside.

She turned to leave when she glanced at him again. How lonely he looked! He did not seem at all happy, especially for a man about to married.

Surely it was not wise to attach too much significance to his attitude. Perhaps it was only that his foot was still troubling him. "My lord?" she ventured quietly, taking a step closer.

"What is it?" he asked, without turning around.

"Are you . . . are you quite well?"

"Yes." Very slowly he faced her, one dark eyebrow raised questioningly. "Is there something else, Gabriella?"

She shook her head.

"Then why do you stay? Are you not afraid to be alone with me again?" How calm his words, as if he were merely commenting on the weather or the season of the year.

He couldn't fool her anymore with that unemotional tone. She saw the loneliness in his eyes and the pain, too. "I'm not afraid of you," she answered truthfully.

He took one step toward her, then halted as if unseen hands held him back. His mouth twisted into a smile. "Perhaps you should be."

She shook her head, knowing in her heart that she would never be afraid of him again, not after he had protected her in the woods. "Is there much to arrange for the wedding?" she asked, trying to tell herself that if she could speak of his marriage, it would soon hurt less to think about it.

"Josephine and Chalfront will see to the details."

"I, um, wish you joy." She attempted to infuse some sincerity into her words, although they were a lie.

"Joy?" he asked quietly. "Why do you think to wish me joy?"

"Because... because you are marrying Lady de Chaney."

He looked startled. "I am not marrying Josephine."

"What?" she whispered, surprised and confused and, beneath it all, delighted, something she commanded herself not to feel. "I thought..." Her words trailed off, her mind warning her not to reveal what she felt.

"She is marrying Robert Chalfront."

He watched her closely, and in his eyes, inscrutable no longer, she thought she saw hope. Hope for what? "Chalfront?" she whispered, her heart thundering in her chest.

"I agree it is not a flattering notion that I am being passed over for another," he continued, his eyes lighting with the smile that played about his lips, making him so attractive she could scarcely refrain from smiling back. "But apparently they are in love. I'm quite happy for Josephine, of course. She deserves to be married. I am happy she has found a husband." His expression grew more somber and he looked away from her. "For I will never marry again." He said the last almost defiantly, as if she had contradicted him before he spoke. His words had a tone of such adamant conviction that all her former joy disappeared like a drop of water on the cobblestones in high summer.

Fool! her mind admonished. *Stupid, stupid fool to care for him! He will never love you.*

"Now I think it would be better if you left and returned another time."

Gabriella did not stand upon the order of her going, but fled. Shame filled her, and her body burned with its heat. She was so weak, with not even pride to give her strength! Even now, she could not ignore him, or the feelings he aroused. All she could think about was that if Josephine de Chaney was no longer his mistress, how long would it be before another took her place? What was worse, she wanted to be the one to share the baron's bed. To share his life and his days, as well as his nights.

What kind of base, weak, immoral creature was she becoming? How much longer could she endure this torture?

She would run away. Now. At once. Leave everything and everyone behind and go away.

She halted confusedly at the bottom of the steps and laid her forehead against the cool stone wall. How could she do that? How could she forget the debt and abandon her honor?

Even if she could ignore the sum she owed, to travel alone and impoverished was too dangerous for a woman. Undoubtedly she would be an easy prey for any thief or brigand, and then *all* her honor would be gone.

But to stay? To live with this agony of desire, knowing it was wrong. How could she bear it?

Then she knew she must find a way to endure, because she could not abandon her honor.

Philippe de Varenne hated the sea. He hated the enormity of it, the power of it, the sight of it and the smell of it. If there had been any other way to get to France, he would have taken it. Unfortunately, there was not, and so he sat in this dim, stinking tavern waiting to sail across the channel, his bandaged leg aching abominably.

Some of his drink had spilled from the cracked chalice and fell upon his soiled, wrinkled tunic, but Philippe didn't notice. He rarely noticed much beyond the most basic bodily needs these days, especially his thirst, and if Sir George and the others had come upon him, they would scarcely have recognized the filthy man as Philippe de Varenne.

It took a lot of wine to subdue the hate burning in Philippe's breast, as well as to dull the sound of the ships creaking at the Dover dockside, lessen his annoyance at the babble of the seamen chattering away in absurd foreign tongues, overcome the scent of the dead fish and seaweed rotting on the pilings and deaden the anger he carried for Baron DeGuerre.

He loathed the baron with his whole heart, or at least all save the bit filled with hatred for his own family, who had refused to help him. His father, the fat fool, had ranted and raved for hours, claiming that it must have been Philippe's fault that the baron had sent him away. Two days of that had been quite enough, and Philippe had gone. Unfortunately, the friends he had sought out did not understand the meaning of hospitality. He had seen their sly looks and heard their parsimonious comments about the price of wine. Greedy dolts, the lot of them! He didn't need them. A man of his capabilities would be more appreciated in Europe anyway.

Alone and sullen, Philippe took another gulp of his wine which barely deserved the name, and watched another man enter. He was young, this stranger, and handsome in a rough, uncouth way. Well pleased with himself, too, judging by his manner as he strode in and smiled as if he owned the earth. The stranger called out for ale, then took the proffered mug thankfully and downed it in a gulp.

Ale, Philippe noted with disdain. The fellow must be a Saxon peasant, for only they drank that disgusting beverage. "Impudent young whelp," he muttered, too far in his cups to realize he spoke aloud.

"Did you address me, sir?" the fellow asked, turning around with the mug of ale still in his hand.

"No, I did not," Philippe replied with a sneer.

"I beg your pardon, then," the stranger replied, and it was then that Philippe saw the scar above his eye—and a distinct resemblance in the features, the wavy brown hair and the fearless brown eyes. What blessing of fortune was this?

"I beg yours, if you be Bryce Frechette," Philippe said with true joy, a delightful plan forming in his wine-soaked mind as he rose unsteadily.

"I am he," the fellow replied with surprise. "How do you know my name?"

"Your sister speaks of you often," Philippe answered. "Are you on your way home?"

"Indeed I am."

Philippe made a sorrowful face. "Too late, I fear."

"Too late!" Frechette cried with alarm. "What do you mean? Explain yourself, sir!"

"Your father is dead—"

Frechette's face grew pale and his hand that held the mug started to tremble. "Dead?" he whispered. "When? How?"

"An illness, or so I understand. He has been dead for many weeks."

Frechette stared at the ground, wrapped in his own thoughts, and Philippe was glad to see that the impertinent smile had been wiped from his face.

"Your sister has suffered much," Philippe went on sorrowfully. "Apparently your father was much in debt when he died."

Frechette glanced up at him sharply. "In debt?"

"Yes, indeed. Chalfront—"

"Chalfront!" Frechette snarled as he brought the mug crashing to the table, where it shattered into several pieces.

"Here now, sir!" the tavern keeper cried. He fell silent and went back to wiping tables when Frechette turned a murderous eye onto him.

"I should have known better than to leave when he was still in charge of Father's money," Frechette said. "I *never* trusted him, never!"

"He is still the bailiff there. Baron DeGuerre confirmed his position."

"Who the devil is Baron DeGuerre to be making such decisions? That should have been for Gabriella to settle, until I came home."

"Ah, but there's the trouble," Philippe said. "It seems nobody knew what had become of you."

A guilty look flashed across the man's face, pleasing Philippe enormously, although he tried to hide his delight. "The king gave your family's estate to Baron Etienne DeGuerre. Your sister has lived to regret that decision," Philippe finished mournfully.

"Gabriella! Why?"

"Well, she was left in a very dubious position, although there were those who sought to help her. Chalfront, for one. He offered to marry her."

Frechette reached for the hilt of his sword. "That little weasel!"

"No need for that," Philippe said slyly. "Chalfront was rebuffed. Now there is another man who wants her, except he will never offer marriage."

"Who?" Frechette demanded, splaying his hands on the scarred tabletop and leaning forward. "Who would dare to make such a base proposition to my sister? Explain yourself."

Philippe couldn't help but notice that Gabriella was more important to him than the loss of his home. Interesting. Stupid, of course, but interesting, because Philippe realized he was going to be able to play this fool like a trout caught on his line.

"Alas," Philippe said with a sigh that seemed to represent the sorrow of the ages, and incidentally increased the delay before he answered, thereby adding to the young man's torture. "Though your sister is currently quite well in body, it is her body, I fear, that will also be her ruin."

Frechette's eyes narrowed. "Baron DeGuerre. I have heard of him. Does he think a noblewoman like my sister would *ever* lower herself to consider a profane liaison with any man, let alone a man of his reputation? I assure you, sir, my sister is made of stronger stuff!"

"Much as I dislike being the bearer of additional bad tidings, I must regretfully tell you she is no longer noble. Nor are you."

"What?" Frechette demanded.

"Your family has lost its title, as well as its estate. Baron DeGuerre forced your sister to become a servant."

"He had no right—!"

"Oh, he did. The king gave the baron that right when he gave him the estate. Baron DeGuerre wanted her to leave, but she wouldn't, so that was the alternative." Philippe lowered his voice. "Of course, she was alone and unprotected, so she had little choice...." He let his words hang in the air suggestively.

How absolutely wonderful it was to watch Bryce Frechette's growing anger and dismay, to rub salt in this arrogant fellow's guilty wounds! "She's a very pretty woman," Philippe continued sorrowfully, "so while she may have resisted him at the beginning, I fear..."

Frechette slammed his fists onto the table and straightened abruptly. "I'll *kill* him if he has touched so much as a hair on her head!" Without waiting for Philippe to say anything more, he marched angrily from the tavern. Outside, he shouted for his horse, and then Philippe heard the rapid clatter of hooves as he galloped away.

Philippe chuckled, the sound more evil than mirthful. "Here, you!" he called to the proprietor. "Clear this mess away and bring me some more wine. And bread. Not that coarse brown stuff, either. The best you've got. I want to celebrate."

"Greetings, my lady!" Mary called out as she bustled into the courtyard of the castle. With a happy smile on her face and shifting the basket of apples she carried on her hip, Mary hurried toward Gabriella, who was about to enter the kitchen. The smile changed into a worried frown. "How are you today, my lady?" she asked solicitously. "Are you feeling ill?"

"I am quite well," Gabriella said, which was not exactly a lie. She was well physically, and if she was troubled because of the recent events in the castle, or her own errant, uncontrollable emotions, that was not something Mary needed to know.

"Well, you look a little peaked to me. They're not starving you, are they?" Mary queried as they entered the kitchen.

Guido overheard the woman's last remark and drew himself up to his full five feet. "Nobody starves in my kitchen!"

"No insult intended, I'm sure," Mary said with a sniff. "I'm having a word with Lady Gabriella," she announced, her stare daring Guido or anyone else in the kitchen to protest. Wisely they did not, and she drew Gabriella aside. "Is it true, what they're sayin'? Is Robert Chalfront really marrying the baron's mistress?"

"His former mistress, yes," Gabriella acknowledged.

"Why?"

"Because they're in love."

Mary gave another derisive sniff. "In love? *Her*— with Robert Chalfront? I don't believe it."

Gabriella shrugged her shoulders.

"A beautiful lady like that, with a fellow like him? Granted he is no pauper, but still!"

"Don't you think love can triumph over such differences in rank?" Gabriella asked, trying not to attach too much significance to the skeptical expression on Mary's face.

"Maybe," she replied grudgingly. "But this business of the wedding feast, from the baron, no less. Is that true, too?"

"Yes."

"By my mother's old gray head! The first thing I says to Elsbeth, if that's true, he's that anxious to be rid of her. Is he?"

Gabriella didn't respond at once. She wondered if Mary's assumption was correct, then told herself it didn't matter. There could never be anything between the baron and herself. Indeed, if he had wanted her in his bed at one time, she could not be sure he desired even that now. He never spoke to her, never looked at her, never seemed to notice she was there. She could well believe, unfortunately, that if the baron had harbored any tender feelings for her, he had since subverted them completely.

And why not, she had asked herself cynically a hundred times. Now he was free to find another mistress. Another beautiful, pliable young woman who was still noble, and who did not value personal honor over the excitement of being deemed worthy by Etienne DeGuerre. Surely there were many such candidates to take Josephine de Chaney's place.

"What does it matter why he's doing it?" she answered at last, with an attempt at casual unconcern. "It's none of our business, except the feast."

Mary clucked her tongue. "None of mine, maybe, but perhaps some of yours. You're a pretty young woman, and he's a man used to having whatever, and *whoever,* he wants. I would take care if I were you, my lady."

"The baron will not want me," she assured Mary.

"Well, if he does, he'll have the whole village after him, that I can tell you. I hear that Philippe fellow got sent packing, too, eh? Good riddance!"

"How do William and the others feel about the baron now?" Gabriella inquired, casually changing the subject. Talk of Philippe inevitably brought back all the feelings she had experienced when the baron had rescued her, feelings that she must repress. "Are they reconciled to him?"

"Better than we ever thought we could be. He seems fair enough, and the raise to the rents wasn't quite as much as we all feared. Chalfront's a changed man, I'll tell you. Goes around singing, true's I live."

"I'm glad to hear it," Gabriella replied sincerely. She was pleased to think that Robert was going to be happy, and sorry for the trouble she had caused him. If she had any regrets about *him,* it was that she hadn't paid more attention to the business of the estate before her father fell ill. That would have prevented much of the hard feelings she had borne him afterward. "Tell me the news of the village." Her tone grew slightly stern. "How are Osric and his mother?"

"Oh, they're all well enough. His mother, poor old soul, is feeling her age this year. Osric's asking for help fixing the thatch on his roof before the snow comes."

Gabriella recalled the "poor old soul's" harsh tone and vulgar curse, as well as the many things both her father and the village members had done for Osric and his mother. "Is that really necessary?" she asked. "Osric makes a good wage as a carpenter, as well as the hayward. Surely he can afford to hire men to thatch the roof."

Mary looked startled. "I . . . I suppose so."

"I would suggest that to William," Gabriella said coolly.

"If you think so," Mary said somewhat dubiously. "Now, is it true that the baron's given Lady de Chaney his bed?"

Gabriella had absolutely no desire to discuss furniture with Mary, even if Mary was right. The baron's large bed and sumptuous linens were in the storeroom at that very moment, and a new bed had recently been put in the baron's bedchamber. It was just as large as his other one, but the linens that had arrived with it were very plain. "If you'll excuse me, I have to get to work," she said, rather abruptly going on her way.

Mary watched Lady Gabriella hurry off into the hall and thought things had gotten to a sorry state when a kind, compassionate young woman like her had grown hard and bitter. "I'd like to strangle that baron myself," she muttered before setting down the apples with a bang in front of a startled Guido and marching from the kitchen.

The wedding of Lady Josephine de Chaney and Robert Chalfront was not a grand affair. The bride, accompanied by her uncle, who was a regal, elderly man reputed to be a clerk to a minor lord, returned to Castle Frechette the day before the ceremony took place and stayed in one of the guest apartments. If the baron or Josephine or even Robert thought there was anything unusual in this arrangement, they didn't indicate it, and certainly none of the baron's men or servants questioned his orders.

As Gabriella helped Josephine prepare in the baron's bedchamber, which he had told her she could use on this occasion, she was forced to admit that Josephine de Chaney was a beautiful bride. Her wedding gown was a lovely garment made of the cloth of gold the merchant had given her the day the baron had returned from his journey. On her head, she wore a plain gold circlet and simple white silk veil. Gabriella realized, however, that Josephine's comeliness was made even more stunning by the beauty of her joy. Gabriella had never seen a woman so delighted to be get-

ting married, and the delight lasted through the
ceremony.

The wedding itself was a short, simple blessing in
the chapel attended by the baron and his knights and
their ladies, followed by a feast in the decorated hall.
The servants were kept busy, for the food was plentiful and elaborate, if not as expensive as that the late
earl served. They, too, were to have a feast the next
day, and the leftovers of both meals were to be given
to the village poor, who were already waiting at the
gate in mouth-watering anticipation of the remnants
of the noble's meal.

Robert Chalfront looked like a man transformed.
Perhaps it was his new clothes, or the happy expression on his face. Whatever it was, he even looked taller
and braver and more worthy of respect, until he stood
beside Baron DeGuerre when the meal was finished
and the music of the minstrels began. Then he was
once again the humble man Gabriella had known before.

As for the baron, Gabriella had wondered what, if
anything, his face would reveal on this day. She might
have spared herself the time lost in such contemplation, for he simply looked as inscrutable as always.
Although it was a special occasion, he wore his customary long black tunic. Nevertheless, he looked more
regal and magnificent in his plain garment than Sir
George, who wore the latest in men's finery, including a dark blue and scarlet brocade tunic with slashed
sleeves that revealed a purple shirt, purple hose, and
scarlet boots.

The feast was a joyous occasion, with Sir George going out of his way to joke. Later he laughingly took the lead in the dancing. Gabriella watched from the entrance to the kitchen as he flitted from partner to partner like a long-legged butterfly. The women took his apparent fickleness in good stride, for who could be annoyed with such a charming fellow?

Then Sir George flitted toward Gabriella. She smiled, waiting for him to pass her, until he unexpectedly halted and bowed. "I would be delighted if you would join me in a round dance," he said with a pleasant and gracious smile, as if she were again a woman of nobility.

"I'm sorry, Sir George," she said with real regret. "I cannot dance with you."

"Why not?" Sir George said, his voice loud over the trilling music of the pipes, *fithele* and tabor. "I'm sure the baron won't mind. A woman as light on her feet as you are will surely be a fine dancer—and it will take a superb dancer to make me look like anything but an ox on two legs!" He was flattering her, of course, and she knew it, but it had been a long time since any man had talked to her like this, and she could not suppress an answering smile, even though she knew she must refuse.

Before she could do so, she glanced at the baron, who had not danced at all.

George saw where she looked. "Baron DeGuerre!" he called, and she wished she could sink through the floor and disappear. She knew her place! A servant would not, and could not, join in the celebrations with the nobility. She never should have let herself pay attention to Sir George.

"Baron DeGuerre," George repeated when the baron looked their way with his cold blue eyes, "do your servants have permission to join in the dancing?"

"No," the baron responded impassively.

Gabriella felt a hot blush flood her face as she looked down at the rush-covered floor and unreasonably blamed Sir George for her embarrassment, even though she knew she was being absurd.

"However, I will make an exception in this servant's case," the baron said. "If she wishes to dance with you, George, she may."

Gabriella had thought she wanted to dance, and that it didn't particularly matter who her partner was. Now she knew she didn't want to dance with any man here except one, just as there was only one man whose hand she wished to touch and whose smile she wished to see.

Nevertheless, it was Sir George who had asked her, and Sir George who held out his hand to escort her to the cleared space, so Gabriella put her hand in his and let him lead her forth.

Chapter Fifteen

As Etienne watched Gabriella dance with George, as graceful and supple as he knew she would be, he tried to turn his mind to other things.

Would Philippe de Varenne make trouble? The scoundrel had been gone a fortnight and he had heard nothing thus far. Or what of the young fool's family? He could well imagine Gerhard de Varenne's reception of a disgraced son, so Philippe had probably kept the reason for his return to himself. On the other hand, Philippe might seek revenge, and ask their help by claiming that Etienne posed some kind of threat to the family. Despite their animosity to one another, the de Varennes were clannish and might agree with Philippe. Unfortunately, there was little he could do until Philippe or his father made a move.

Poaching continued to be troublesome. His men had found more snares and traps but, so far, had no suspects. He had doubled the foot patrols in the forest, and given orders that they were to investigate any clue, no matter how insignificant.

Gabriella's hair swirled around her flushed, smiling face as she went by the high table. Despite his efforts not to, Etienne watched her pass. How lovely she was! How that simple gown suited her, but how easy it was to envision her in something more befitting her regal nature, something in a deep blue, with gold and silver trim, made of velvet, or another soft fabric that begged to be caressed. Blue ribbons braided in her thick hair. Dainty silver slippers on her dancing feet.

He must not look at her again.

He wondered if Donald and Seldon had achieved any success in their quest to find Bryce Frechette. Apparently not, for they had not returned. Or perhaps they had found some clue and decided to follow it. He had given them plenty of money and a free hand to search until they either found the young man, or the trail went completely cold.

Donald Bouchard was a fine young man. Etienne decided it was time to think about giving him a manor. He deserved it. Then Donald could marry.

George should marry, too. Etienne's hand tightened on his chalice as the couple whirled past him again. George was smiling far too pleasantly at Gabriella, who was but a servant, after all.

Suddenly the hall seemed stiflingly hot and unbearably stuffy.

Etienne stood swiftly, and the music immediately ceased.

"My lord?" one of the minstrels asked humbly.

"Nothing, it's nothing," Etienne said. "Keep playing."

He left the hall without looking back at the whirling, laughing dancers. He needed some fresh air. He had to get his wayward emotions under control. He had to remember that he was never going to marry again. He was all alone in the world and always would be. That was simply the way it was.

Once he was in the courtyard, he became aware of a commotion at the castle gates on the other side of the lowered portcullis. At first he thought some of the paupers waiting there for the remains of the feast had gotten into an argument, then he realized that several of his foot soldiers were trying to push their way toward the portcullis through the crowd while keeping hold of a man in their midst.

He quickly marched toward them, halting with his legs apart and his arms akimbo. "Fetch some torches," he commanded one of the gatekeepers. He glared at the fearful soldiers at the gatehouse. "Why is the portcullis down?" he demanded.

"Well, my lord," one of them said shakily, "you can hear the ruckus on the other side. It's not safe, I don't think—"

"Open it," Etienne ordered.

The portcullis slowly rattled upward. Those at the front of the crowd of peasants, catching sight of Etienne, fell back at once. The soldiers outside forced the rest of the mob out of their way.

Pushing through the unruly crowd with the tips of their swords, his soldiers came inside, bearing the peasant in custody with them. Other men from inside the castle appeared with torches, and the crowd fell further back.

The man in the midst of the soldiers stumbled and fell. The sergeant at arms, who held an incriminating bundle of pelts in his left hand, roughly lifted the fellow by his collar, and the malefactor's face became visible in the flickering flames.

It was the hayward, Osric.

By now, the wedding guests and the servants had heard the tumult in the courtyard and come outside. Etienne paid them no heed. All except one. A quick glance had shown him Gabriella standing off to one side, watching.

Etienne ignored the man and turned to those who had come from the hall. "Please, return to the feast. I will deal with this."

They did as he requested. All except one, who stood off to one side, watching.

"It's Osric, is it not?" Etienne asked, turning his attention to the matter at hand. He spoke calmly despite his anger, for he could well guess what the sergeant's booty meant.

"My lord, it's a mistake," Osric spluttered, his eyes wide with fright. "I was walkin' in the woods and I—"

"Sergeant, tell me what happened," Etienne said, realizing that the hayward stupidly planned to lie.

"We were searching the forest for signs of poachers, as you ordered, my lord," the sergeant explained, "and we found a hut hidden in the woods. It was covered with branches, disguised like, and full of racks with skins dryin' on 'em. So we decided to set a watch on it and sure enough, this fellow comes sneaking along. So we grabbed him."

"My lord, please, it's all a terrible mistake," Osric pleaded. "I found the hut the same as your men. They... they didn't let me explain."

"I see. Now you may have your chance to explain," Etienne said. "Explain to me what you were doing in the woods at this late hour of the night. Explain to me why you were 'sneaking along.' Tell me where these pelts come from."

"I was... in the woods because..."

"Yes?" Etienne inquired coolly as the man struggled to think of a plausible lie.

Osric looked about wildly. "Lady Gabriella, help me!"

Etienne steeled himself to resist her pleas on behalf of this thief. "She has no standing here," Etienne said firmly. "I am the law and the justice. I know about you, Osric. I know from the earl's records that you have been brought before him three times for poaching, and each time he let you go with a warning.

"I am not as lenient as the earl. I believe the evidence of my sergeant, and the pelts in his hand."

"My lady, for your good father's sake, help me!" Osric pleaded, falling to his knees. "Oh, have mercy, my lord! Think of my poor old mother!"

Gabriella took one hesitant step forward.

"Do you know the penalty for poaching?" Etienne demanded of the criminal, willing Gabriella to leave the courtyard, determined to uphold the law, as was his sworn duty. "The first time, a man loses his thumb and bow fingers. The second, his sight. The third, his life."

Osric shook his head, his body shaking with sobs. "Oh, mercy, my lord! Please, I beg you!"

"Luckily for you, this is the first time you have been brought before *me,*" Etienne said. "Sergeant, his fingers are the price he will pay."

The sergeant nodded grimly while Osric's screams grew louder and more piercing.

"Do it on the village green, so that all will learn that no man should dare to steal from the king. Or from me," Etienne ordered.

Etienne's resolute gaze met Gabriella's briefly, before she bowed her head and hurried toward the chapel. He could not tell what she was thinking from her large brown eyes, but he thought he could make a very good guess.

She despised him.

It was weakness to care what she thought. It was foolishness to feel the pain he experienced as he watched her go. It would be an admission of her power over him if he went after her to explain.

All these things he thought as he stood in the courtyard, knowing the truth of them.

But he simply could not bear to have her hate him, so when the courtyard was empty once again, he followed her.

Gabriella hurried into the chapel, wanting to be alone. Away from the baron. Away from the wedding. Away from everything.

She sank onto the bench nearest the altar, every limb quivering. The lights from the many small candles flickered and danced, casting elusive shadows on the walls. The air was cold and incense-scented, the bench hard and unyielding.

Gabriella noticed almost nothing of this. Her thoughts were focused solely upon her reaction to what had just transpired.

Although the punishment was harsh, Osric had broken the law many times and never been caught; now he had, and now he must pay. Indeed, the baron had applied justice with more mercy than he had to. He was not the unjust lord she had feared. He was ambitious and fiercely protective of his property, but he was no monster.

He was a man, and she loved him.

Hopelessly, she knew, and so she must leave this place while she could yet contemplate going where he was not. Before she was tempted to forget her up-bringing, and who she was.

She must leave Castle Frechette, which was no longer a home but a place of torment, and forget that she had ever seen Baron DeGuerre. She would ask Mary to take her in, until she could figure out where to go next.

Then she realized she was not alone. Slowly she turned to see the shadow of a man cast by the light shining in through the stained-glass window, a tall, muscular man who wore a long robe.

She rose quickly.

"I will . . . I will leave you to your contemplation," the baron said, his voice sounding loud yet hesitant in the stillness.

"No, I will go," she said quickly, moving toward him and the door, more confused than ever by his apparent uncertainty.

"I have not come to pray for forgiveness," he said with an obvious attempt to sound defiant. Was that dismay she saw wrinkling his brow? Was the always confident Etienne DeGuerre questioning his decision?

More importantly, if that was so, why did he seek *her* out?

"It is Osric who should be asking for forgiveness," she replied at last, a hope she dared not harbor growing in her heart. "Why did you follow me here? Was it to explain to me that you were merely an agent of the law? A lord with a responsibility to punish wrongdoers? That you were only doing your duty?"

His eyes narrowed, as if he wondered what she meant by her words. "I have no need to explain my decisions to anyone."

"No, you do not. Because what you did was what you felt you had to do. I am the daughter of an earl, my lord. If my father was a lenient man, some of his friends were not. I have met unjust men in my life. You are not of their ilk, no matter what others may say."

His pale blue eyes seemed to glow in the darkness from some kind of inner struggle being waged within him. "You flatter me," he remarked.

"That was not my intention," she answered. "I do *not* need an explanation for your decision about Osric, because I agree with it." She hesitated, then decided to tell what she had discovered, to prove that he had not erred in what he had been forced to do. "I knew about Osric before."

"So I understood."

"Since my father's death, I mean. I overheard him speaking with his mother. I could have said something to William, or Mary, or even Osric himself, to warn him to leave the village, but I was angry and upset at them, and—" she lowered her voice as she made her admission "—at you, for being right."

"Then you understand that I only did what I had to do tonight?" he asked, and she knew with sudden certainty that her answer truly mattered to him.

She nodded slowly as he came toward her.

"Do you hate me, Gabriella?" The question was posed softly, yet she heard the need in his voice.

"No," she whispered.

"Perhaps you should. I am a man who takes what he wants." Despite his bold attempt to appear cold and unfeeling, she saw a mixture of hope, desire and despair in his eyes, like those of a man beholding something he wants very much but fears he can never have.

"What do you want?" she asked softly, half-afraid to pose the question, and more afraid not to.

"I want you." His voice grew hard again. "I am in need of another mistress, after all."

"I don't believe you have so little respect for me that you mean such an iniquitous proposal," she said. "You care too much for me."

His eyes widened for the briefest of moments, and another flicker of pain passed through them. "As you have already discovered, Gabriella, there is but one way I love," he answered, reaching for her and pulling her into his arms. His lips swooped down upon hers in a burning, heated kiss that left her dizzy and breathless before he pulled back and ran his searching gaze over her face. "Would you take Josephine's place?"

"No," she answered, twisting away from him and planting her feet apart. "I will not dishonor myself, not even for love."

"I don't *love* you," the baron replied with forced arrogance. "I don't love anybody. I simply desire you. I will use you and, when I see another woman who catches my fancy, I will send you from my bed."

"You think to frighten me away from you," she charged, "but it is already too late to do that." He was trying so hard to hide his true feelings! Yet his desperate words could not mask his agony, and love for him filled her. She went and stood directly in front of him, so that he would be forced to see her. "You already care for me, or you would not be trying to scare me away."

"Are you a mind reader, then?" he demanded scornfully.

"No. I know—" She took a deep breath "—because I feel the same for you."

He stared at her with an expression that was, she realized with great dismay, one of horror. That was not what she had thought to see. "What has happened to you?" she cried anxiously. "What has made you so afraid to love?"

His horror disappeared, replaced with his usual cold impartiality so quickly that she marveled at his self-control. And cursed it. "I do not need your help to find the answers to such ridiculous questions," he replied.

"Are you going to shut me out?" she asked. "Are you going to lock your heart away again, behind that wall of reserve? Then why did you come here?"

"I was momentarily...weak," he said harshly. "Now you may go back to the dancing and leave me alone."

"I won't, any more than I would leave a wounded man on the road. Whatever has happened to you in the past has left a poison in your heart. Let the poison drain, before it festers and kills you."

He gazed at her, still struggling with his wounded heart. "I do not need your physic, you who had parents and a brother who loved you. You would never understand!"

She reached out to take his hand in hers. "I can try, and I can listen," she said softly. "I will not go from here until you tell me who has hurt you so badly, unless you pick me up and throw me out that door."

He looked as if he would indeed do that, and then, his shoulders slumped and he shrugged as he sat wearily on the bench. "You are a stubborn woman, Gabriella Frechette. If you want to hear about me, I will tell you—if only to convince you that I can never love you, or anybody else." He spoke almost to himself, or as if he were addressing the spirit of the air and not a flesh-and-blood woman. "I was born a bastard, the son of a knight my mother loved with all her heart. He died before I was born. My mother always believed he was returning to marry her when he met with his fatal accident.

"She loved him so much that there was little, if any, love left for her child, except as the reminder of the man. Ever since I could take my first steps, she told me of my father's greatness. His battle prowess, his skill, his manners, his looks—they were my bedtime stories, along with the exhortation to be worthy of him, a man I had never known. Oh, the goals my mother set for me!" he said wryly, but it was a tortured attempt at lightness that touched her more than another man's tears might have. "It was not enough to be good at fighting. I had to be the best."

Here, then, was the root of his ambition. It was not to achieve power or glory or wealth for himself alone, but to be worthy of an ideal. Suddenly she saw not the great Baron DeGuerre sitting before her, but a lonely little boy trying to win his mother's love.

The baron sighed heavily and rubbed his forehead as if he would blot out his memories. "I left home and began to earn rewards at tournaments and the notice of great lords. I became the best, for my mother's sake." His estimation was said without arrogance or undue pride. "I saved most of what I got, to provide for her. I bought her a fine house and horses, and hired her servants.

"Still not enough. I must be even better. Richer. More powerful. By this time," he said, glancing at Gabriella with a sad, ironic smile, "I enjoyed what I had become. It was no longer for my mother's sake that I strove, but my own.

"Then my mother fell seriously ill. I rushed to her bedside and saw to it that she had the best of care.

"Yet all she ever spoke of was my father. His name was the one always on her lips when she was able to speak." His voice became ragged and low. "Not one word did she spare for me. I should have told her what I knew," he continued bitterly, "what I found out when I was earning my rewards in tournaments and heard my father's name mentioned. He wasn't coming back to her when he died. He was on his way to be married, to *somebody else*."

"Why didn't you tell her?" Gabriella prompted gently, although she thought she could guess the answer.

"Because even then, I think I was trying to ease my mother's pain," he replied, confirming what she suspected as he sighed once more. "At any rate, she died."

"And you were left alone."

He looked surprised. "I was free."

"What kind of woman could not love her only child?" Gabriella wondered aloud.

He regarded her steadily. "Don't you know? A woman who has succumbed to the domination of love," he answered. "She set her heart on one human being who was gone and did not see the child at her knee."

Gabriella nodded pensively.

"Is it so surprising that I should try to understand her?" he asked as if he had heard her unspoken thought. "For years she was the only person in my life, and I studied her well. But now you know why I do not want anyone's love," he warned. "Love is a snare and a weakness, and I will have no part of it. I am content to be alone.''

"No, you are not content,'' Gabriella protested fervently, her heart full of love for the abandoned, vulnerable man. "You are lonely and your heart is full of bitter pain. Nobody wants to be alone.''

"I don't want your love!'' Etienne said sternly, rising abruptly.

"Whether you want it or not, you have it,'' she said gently, and with all the determination of her stubborn nature, revealing what she had been uselessly trying to fight, and what she wouldn't fight anymore.

She walked toward him slowly. Now was the time to decide. What was more important, her honor or this man? Could she deny that undisguised look of longing in his eyes, or ignore his loneliness? If she did, would she not rue it the rest of her life?

She was Gabriella Frechette, daughter of earls and lords. She had nothing but her honor left.

And she had no other gift, save that, to prove her love. Here, now, she would make a new decision.

He did not move. He did not speak, not even when she put her arms around him and kissed him.

She felt the tension in his body, like the string of a bow drawn overly tight. Then slowly, as her kiss continued, he moved to embrace her delicately, as if he were afraid she might break in his grasp. Or as if he feared she did not mean what her actions implied.

She drew back and smiled her love. He wasn't the bold, brave baron now, but a lover uncertain, and she would convince him that she would not regret her decision. Still smiling, although her heart raced, she began to untie the laces at the neck of his long tunic. She sensed that he would not take command here, that it was her place to lead.

With sudden understanding and a look of such hopeful delight that Gabriella knew she would never, ever be sorry for what they were about to do, he grabbed her hand and pressed fervent kisses on her fingers.

Then she was in his arms, surrounded and held tight against him while their lips met in passionate delight. With one accord they sank to their knees as their kiss deepened, unmindful of the hard stones.

Her fingers worked the lacings until she could reach one hand inside his tunic to feel the warm, hard flesh of his chest.

She withdrew her hand and pulled away, so that she could see the buckle of his belt. Breathing rapidly, she had it undone quickly, but as it fell to the ground, he pulled her to him with a low growl of desire and kissed the tops of her breasts. She gasped and leaned back as his chin nuzzled down the fabric of her bodice until her breasts were exposed to his lips and teasing tongue.

Her hands clutched his long hair and she couldn't suppress the moan of pleasure as he continued. What he was doing was so astoundingly wonderful she had an urgent need to return the pleasure. She tore at his tunic until she widened the gap enough to reach his nipples with her mouth. As he had done, she kissed and suckled and lightly brushed each hardened nub with her tongue.

He put his hands on her shoulders and gently pushed her backward until she lay on the floor. His eyes full of primitive desire, he knelt between her legs and leaned forward. While he kissed her, one hand raised her skirt and caressed her thigh, the other supported his weight. His lean, strong fingers, cold at first, grew warm as they continued to probe. She closed her eyes, awash with sensation and craving more.

He thrust his tongue gently inside the soft confines of her mouth, and his fingers continued to work their magic. Incredible sensations swept over her, each more powerful than the next. Tension built and ebbed and built again, until she was whimpering with need.

Then she felt him enter her. A brief pain soon passed away as he began to move, thrusting rhythmically. She clutched his muscular arms while his lips moved over her until she thought she would faint with pleasure. His breathing grew ragged, nearly as ragged as her own.

The tension continued to build, and her knuckles grew white as she held him in exquisite agony.

And then she felt an incredible release of pleasure that made her cry out with sheer unbridled delight. He groaned and she slowly realized that he, too, had experienced release.

He lifted himself away from her and rose, his tunic falling into place as he gazed down at her, his pale blue eyes telling her...nothing. Then he turned and left her there.

Without saying a single word.

Chapter Sixteen

Bryce begrudged having to let his lame horse walk the last few miles toward home. He wanted to reach Castle Frechette as soon as he could, which had been his aim since he had left Dover. Unfortunately, the lameness of his horse was but another in a series of troubles that had delayed him.

Not for the first time he cursed his angry haste at leaving his home. Long chafing at what he perceived as a lack of independence, the confrontation with his father over Chalfront had seemed the final straw. But if he had known he would never see his father alive again—!

To his infinite regret, he had not considered such an event, and so had gone away, too upset to linger to explain his mistrust of Chalfront to Gabriella, supposing he had even been able to put it into words. He had no evidence beyond his own distaste for the obsequious man who couldn't be made to see that a nobleman had certain expenses that could not be ignored or deferred.

As time had passed, and Bryce had grown wiser and seen more of truly dishonest men, he had come to doubt his suspicions of Chalfront. If the bailiff had been dishonest, would his father not have suspected, too?

Still the days had passed, and he, proud and stubborn, had waited for his father to try to find him. When he did not, pride and stubbornness kept him away. Why, even the trip to Dover had been based upon the whim to taste good English ale.

Thank God for that whim, if that was all it was, and not a divine inspiration. And how fortunate it was that he had met that fellow in the tavern. If he had not, Gabriella's sufferings might have been prolonged. As it was, they would end soon.

As anxious as Bryce was to get home, the leisurely pace allowed him to savor his return, at least a little. Each step of the way brought back some memory of his past, both good and ill.

Here was the apple tree he used to climb as a boy, where he could watch the traffic on the roadway—and throw apples at unsuspecting travelers. Here was the stream he and his companions used to bathe in during the hot summer months, splashing and screaming with delight. There was the tumbledown cottage he had gone to with Edith, a buxom lass far more mature than he, and where he had joyfully lost his virginity. He smiled to himself thinking of the delightful sensations she had introduced him to in that ruined place and sighed. She had married before he left and probably had several children by this time. Perhaps the remnants of that old blanket were still in the cottage, though, or the blackened coals from the fire he had made when the blanket proved insufficient to keep them warm.

How angry Edith had been when she had found him there with another girl! He felt a twinge of guilt at the memory of Edith's wrath. What a callous youth he had been, far more concerned with satisfying his own needs than giving any thought to the girls, for there had been several more after Edith. One or two had even been very willing daughters of noblemen, eager and surprisingly experienced.

He felt another pang of remorse when he passed the mill. Did anyone still suspect him of beating the miller under cover of darkness? They certainly had at the time, and he had neither defended nor excused himself, for he had done it, of course. He had been convinced the man was a cheat and a liar despite his smiles and compliments. Like Chalfront.

Bryce scowled darkly. Chalfront! Even if the bailiff was an honest man, he should have beaten *him* before he went away, or at least threatened him with such a fate if he ever dared to so much as look at Gabriella!

It would have been so much better if he had never gone, he admitted to himself. But the shame he had felt when his father continued to listen to Chalfront, taking the bailiff's opinion over that of his own son, had sown the seeds of his discontent.

They had said so many harsh things to each other that day! Perhaps the most galling had been his father's complaint about Bryce's penchant for hunting and sport when he should have been attending to his studies. Coming from his father, who hated any kind of book work and left it all to Chalfront, that had struck Bryce as the height of injustice.

Now that he was older, he often wondered if his father, with his slightly wistful expression, hadn't been hoping his son would do better in that regard.

If only he could ask him! But now he was too late.

Too late for that, but not too late to help Gabriella. God's wounds, if that fellow's words had a grain of truth in them, if Baron DeGuerre had harmed her or taken her against her will, or if he had even touched her, that man would regret it! *"I swear it,"* Bryce muttered aloud.

Then the road went over the ridge and he could see his family's land stretching before him. He scanned the woodlands, barren with the approach of winter. Beyond that was the castle, his father's lifelong passion. It *did* look magnificent, Bryce thought proudly, although even now he couldn't understand why his father would get so excited about stones and designs and carving, just as his father couldn't understand his son's need to fight and hunt and be away from the stuffy confines of hall and home.

The sun was high overhead when Bryce finally arrived at the village. It seemed deserted, until he heard the lowing of cattle and bleating of sheep. Of course. The men were rounding up the animals for the fall slaughter and separating them based on their condition.

He passed Osric's cottage and noticed Osric sitting behind it in the sun, his right hand bandaged. An injury, or had he finally been punished for his poaching? Perhaps the baron was not nearly so sanguine about such activity, which was not something Bryce would hold against the man. He had often quarreled with his father about Osric, too.

A window in one of the largest houses stood open, and from it came the sweet sounds of a feminine voice. A woman moved to close it and Bryce's breath caught in his throat.

She was the most astonishingly lovely woman he had ever seen in his life. Indeed, he suspected she was surely the most beautiful woman in the world, with her long, unbound golden hair, pale skin, slender throat and lips half parted as she drew the shutter closed.

He suddenly had even more reason to be glad he had decided to return home.

And then, just as suddenly, his lip curled with hate, for Robert Chalfront came bustling down the road toward him.

"Greetings, Robert," Bryce called out as he stepped into the road and blocked the man's way.

Robert Chalfront's mouth dropped open. "You!" he gasped.

Bryce bounded forward and took hold of Chalfront's garments by the neck, lifting him so that the bailiff's feet barely touched the ground. "Come now, man. We can't have you falling on the road in a faint, can we?"

"What...what are you doing here?" Chalfront rasped.

"I daresay you wish I wasn't. Stolen any more money lately, Chalfront? Threatened any widows with dispossession?"

"I never—"

"No, but you wanted my father to."

Bryce let go and Chalfront stumbled, then righted himself. "You have no right to accost me in such a manner," Chalfront said with unexpected warmth.

"Where is Gabriella?"

"In the . . . in the castle, of course," he answered, drawing himself up to his full height, which meant that he came even with Bryce's chin.

"I knew my father was a fool to trust his money to you!"

"It has been proven otherwise," Chalfront retorted. "The baron—"

"Ah, yes. The baron. He's next on my list of people to visit. He'll be sorry I've come back, too."

"Robert? What is it, Robert? What's happening?" a woman's voice called from the door of the large house, and the beautiful creature Bryce had seen before stood there. "Who are *you?*" she demanded haughtily. "What do you want?"

"I am sorry to disturb you, dear lady," Bryce said with a courteous bow. "I have business with this simpleton."

"That *simpleton* is my husband, and the bailiff here. If you have business with him, I suggest it can wait until later. He has much to do today."

Bryce could hardly believe his ears. Robert Chalfront was married to this beauty? It seemed incredible, although it might go a long way to explain the alteration in the man's manner. Bryce had expected him to cower with fear, not upbraid him.

He scowled at Chalfront. "Out of respect for your wife, I will wait to speak of these matters another day." He walked close to Chalfront. "Sleep well, knowing that I will come to you soon and you will have much explaining to do, for I know what you did to my sister."

"Me?" Chalfront squeaked. "It was the baron—"

"Robert!" his wife called out. "Enough. You should not be discussing such things in the street."

"Yes, my love," Chalfront answered. He gave Bryce a condescending look. "You will find much has changed since you were last here, Bryce Frechette, and I would prepare to be humble, if I were you. If Gabriella had been less haughty, she would have spared herself much trouble." He took a look at Bryce's face and wisely said no more, but hurried inside his house and slammed the door shut.

Bryce heard the bar slide home. Then he grabbed his horse's reins and marched off to find his sister.

As Etienne walked alone through the belt of woodland on his estate, he told himself he was checking the condition of the game in the forest before the winter set in, and to ensure that Osric's punishment had served as a deterrent. His gaze roved over the ground and the underbrush, much of the branches bare in anticipation of winter. Still, the limbs grew thick and close together, and there were patches of evergreens such as holly that could hide a trap. Vigilance would be necessary to overcome the long years of the late earl's deficiency in enforcing the law.

That did not explain why Etienne was alone. He should have brought his forester, or his huntsman, or any one of his knights for safety, if nothing else. However, he had told George that he could walk faster if he was by himself, which was true, and wisely George did not repeat his request to accompany his lord.

Etienne was, in actuality, walking at a slower pace than his usual brisk stride because he had come to the solitude of the forest to think.

No, not even to think. To give himself up to an uncharacteristic bout of self-pity, brought on by the hopelessness of his regard for Gabriella Frechette.

God's wounds, how he wanted her! If someone had asked him a few weeks ago what he might feel if he sent Gabriella away, he would have *said* nothing at all, and would have told himself that he would miss her a little. He would have convinced himself that it was not her loss he regretted as much as the lost opportunity to make love with her. If they had asked about Josephine, he would have said, with a straight face but a touch of amusement, that of course he would miss her in his bed.

Instead, he had discovered that he missed Josephine not at all, and if he bemoaned his empty bed, it was because Gabriella was not in it. He had never known such bliss as he had experienced that night in the chapel with Gabriella. Never before had his heart been so engaged, his emotions so in tune with the desire of his body.

Never had he been able to talk to anyone as he had talked to her. For years he had hoarded the story of his past, locking it away, until she drew it out of him, like a *medicus* drawing poison from a wound, as she herself had said. She was like medicine to him; with her to listen, he had felt whole.

He had been alone all his life, lonely and lost, until a young woman with soft brown eyes offered him her love. How much he had wanted to describe his feelings for her, of his passion and joy, his hope and love.

He could not. He did not have the skill, could not find the words. He had risen from the floor beside her and looked at her, loving her. Then, suddenly, he had grown afraid, more afraid than he had ever been in his life. He was terrified of her, and the power of the emotions she stirred within him. He remembered the overwhelming potency of love that could sweep everything before it like chaff in the breeze, including honor, self-confidence and strength.

His first impulse had been to tell her of his fear, but abashed before her, ignorant of the words he needed to say, afraid of the control love could exert over him, he instead had obeyed the impulse for self-protection.

He had walked away. Like a coward.

He had gone to the battlements and stood on the wall walk for how long he didn't know, as he fought a battle between a desire to acknowledge his feelings and his ancient need to protect his already crippled heart. Then he discovered there was a worse thing than surrendering to love, and that was to reject it.

He had returned to the chapel, but Gabriella was already gone.

He could not blame her for fleeing. He blamed himself for taking too long to understand his own heart, and for being so long unused to having any regard for the feelings of others. Indeed, he had tried to ensure that he did not have to consider anyone but himself for many years.

He set about searching for her at once, but he soon realized she had either fled the castle, or was hiding from him. At dawn he had considered rousing his men to help him look for her, but his pride had silenced him. What would he say to them? That Gabriella had run away after making love with him in the chapel? What would they think of *her?*

He had decided to wait, hoping she would come back to him of her own will. That she would humble herself, so that he did not have to.

She did not return, and then he feared the time for explanations had passed. Two days had gone by, and in that time he had come to fear that she deeply regretted what they had shared.

Perhaps it was better for Gabriella to learn that his love was weaker than his selfish need to protect his pride.

With such unhappy thoughts for company, Etienne turned his weary steps for home.

Seated in Mary's cottage, Gabriella's heart felt like a lump of ice in her chest. Her arms were wrapped protectively about her, as if by doing so she could protect what remained of her self-esteem. She had lost most of it when Etienne DeGuerre had taken his pleasure of her and then left her lying on the floor of the chapel like a discarded weapon.

Stunned by his action, she had lain motionless for what seemed a very long time, waiting for him to return.

Then, as the moments passed and he did not come back, a growing sense of shame and degradation had crept over her. Despite her deeply felt belief that she would have no regrets about giving herself to him, it had taken only those few moments to destroy that faith. Regret? She felt it keenly. And shame. She had weakened, lulled by his apparent need, and she had let him triumph. She must have imagined that vulnerability in his eyes and been deceived by a man clever in the ways of seduction.

Soon enough, her pride had reasserted itself, galvanizing her to action. If he wanted to treat her like his whore, she would let him—this once! She would leave the castle immediately, for she had paid her debt, by God—with her body and her honor. Let him try to tell her otherwise!

She had hurried from the chapel, pushing past the gate house guards, who wisely did not try to stop her, and had run to Mary's cottage.

Mary, sensing that all was far from well, took her in without a word or question. Even now, though she glanced at her guest often with worried eyes while she stirred her pot of dye, she remained blessedly silent.

And here Gabriella would stay, until she could earn enough to get away from this village. To go some place, any place, where she could forget she had ever loved Baron DeGuerre.

If she could ever forget she had loved him.

With a low moan like a wounded beast, she covered her face with her hands.

"Gabriella!" someone shouted, by the sound, standing in the middle of the village green.

She sat up as if stabbed, the familiar voice shocking her.

"Who's that?" Mary demanded, looking up from the bubbling pot of bright orange. "He's calling your name like a fishwife at market."

Gabriella didn't answer as she leapt to her feet and ran out of the cottage toward the green.

"Bryce!" she cried, throwing herself into her brother's arms. "You're safe! You're home!"

He hugged her tightly, returning her fervent embrace. "I'm sorry I wasn't here sooner, Gabriella," he whispered. "I didn't know about Father, or the rest of it, or I would have come back at once, I promise you."

She drew back and surveyed him anxiously, wiping the happy tears from her cheeks as she devoured him with her eyes. He had always been handsome, tall and muscular; now, though, there was a leanness and maturity to his features that he had never possessed before. His tunic and chausses were plain and of inexpensive fabric, but they suited him. He still wore the sword their father had given him the day he had taken part in his first tournament. How long ago that seemed, and yet it felt like yesterday, too.

She wondered if he saw similar changes in herself. He probably did. But that didn't matter, now that he was home. "Are you well? When did you get back to England?"

"I should not have stayed away," he said softly. "I was a selfish fool. Can you ever forgive me?"

"I can and I do," she replied sincerely. "Has it been difficult for you, Bryce?" she asked, ignorant of the crowd gathering around the green, watching them.

He shrugged his shoulders and frowned deeply, looking so like their father that she felt renewed pain for the loss of him. "Somewhat, but not so difficult as it has been for you, I take it." He took her hand in his and regarded her pensively.

"What...what have you heard?" she asked, flushing deeply. The truth was not pleasant; depending upon whom he had spoken with, rumors might be even worse.

"I curse myself for being so long!" he said between clenched teeth. He reached into his belt and produced a purse heavy with coins, and his expression softened. "I saved nearly everything I won or earned, because I knew Father would have need of it someday. But I waited too long, for him and for you. I am so sorry, Gabriella!"

"It's all right, now," she answered truthfully, for his anguish was clear to see. "I confess I was upset that you weren't here. I thought...well, it seemed you had abandoned me."

"And left you at the mercy of this Baron De-Guerre." He regarded her steadily, anger brooding in his eyes. "Has he harmed you, Gabriella?"

She didn't know what to answer. What did it mean, "harm." That her life had been changed forever, she could not deny.

Then she realized Bryce wasn't looking at her any-more. He was staring over her shoulder at something behind her, his eyes narrowing with a fierce and an-gry look.

She twisted to glance over her shoulder. Baron DeGuerre, his blue eyes gleaming like two jewels, marched toward them.

"Gabriella, what is the meaning of this? Who is this man?" the baron asked, more agitated than she had ever seen him.

She commanded herself to ignore him, to pay no attention to the desire overwhelming her despite her resolutions, to attach no significance to his expres-sion, or the unusual anxious tension in his body.

Bryce gently pushed her away and faced Baron DeGuerre with a purposeful stance. "I am her brother, the Earl of Westborough."

Did the baron sigh? She couldn't be sure. She couldn't care. She must think of Bryce now.

"Her brother you may be," the baron replied, run-ning his gaze over Bryce, "and indeed, I do see a re-semblance. I am the Baron DeGuerre."

With trepidation, Gabriella saw her brother's hands curl into fists. "Bryce—" she cautioned.

Her brother ignored her. "I know what you've done," he accused.

"Bryce, he hasn't hurt me," she protested, afraid for her brother. She well remembered the cold, fierce menace in the baron's eyes when he had dragged Philippe de Varenne past her, and she could guess how he might respond to a false accusation.

Bryce glanced at her, his eyes flashing with anger. "He thought to dishonor you!" He turned back to Baron DeGuerre. "You base, disgusting bastard!"

"I myself prefer 'spawn of the devil,' " Etienne replied, controlling his torment and his fear as best he could. Nevertheless, a sense of fatality crushed him, for he spied the pouch of money in Bryce Frechette's hand and knew what it meant. This man could pay the debt and take Gabriella away.

"I am going to plead my case with the king, DeGuerre," Bryce Frechette said. "I can pay my father's debt, and my family has more right to this land than you. Come, Gabriella. You are leaving here at once!"

Gabriella looked at Etienne, and suddenly, he knew he could not let her go, not this way. In the face of his undeniable love, everything he had accomplished was ultimately worthless. His titles, his estates, even his dignity—all were nothing if he did not have Gabriella.

"Gabriella!" he cried with heartfelt anguish, his voice revealing the passion he had tried unsuccessfully to conquer for so long. "Gabriella, I left you because I was afraid. Afraid of you—and the power of the love I felt for you. I...I was afraid to submit to it, to even acknowledge that I could love. Nor have I wanted to, until I met you. I had no one to teach me how to love, until I met you." He paused, searching for the way to show her that he cared for her far more than for himself, or anyone else. "Your family may have your home back. I return this castle, this estate.

It means nothing to me. Nothing I possess means anything to me if you leave.''

Then the proud, the strong, the infamous Baron Etienne DeGuerre sank to his knees in front of Gabriella, her brother and everyone else watching. ''I love you, Gabriella,'' he said, all the restraint of years vanishing as he spoke, taking her hand in his. ''My life will be empty without you. Please, would you do me the great honor of becoming my wife?''

Chapter Seventeen

Gabriella's gaze searched the baron's imploring face, seeking the truth.

She knew his admission made here, in front of everyone, cost him dear. No other confirmation did she need to gauge the depth of his feeling than that, and the love looking back at her from his blue eyes.

"How *dare* you!" Bryce cried, slapping her hand away from the baron and glaring at him. "You cannot marry my sister."

"Bryce!" Gabriella cried, reminded only now of his presence. "It is not for you to make any decisions about my life. You gave up that right when you left home before our father died."

"I love her," Baron DeGuerre said in his calm, deep voice as he rose, once more in command of himself, yet looking at her with eyes full of love and need.

"That's impossible!" Bryce growled before she could respond. "You took away our home."

"Bryce, be *quiet*," she said, trying to silence him. "You don't understand."

· "I forbid you to even speak my sister's name again, you base bastard!" Bryce declared, drawing his sword from its sheath. "As for understanding, I understand well enough," he said scornfully. "I have eyes. I can see how low he has brought you. Wife? Don't be a fool, Gabriella." He stared at her with all the intensity of his passionate nature. "He only wants you in his bed, and once he has you there, I daresay all talk of marriage will disappear. This grasping, ambitious lout claims he will return our property—and you *believe* him? You have suffered much, Gabriella, for which I blame myself, but you cannot love the man who has taken away our home, treated you like a servant and who is surely lying, saying whatever he thinks you want to hear to lure you to his side."

"She loves you still and you deserted her," the baron observed coldly.

"Please, be quiet, both of you!" Gabriella cried in exasperation, stepping to stand between the two men she cared for above all else. "Bryce, you are the head of our family, and as such, I should respect your opinion."

He began to nod in agreement, but she held up her hand. "That does not mean I intend to abide by it. You have been gone a long time—"

"I didn't know—"

"I understand. But you cannot appreciate what has happened, or Baron DeGuerre, either. Yes, he took possession of our home, but it was lost before he was given it."

"Chalfront, that weasel—"

"Had nothing to do with it, either. He tried to prevent it."

"Has *he* fooled you, too?" Bryce demanded.

"You won't concede that you could be wrong, will you, or that perhaps Chalfront was right? I know you disagreed with him, but you disagreed with Father, too. I thought as you did, until I learned otherwise. The baron's steward examined the records and found nothing, *absolutely nothing,* amiss."

"I'm not taking *his* steward's word for anything," Bryce replied, jabbing his finger toward the motionless baron.

"Then take mine. We both misjudged Chalfront. Father was too extravagant and too lenient. Surely you must agree with *that.*"

"Too lenient, yes. As for extravagant, perhaps. But that is no reason for you to marry this man. I can support us both." He flushed and swallowed hard, then planted his feet defiantly. "I have long dreamed of coming home again. Now that home no longer exists, except in you, my dear sister. We can find a new home together."

Gabriella saw his regret and loneliness beneath the bravado. Then she looked at Etienne. To a stranger, he would have been unreadable, but she saw the hopeful yearning and almost hidden dread in his eyes. She loved both of these men, and had no wish to carry on this painful discussion in public; nevertheless, she knew this was the time to make her decision. "I have a home, Bryce," she said quietly, reaching out to take the baron's hand. "It is here, with this man, because I love him."

"Gabriella!" Etienne pulled her into his arms and held her tight. The back of his tunic was cold and damp, as if he had been sweating, and his heart was beating wildly. With fear? That she would not stay with him? She drew back and looked into his face. "I would not leave you, my love."

The baron smiled, a broad smile of great joy such as she had never seen him make. She looked beseechingly at Bryce. "You cannot understand, Bryce, I know. But you will have to trust that I am making the right decision."

He didn't answer at once, but stared at her with disbelief for a long moment before he shrugged his shoulders. "I will try," he said with no sincerity before he turned on his heel and marched away.

Etienne gently turned her to face him. He didn't speak, but his worried gaze searched her face.

"I have made my decision," she said with a wan, yet defiant smile. "Surely someday he will understand."

If Etienne doubted that a man like Bryce Frechette would ever sympathize with the choice his sister had made, he kept it to himself. All that truly mattered was that Gabriella was going to be his wife.

"I don't understand it," Donald said pensively several days later, surveying the village from the ridge. Castle Frechette was abloom with pennants and flags in a manner that took Donald's breath away. It was quite unlike Baron DeGuerre to go in for such frivolous display.

Seldon nodded his head in agreement. "It's not market day, or a saint's day, or any festival that I know of. Where's all the villagers going? To the castle?''

"Perhaps someone of importance has arrived," Donald mused. "Or maybe the harvest was better than the baron hoped and he has decided to celebrate."

"I hope so, since we don't return with good news," Seldon replied. "Well, I suppose we do, in a way. The baron will be relieved to hear that Philippe de Varenne won't trouble him anymore. And maybe that was Bryce Frechette in Dover, after all."

"I would like to think we could trust the tavern keeper's description," Donald said. "The young man he spoke of certainly sounded like Bryce Frechette."

"Maybe it's him come here, eh?" Seldon asked hopefully. "Maybe that's why the flags are flying."

"I don't think Baron DeGuerre would do that for the late earl's son, do you?''

"No, no, I suppose not."

"Well, we had better not sit here all day," Donald said, stifling a sigh. "Might as well make our report and get it over with.''

"Stop fidgeting, my lady!" Mary admonished as she tried to tie the lacings at the back of Gabriella's wedding dress.

It was a lovely gown of blue velvet trimmed with gold and silver. Her hair hung loose about her shoulders, crowned with a garland of dried red roses and baby's breath that Mary had made for her. Josephine had sent a slender gold necklace, and a shift of soft thin silk that was almost transparent. Gabriella had blushed deeply when she put it on, until she realized that after what had happened in the chapel, there was little cause for maidenly modesty with her future husband.

"Hold still, or that garland's going to fall right off and land on the candle and start burning!" Mary chided. "Holy heart of Saint Agatha! You're as jumpy as a flea."

"I'm...excited," Gabriella explained unnecessarily. "I've never gotten married before."

"No!" Mary cried in mock astonishment. Then she grinned. "I understand, although I've never had the pleasure of being a bride myself."

"You may yet," Gabriella noted.

Mary snorted derisively. "Small chance of that. As if I'd let a man lay his hands on my money—or anything else!" she said firmly. "Big hulking brutes, the lot of them. Or sniveling babies wanting a mother, not a wife."

"Which would you say the baron is?" Gabriella asked innocently as she suppressed a smile.

"Big hulking brute," Mary replied matter-of-factly. Then she blushed beet red. "Of course, he's a *rich* big hulking brute." A wide grin slashed her careworn face.

"Are you sure I can't persuade you to come to the castle to work?" Gabriella asked.

Mary shook her head. "No, that Lady Josephine would be lost without me to help her. She's beautiful, all right, and knows how to give orders, but she hasn't ever had to do any work herself, poor creature. You should have seen the mess she made of the washing!"

"She does that?"

"Enjoys it, she says. Makes her feel more useful than she's ever been in her life. They're very happy, those two, I must say. I had my doubts, I don't mind confessing."

"I'm so happy myself, I'm glad others are as fortunate." Gabriella stepped to the window of the apartment she had occupied since Etienne had asked her to be his wife.

She hoped Bryce would come. Yesterday she had asked him again to attend her wedding, but his response had been sullen and noncommittal. She knew he blamed himself for being absent at a crucial time, and she had tried and tried in the past several days to show him that it was all right. He refused to be consoled, despite her obvious happiness.

Now, and to her considerable relief, she spotted Bryce walking along the road toward the castle. He must have realized at last that she truly loved Etienne and had changed his mind about seeing his sister married.

She watched him striding across the courtyard with his head lowered in thought, his sword striking his thigh. He was a head taller than most of the people already assembled there, and it suddenly struck her that her brother looked as alone and isolated as she had ever felt. Or as Etienne had appeared that first day when he rode into the courtyard of the castle.

Nor did he look happy, as would befit the brother of a bride marrying the man she loved. He looked stubborn and determined, the way he always did when he was prepared to fight.

She would not allow Bryce to destroy her happiness this day, Gabriella vowed as she turned away from the window, her expression identical to that she had just seen on her brother's face.

"My lady, what is it?" Mary cried, hurrying to look out the window. "What's happened?"

Gabriella didn't answer as she hurried from the room. She was too busy focusing all her energy on what she believed would be a catastrophic argument. She rushed through the gaily decorated hall and paused on the threshold of the courtyard to survey the waiting crowd. Many smiled and voiced their good wishes, which she acknowledged with a curt nod. Then she saw him.

"Bryce!" she called, getting his attention. She turned and went inside, where she waited for him to join her. Once he did, she took a deep breath and faced him. "I hope you have come to give me your blessing," she said, her words a challenge.

"I couldn't allow my only sister to be married without me to give her away," he said grimly. "You were always stubborn, Gabriella. I just hope you will be happy with the choice you have made."

"I will," she assured him.

His expression softened into one of concern. "Are you sure—"

"Absolutely," she said firmly.

Suddenly his gaze faltered. "I do mean it when I say I hope you'll be happy. I will see that you are never unsure of my whereabouts again." He cleared his throat awkwardly. "If he ever hurts you in any way, you must come to me at once. Give me your word that you will."

"Although I seriously doubt that I will ever need to seek you for a refuge, Bryce," she replied, "I am glad that you will let me know that you are safe and well."

She reached out and took his hands in hers. "Won't you stay here? We could be a family again."

"No. You and your baron belong here more than I do, now," he said with a shake of his head. He raised his eyes to look at her again. "I don't blame anyone but myself for that. I chose my course when I left." He smiled wryly, and she was finally convinced that he was resigned to her marriage, if not delighted by it. "You know I have no gift for hiding my thoughts from others. In time, I might say or do something to make you regret your invitation. So, thank you again, but I will not stay."

She nodded reluctantly. "But do I have your blessing on my wedding day?"

"Of course you do. You are the only sister I have." He put his arm around her and pressed a brotherly kiss on her cheek. "I hope he is deserving of you," he whispered huskily, with suspicious moisture in his eyes that Gabriella knew he would deny.

"And I of him, Bryce. And I of him."

Baron DeGuerre stood in his bedchamber, anxiously surveying his clothing. George, leaning against the wall languidly with an indulgent smile on his genial face, said, "You look quite fine enough, Baron DeGuerre. I don't recall you ever fretting about how you looked in all the years I've known you."

Etienne put on a frown at the astute observation. "You are a fine one to chid about vanity, George. How much did that tunic cost you?" He nodded toward the elaborate scarlet-and-gold brocade garment George wore.

"Too much, I fear," he replied, attempting to look downcast and failing miserably. "I thought I should look good, for the pride of my lord."

"People will think you're the bridegroom," Etienne observed, wondering if he should wear something more colorful. He had worn black for so long, he had thought he would feel like a jester in anything brighter, so he had chosen another black tunic, albeit one of the finest wool.

"Oh, I don't think there will be much confusion on that point."

Etienne brushed his shoulders with his hands. "Why?"

"The expression in those usually inscrutable orbs of yours leave no doubt which man here is in love."

"You are getting to be a most impertinent fellow," Etienne warned, his tone serious.

"You cannot tell me you don't like impertinence. Why, you're marrying the most impertinent woman I've ever met in my life."

"She's a lot prettier than you," Etienne noted gravely.

George threw back his head and laughed. When he sobered, he said, "By God, this is wonderful."

"What?" Etienne asked suspiciously.

"With all due respect, my lord, I don't recall you ever making a joke under duress. I believe this marriage will be the making of you."

"I heartily agree," Etienne said with a warm smile.

The murmur from the courtyard had been growing steadily since Etienne had come to dress for the ceremony, and it was now quite noisy. He went to the window and glanced out. "It must be nearly time. God's wounds, I haven't been this nervous since . . . I don't think I've *ever* been this nervous. My hands are sweating!" Such a reaction had never occurred before his other marriages, but perhaps, Etienne thought, that was because he had never been in love before.

"Have you seen your betrothed's brother today?" George asked, trying to sound nonchalant.

"No." A cloud appeared on the sunshine of Etienne's wedding day. "I hope he comes for the ceremony, for Gabriella's sake. He's made it very obvious that he still doesn't approve."

"It hasn't changed her mind any," George observed.

"No, thank God." Etienne straightened his shoulders. "Well, let's go."

"No need to look so worried," George said, clapping his hand on the baron's shoulder in a friendly gesture he never would have attempted before. "All will be well. There's a little time yet. Why don't you wait here and try to regain your customary calm. I shall see if the wine has arrived."

George strolled from the room, leaving Etienne staring thoughtfully out the window. He was almost unbearably happy; nevertheless, he could not rid himself of the fear that he would somehow find his joy obstructed before the day was out.

Donald and Seldon joined the people heading through the gates of the castle. They rode under the portcullis into the courtyard, halting their horses as close to the stable as they could get because of the boisterous crowd before dismounting.

"Donald!" George called out, sauntering toward them with a bright smile. "And Seldon. How was your journey? You've timed your return impeccably."

"What is happening?" Donald asked, his gesture encompassing the waiting crowd.

"A wedding," George replied cheerfully. "The baron's getting married to Gabriella Frechette."

"Truly?" Donald asked, obviously shocked and skeptical. "Or is this another one of your jokes?"

"It can't be," Seldon scoffed. "She's too skinny."

"Truly," George replied, his serious tone adding credence to his words. He gave Seldon a slightly disgusted frown. "Today, at noon. Here, come to the kitchen and have some ale before we go for the ceremony, and the feast. The baron's spent a fortune on the food and wine, Chalfront says. The poor man looks to have a fit every time he leaves the castle, but the baron said money was not to be spared."

"Well..." Donald had intended to go at once to the baron and recount what he had learned. But this was a festive occasion, and when he thought of being the bearer of bad tidings for the bride, he decided his news could wait. The two young men followed George into the kitchen, which was a scene of mass confusion presided over by Guido, who had apparently finally been driven to madness, for he shouted at everyone and waved his arms as if he were demented.

George ignored the uproar, and the harried servants ignored the noblemen. "I tell you, all this wedding business makes a man think of getting married himself, eh?" George said philosophically, corralling a startled Alda whose arms were full of linen and giving the wench a hearty kiss on the cheek. She blushed and spun out of his grasp, then reeled toward the hall. "Meet any likely candidates on your travels?"

"I was on an errand for the baron, not looking for a wife," Donald said severely.

"Might have done both," Seldon noted with a slow grin. "Might have had better luck."

The baron had sworn Donald and Seldon to secrecy, so Donald shot his companion a warning look.

"No need to inform me of your doings," George said cheerfully. If he surmised he was to be kept in the dark concerning the purpose of their journey, he was obviously not offended. "You've missed plenty of excitement here, I'll tell you."

"Obviously," Donald observed. "I never would have guessed we'd be coming home to a wedding."

"You're not the only one. Bryce Frechette didn't expect it, either, I daresay."

"What?" Donald demanded. "Bryce Frechette came here? When?"

"After Osric got caught poaching and lost his fingers."

"You'd better start from the beginning," Donald said gravely. "And when you're finished, I'll tell you about Philippe."

"I take it the news is not good?"

Donald and Seldon glanced at each other.

"You are going to leave me in suspense?"

The two young men nodded. "What you have to say is surely more enjoyable," Donald said with a slight smile.

"I quite agree," George said, and he proceeded to recount what had recently transpired in Castle Frechette.

"I'm glad for the lady's sake," Donald said when George finished, "although it seems the baron sent us away for nothing."

"Now tell me about Philippe de Varenne," George replied.

"He's dead," Seldon announced with his customary lack of embellishment.

"Dead?" George asked incredulously.

"Dead," Donald confirmed. "He got drunk and fell off a pier at Dover, or so they say. It could be someone tried to rob him. Either way, he drowned."

"He never should have tried to make trouble," Seldon noted with a distinct lack of compassion. "Ambitious fool! Where's it all got him, eh?"

Chapter Eighteen

Despite Etienne's pessimistic misgivings, nothing happened to prevent his marriage.

George returned with Donald and Seldon, who reported their news of Philippe de Varenne, and Etienne could even find it in his heart to regret the loss of one so young and so corrupted. He could not help but wonder what part Philippe's family had played in the man's ruin, or if, with better men to guide his early years, Philippe might have turned out better.

If he should become a father—a new and now welcome possibility!—he would remember well the influence a parent could wield, for good or ill.

At the appropriate time they went to the chapel and when Etienne saw Gabriella awaiting him, her eyes shining with love and trust, he discovered that he could also find some sympathy for his mother. Full of love himself, he no longer blamed her for falling in love with a man unworthy of her devotion, as he had so often done before, and although he did not forgive her neglect of him, he could at least comprehend it.

Then he spotted Bryce Frechette trying not to scowl at him. The impudent fellow was no cipher, and it was clear he did not like the man his sister had chosen, yet Frechette wisely did not make any protest or try to prevent the ceremony.

Gabriella was so obviously delighted by her brother's presence that when the ceremony was over, and Etienne had bestowed a kiss on his beautiful bride, Bryce Frechette even received one of the baron's rare smiles, albeit not one nearly as warm and happy as the one the baron bestowed on his wife.

Merry and long was the wedding feast that followed the ceremony, with fine food, excellent wine and delightful music. The hall was decorated with so many evergreen branches and late-blooming flowers that it looked like an enchanted bower. The servants darted about ensuring a plentiful supply of food for everyone, and the several guests laughed and talked and jested until long after the sun went down. George particularly outdid himself making witty remarks, and his reward was the attention of a certain lovely young lady who was, to his very pleasant surprise, unmarried and unpromised. Her pretty face and appreciation for his intelligence were certainly enough to give a man pause, even one so unused to serious speculation.

Donald and Seldon enjoyed the meal and George's comments in their own particular fashions. Donald was alternately driven to helpless laughter and embarrassed horror by George's irreverent remarks. Seldon didn't understand a lot of them, and didn't pay attention to many more, for there was too much food spread before him to consider inconsequential matters.

It was later noted by many that the baron seemed to be mellowing with age, for no one could recall him ever smiling or laughing so much. Indeed, Etienne himself could not remember a time in his life when he felt so happy and carefree, and he thanked God for sending him his lovely bride.

Gabriella smiled much and said little, but her joy shone in her face. In the spring and summer, she had thought she could never be happy again. Now Bryce had come home safe and sound, she would always be able to retain her home and most importantly, she was married to the man she loved.

Chalfront revealed that Osric and his mother had left the village, sneaking away in the night and taking with them several tools that they did not own. William had organized a group to give chase, but the hayward and his mother had eluded them. As for Chalfront and Josephine, the bailiff looked so pleased when he led his beautiful wife into the hall, Gabriella thought he might explode from the warring combination of pride and humility he was obviously experiencing.

He could not have been any happier than Gabriella, though, nor was she nearly as sanguine as she appeared. How could she be, with Etienne seated so close beside her, his hand straying to caress hers at what seemed every available opportunity?

Not that she wanted him to stop. She quite shamelessly wanted him to continue, and begrudged the absence when he took his hand away.

At last the feast was concluded, and minstrels entered the hall from the kitchen, by their contented expression well pleased with the meal they had enjoyed there. "What is your pleasure, my lord?" the leader asked as he tuned his harp. "A ballad? Or a dance?"

"I think a ballad," Etienne began. Then he hesitated and said with pensive gravity, "No, I believe a dance." He rose majestically. "Gabriella?"

She tried to maintain an equally dignified demeanor as she stood to join him. "I would be delighted, my lor...husband."

She put her hand in his, and even that simple contact made her blush.

He was a surprisingly good dancer, she realized at once, then knew she should have guessed that. Any man who could move with his customary grace *should* be an exceptional dancer.

It seemed she was not the only one who enjoyed watching Etienne, for nobody rose to join them. "I believe I am making a spectacle of myself," Etienne whispered sardonically as she passed in front of him to take his other upheld hand.

She shook her head, smiling. "They are all simply astounded by your agility," she answered.

"Perhaps I should do something completely unexpected," he whispered next with a roguish grin that made her heart race.

"What did you have in mind?" she replied breathlessly.

He halted abruptly, jerking her to a stop. The amazed minstrels ceased playing, and then the assembly gasped as Etienne pulled her into his arms and gave her a passionate kiss that sent the heat pulsing through her body. His lips moved over hers lazily, seductively, until her knees felt weak.

"My lord!" George called out, bringing her back to reality with a suddenness that took away what little breath she had left. "I believe you are under a serious delusion."

Etienne stepped away, and together they turned to George, who was looking very serious. "This is *not* your bedchamber," he told them.

Gabriella flushed warmly and felt a most undignified urge to giggle, because she had completely forgotten the existence of anyone except Etienne.

"I thank you for pointing that out," Etienne said just as gravely as George. "If you all will excuse us, I believe my wife and I shall retire to the proper room."

In the next moment, Etienne swept Gabriella up in his arms and started to carry her toward the tower stairs. "I hope I'm not too heavy," she said with mock gravity as he began to climb the steps.

"And I hope I don't stumble," Etienne replied. His tone was so unemotional, she started to wonder if he meant his words.

"I wouldn't want you to strain yourself," she said. "You may put me down."

"Oh, I will," he said with a low chuckle. "When I get you to our bedchamber."

He reached the bedchamber and kicked open the door. Once across the threshold, he set her down quickly, then turned and shoved the door closed. Gabriella didn't know quite what to do, between her excitement, her nervous anxiety and the fact that she was alone with the man she desired with all her heart, so she went to the table as fast as her weakened knees could carry her, sat on the stool and started to remove her veil with trembling fingers.

Etienne didn't do anything except watch her.

"It was a very good feast," she said brightly, thinking she sounded like a very silly and very young girl. "Everyone seemed to be enjoying themselves. George had better be careful, or he'll make Emmeline D'Arcy fall in love with him." She got the veil and headdress off.

Was he simply going to stand there and do nothing? Was there something she was supposed to do? "I was so happy Bryce gave me his blessing," she babbled. "I hope he'll stay for a little while, at least."

Etienne moved at last and she sighed with relief, although she nearly jumped out of her skin when he placed his two hands on her shoulders. "Gabriella," he said wistfully, "there's so much I want to say, and I do not have the words."

She rose and faced him, touched by his humble tone. "I do not need words," she said truthfully. "I have you."

He smiled, but he still didn't seem quite convinced. "I want to explain something. That night in the chapel, when I frightened you . . . I was trying to show you how much I cared for you, in the only way I knew how."

She smiled and nodded. "I understand, Etienne. You had no teacher for any other way, but truly, I do not need flowery flattery and empty eloquence. You told me everything when you told me about your past." She splayed her hands on his broad chest. "*Show* me how much you love me, and I will do my best to show you how much I return that love." She kissed him and rejoiced as his arms closed around her and drew her close. Nestling against his chest, she whispered, "Who needs words, when our lips can speak so eloquently without them?"

She became aware that he was untying the lacing of her gown, and her heart began to race with renewed excitement, all the more so because they were husband and wife, their union sanctified by church and state. No shame would attach itself to the glory they were about to share.

His hand slipped inside her gown and stroked her back. She tilted her head for another kiss, this time imbuing it with all the passion she felt.

Etienne responded with equal passion, his tongue making forays into the waiting warmth of her mouth and sensuously entwining with her own. Just as anxious to feel his naked flesh, she fumbled for his lacings.

"I want you so much," he murmured with closed eyes when she succeeded and pressed her hand along his hardened muscles. "I need you so much."

He opened his eyes, which gleamed with desire. With a low growl, he picked her up and carried her to their bed. Once he had placed her there, he stepped away and yanked off his tunic, then tossed it aside and took off his chausses.

How magnificent he was! she thought as he crawled onto the end of the bed, his movements as lithe and graceful as a cat's. She wanted to feel his lips upon hers and closed her eyes in anticipation.

His lips touched her, but not upon her mouth. His hand moved slowly along her leg, pushing up her skirt, his kisses trailing behind, up and up and up, creating an incredible suspense.

"What are you—" she gasped.

"Showing you how many ways I can love you," he replied huskily, still making his slow progress, which stopped just short. He looked up at her with a wicked grin.

Throbbing with desire, she begged, "Take me now, Etienne, please," and sat up, pressing hot kisses over his chest and reaching for his waist.

"No, not yet," he protested softly, with a shake of his head. He gently pushed her back and positioned himself between her legs. With agonizing slowness he helped her remove her gown and shift. With even more agonizing slowness, he bent down to tease and caressed her with his hands and tongue until she thought she would die with pleasure.

Instinctively undulating beneath him, she could not wait. Her eager fingers found his hardened manhood and guided it to her. Gasping, he pressed gently inside. The tempo of their movements increased, building into a tension of incredible proportion. She grabbed his shoulders, her fingers biting into the flesh, until he threw back his head and groaned just as the tension burst within her.

Who could put a word to this feeling? she thought as wave after wave of pleasure rippled through her and she cradled Etienne against the softness of her breasts.

After a long moment of blissful rest, he disengaged himself and lay beside her, panting. Then he smiled at her, his chest still slick from the frenzy of their passion.

She reached out to touch his hair. "Here is something I've been curious about," she said pensively, her eyes dancing. "Why is your hair so long?"

"Do you think I look like a woman?" he demanded, half-serious.

"You?" She ran her gaze over his naked body. "Never. But it is so unusual."

He lifted one of her own tresses and began to brush the end across her cheek. "When I was young, I could not afford to hire a body servant, or a squire, nor could I afford to have my hair properly trimmed. So I let it grow and ignored the stares and taunts of others. And then a very interesting thing happened. After I had won a few tournaments, I noticed that some of those I had fought were arriving at tournaments with longer hair. I heard a few remarks about 'Samson.'" He smiled at the memory. "After that, I saw no need to cut my hair." He kissed her forehead. "If you wish it, I will have it trimmed tomorrow."

"Oh, no, I like it, although at first I thought you looked quite savage."

"I am," he said with a wicked smile. "You didn't let me finish showing you what I wanted to," he remarked, slipping lower on the bed. "I do not like to be interrupted, as you well know."

"I lack patience," she replied.

"So I gather. Fortunately, I have patience enough for both. Because," he said, lazily pressing kisses along her belly toward her thighs, "this time I am going to take my time, I promise you."

"Then I had better move this gown," she said hurriedly, suddenly tense as she rose to remove her crushed and wrinkled wedding dress from beneath them.

He smiled dreamily, imagining a few of the many delights they would share. Then he noticed the frown on her face. "What is it? I didn't mean to criticize."

She glanced at him over her smooth, naked shoulder. "I know."

"Then what is troubling you?" He almost forgot his question as he watched her, seeing her body completely for the first time. How splendid she was—all the more so because of the feelings of love and tenderness she invoked within him.

May he always be worthy of those feelings! he thought as she went to the chest of her garments now standing beside his own and pulled out a robe he had given her for a wedding gift. It was rich red velvet, lined with soft rabbits' fur. She had protested that it was too expensive, but he had assured her that he knew quite well the state of his purse, and that even Chalfront had approved of the purchase. Right at the moment, he thought he had never bought anything so delightful in his life.

"It's just that . . . you've had so many women and I . . . I am so ignorant of . . . in the bed . . . and . . ." she said haltingly, hiding her face in a manner that was astonishingly provocative.

He was out of the bed in an instant, gathering her in his arms, the fur tickling his nostrils. "No other woman has ever mattered to me as you do," he said. "I liked them and enjoyed their company, but I didn't love them. How could I, when I didn't know how to love until I found you?"

"Are you sure?"

He laughed, a hearty, full-throated laugh that filled the chamber. "I am absolutely sure, my beloved." His eyes took on the hungry gleam Gabriella was beginning to appreciate. "Come back to bed, wife."

"I thought you were a patient man, Baron De-Guerre," she chided, flushing to the roots of her hair, her body tingling with expectation and her flesh aroused by the softness of the fur.

He started to chuckle, his chest rumbling with the laughter. "My name is Etienne. All things considered, I think you have every right to use it."

"Etienne." She sighed, snuggling up to him and toying with a lock of his hair. "You love me."

"I love you," he whispered. "I love you, Gabriella."

Her answering expression and kiss confirmed that he had made no mistake taking her for his wife. She was perfect, and he would never be alone again. "Although I am patient, I am only mortal," he said huskily as he took her hand and led her to the bed.

* * *

Etienne awoke as the first faint streaks of light began coloring the eastern sky with the bright gold, orange and fuchsia of morning. For several minutes he lay still, enjoying the delightful sensation of Gabriella slumbering so peacefully in his arms. She would surely want to sleep late this morning, he thought with a satisfied smile.

Then he heard voices outside in the courtyard. Very gently he moved away from Gabriella, for he should go down and bid farewell to any guest leaving at this hour. He went to the window and looked out.

It was Bryce Frechette, who had apparently spent the night in the hall, probably too tired or drunk to return to the village inn. Did that young hothead think he was going to leave the castle without saying goodbye to his sister, after all the worrying she had done over him?

Etienne grabbed his tunic from the floor and threw it over his head, then ran down the stairs, the stones frigid on his naked feet. He ignored the knights and squires sleeping in the hall and strode out into the courtyard. "Frechette!" he called.

Bryce halted on his way to the gate and turned. "Baron DeGuerre," he acknowledged with a courteous bow and a smile that reminded Etienne of Gabriella.

Etienne was not a man easily won over by superficial charm, so he crossed his arms and surveyed the young man with his forceful glare. "I trust you were not planning to leave without saying goodbye to your sister."

"I'm sorry if I have roused you from your slumber," Bryce said unrepentantly. "I didn't see any reason to disturb Gabriella."

Etienne struggled to control his annoyance. What a selfish knave this fellow was! If he was not his dear wife's beloved brother, he would take great joy in teaching him a lesson in courtesy. However, since Bryce was, he contented himself with a brief shake of his head and said, "I must insist you remain until you can bid her a proper farewell."

Bryce cocked his head and his smile was curiously indulgent, considering the tone of voice the baron had used. "Aren't your feet getting cold?"

All at once, Etienne realized how ridiculous he must look, with his bare feet, unlaced tunic and disheveled hair. A fast glance at a gaping stable boy seemed to confirm his dread. "Then come inside and eat," he said gruffly, heading for the hall, barely subduing the urge to make certain the fellow was following, and trying not to hear the muffled chortles of the stable boy.

Etienne had his reward for his frozen feet later when he watched his wife bid her brother a poignant farewell in the courtyard. The day was overcast and the sky threatened rain, or perhaps even snow. Not the most auspicious day to start a journey, but Bryce was quite firm in his decision to leave. A stubborn adherence to abide by resolutions seemed to be a family trait of the Frechettes.

Etienne stayed out of earshot, not wishing to intrude upon their familial leave-taking. He watched his pretty bride, looking like a wood sprite with her long brown hair, rosy complexion, and dressed in a blue cloak trimmed with fox fur that had been a wedding gift from George.

Gabriella gestured for him to join them. When he did, her hand slipped possessively about Etienne's waist, and the gesture was so new and delightful that he forgot to be annoyed at Bryce. "God go with you, Bryce," he said. "Be sure to let us know where you are."

"I've already promised Gabriella I would, several times," the young man replied with a smile. He grew somber and in his eyes appeared the same defiant look Etienne had seen so often in Gabriella's. "Take good care of her, Baron DeGuerre."

"You have my solemn oath and promise," Etienne replied.

Gabriella let go of her husband to embrace her brother once more. "God go with you!" she whispered fervently and there were tears in her eyes.

"Until my return," Bryce said. Then, with a jaunty wave of his hand, he strode across the courtyard and through the gate.

At nearly the same instant, Chalfront appeared, bustling under the portcullis with several scrolls under his arm and a worried frown on his round face as he hurried toward the hall, his gaze fastened intently on the cobblestones.

Before Chalfront spotted him, Etienne put his arm around Gabriella and turned her toward the hall. "Let us go to the hall. It's cold out here."

She nodded, and together they went inside. A blazing fire was burning in the huge hearth, dispelling the November chill. George was sitting on a bench beside it, gossiping with some of the noble guests, his gaze often straying to Emmeline D'Arcy, who was pretending she didn't notice his attempts to engage her attention as she sewed at a tapestry with some of the other visiting noblewomen. Donald, serious as always, looked on with apparent distaste for George's frivolous words, yet he didn't move away from his place near the industrious women. Seldon was too busy eating the heel of a loaf to take much notice of anybody, except when a blushing, prettily bashful Alda brought more bread. Etienne perceived that although he had married off one troublesome serving wench—to a very fine fellow, of course—there might be trouble brewing with another.

Suddenly he started to laugh.

"What is it?" Gabriella asked, smiling to see him so happy, which took away the pain of Bryce's departure.

"I declare I am the happiest man in all of England," he said, looking at her with love shining in his eyes. Unmindful of the others in the hall, he gave her a long, lingering kiss. "I have finally found the end of my quest."

"What is that?" she asked.

Etienne lightly kissed away the furrow that appeared between Gabriella's lovely brown eyes.

"You, my beloved. You."

* * * * *

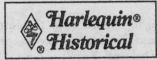

Harlequin® Historical

Bestselling author **RUTH LANGAN** brings you nonstop
adventure and romance with her new Western series
from Harlequin Historicals

The Jewels of Texas

DIAMOND	February 1996
PEARL	August 1996
JADE	February 1997
RUBY	June 1997

Don't miss these exciting stories of four sisters as wild
and vibrant as the untamed land they're fighting to protect!

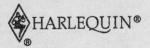

HARLEQUIN®

Look us up on-line at: http://www.romance.net

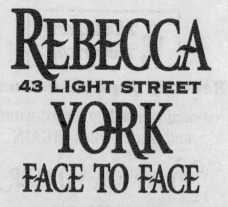

REBECCA

43 LIGHT STREET

YORK

FACE TO FACE

*Bestselling author Rebecca York returns to "43 Light Street"
for an original story of past secrets, deadly deceptions—and
the most intimate betrayal.*

She woke in a hospital—with amnesia…and with child.
According to her rescuer, whose striking face is the last
image she remembers, she's Justine Hollingsworth. But
nothing about her life seems to fit, except for the baby
inside her and Mike Lancer's arms around her. Consumed
by forbidden passion and racked by nameless fear, she
must discover if she is Justine…or the victim of some mind
game. Her life—and her unborn child's—depends on it….

Don't miss *Face To Face*—Available in October, wherever
Harlequin books are sold.

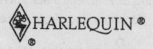

HARLEQUIN ®

®

43FTF

Look us up on-line at: http://www.romance.net

Harlequin® Historical

Back by popular demand!

National bestselling award-winning
author of **THE BARGAIN**

Veronica Sattler

presents

JESSE'S LADY

Where a dashing guardian and his fiery ward
discover a forbidden passion....

Don't miss this *sizzling* romance novel
available in September wherever
Harlequin Historicals are sold!

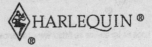

HARLEQUIN ®

Harlequin® Historical

If you're a serious fan of historical romance, then you're in luck!

Harlequin Historicals brings you stories by bestselling authors, rising new stars and talented first-timers.

Ruth Langan & Theresa Michaels
Mary McBride & Cheryl St. John
Margaret Moore & Merline Lovelace
Julie Tetel & Nina Beaumont
Susan Amarillas & Ana Seymour
Deborah Simmons & Linda Castle
Cassandra Austin & Emily French
Miranda Jarrett & Suzanne Barclay
DeLoras Scott & Laurie Grant...

You'll never run out of favorites.

Harlequin Historicals...they're too good to miss!

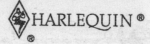